IN THE
COMPANY
OF WOLVES

PAIGE TYLER

sourcebooks
casablanca

Published by Sourcebooks Casablanca, an imprint of Sourcebooks, Inc.
P.O. Box 4410, Naperville, Illinois 60567-4410
(630) 961-3900
Fax: (630) 961-2168
www.sourcebooks.com

Printed and bound in Canada.
MBP 10 9 8 7 6 5 4 3 2 1

With special thanks to my extremely patient and understanding husband. Without your help and support, I couldn't have pursued my dream job of becoming a writer. You're my sounding board, my idea man, my critique partner, and the absolute best research assistant any girl could ask for.

Love you!

Prologue

East Side Detroit, September, 2010

JAYNA WINSTON FLINCHED AT THE SOUND OF THE DOOR slamming against the cheap plaster wall of the apartment's tiny entryway. *Crap*. Her stepdad was drunk again. No surprise there. These days, Darren came home drunk almost every night. He was supposed to be looking for work, but unless there was a job hiding under a bar stool down at Hoolie's, he wasn't likely to find one anytime soon.

She glanced at her partially opened bedroom window that exited out onto the fire escape. Maybe she should bail and see if she could crash at a friend's for the night. She didn't like the idea of walking the streets of Detroit's East Side this late, but she really wasn't in the mood to listen to Darren and her mom get in another fight over money and his drinking habits. Darren was a mean drunk, and when her mom started screaming at him about wasting what little money they had, things usually got ugly fast.

Not that her mom was any kind of saint when it came to saving money. The reason she got so pissed about Darren blowing through all the cash was because it hardly left her any to spend on her own vices—lottery tickets with a little crystal meth on the side.

Jayna scrambled off the bed and started for the

window, but then hesitated. Darren got pissed when she used the fire escape to leave their third-floor apartment. He said it made her look like a dirty hoodlum, sliding down the ladder like that. Not that she cared what people around here thought, but the last time he'd caught her slipping out the window, he'd thrashed her with his belt right out on the street while the neighbors watched.

She was still weighing the odds when she heard Darren swear, immediately followed by her mom's voice, roughened by a lifetime of smoking unfiltered cigarettes, cussing right back at him.

"Don't turn your face away from me, you stupid bitch!" Darren's deep voice was so heavily slurred, it would have been impossible to understand if she didn't have so much experience at interpreting his drunken rants. "You think you're too good for me or something? You're nothing but a meth whore. Get over here!"

"Double crap," Jayna muttered as she headed for the window.

She was getting the hell out of there. Darren wasn't only violent when he was drunk; sometimes he was horny too, and now seemed like one of those times. Her stepdad never had a problem smacking her around whenever he felt she deserved it—which was frequently—but he'd never tried anything else. Since she'd turned seventeen a couple weeks ago, he'd started looking at her in a way that made her feel really queasy. Jayna knew that sooner or later, he was going to come sniffing around her. She wasn't going to hang around and give him a chance to do it tonight.

She was yanking on the window, which got stuck more often than not, when a loud thud resonated from the living room, immediately followed by a sharp cry of pain. She hesitated, but not for long. She'd tried to come to her mom's defense a few months ago, putting herself in front of Darren and rocking his head back with a slap across his face, only to end up getting hit on the head with a heavy glass ashtray by her mom, who then shouted at Jayna for touching "her man."

Jayna didn't think of herself as all that smart—she was barely making it in school—but there were some lessons she only had to learn once. That night had been the last time she ever tried to get between her mom and Darren. Her mom wanted him; she could keep him.

Ignoring the sobbing outside her bedroom door, Jayna tugged on the window again. It broke loose without a sound, and she already had one leg halfway over the sill before she remembered her cell phone.

"Crap."

She pulled her leg back in and darted for her dresser, where her old, battered Nokia was charging. She hated wasting time getting the thing. It had crappy service most of the time anyway. But if she was going to find a place to crash tonight, she'd need her cell. It wasn't like she'd find a working pay phone around this part of town.

Jayna was shoving the phone in her jeans back pocket when her bedroom door flew open so violently the knob smashed a hole in the wall and sent a cloud of white dust flying. She took one look at Darren's pissed-off expression and ran for the window as fast as she could. Angry might have been his default expression, but this was different. This time, he looked…hungry.

She didn't make it far before a heavy hand caught her shoulder. Darren spun her around and gave her a shove, bouncing her off the cheap mirror attached to the wall beside the window. Her right elbow and forearm absorbed most of the impact, hitting the mirror hard enough to shatter it. Something shattered in her arm too, and the stab of pain that shot through it was enough to make tears spring to her eyes.

But she didn't cry. She'd found out a while ago that crying only made it worse. Darren liked to hear women cry.

Gritting her teeth against the pain, Jayna glared at the piece of crap her mom had brought into their lives. "What do you want?"

Darren eyed her from under heavy lids. "I want you to start pulling your weight around here, girl, that's what I want."

Her heart pounded as he moved closer, and she knew this had nothing to do with her cleaning the toilet or taking out the trash. Darren had wanted something else from her for a while, and tonight, he was apparently drunk enough to try to take it. That was never going to happen. She'd die first.

She edged closer to the window. "Stay the hell away from me, you pig!"

If she could get a lead on him, she could get out the window and onto the fire escape. He'd never catch her once she got outside. She was too fast, and he was too clumsy.

But he closed the distance between them faster than she'd ever seen him move, making her wonder just how drunk he really was. Before she could even take a breath to scream, he had his big hand around her throat and was shoving her against the wall. The back of her head bounced off the edge of the mirror frame, and she felt shards of loose glass dig into her back at the same time stars exploded in her vision.

Jayna was still fighting off a creeping wave of blackness when his lips came down on hers and he forced his tongue into her mouth. He tasted of cheap beer and cigarettes, and she bit down hard, jerking away. He bellowed like an angry bear and backhanded her. She fell over the broken remains of her mirror in a heap, pieces of the razor-sharp glass stabbing into her in a dozen different places.

She cried out, kicking at him with her tennis shoes as Darren roughly flipped her over on her back. He ignored her feeble kicks the same way he ignored her wild punches. She screamed then, as loud as she could — not because she thought someone might come to help, but simply because she wasn't going to let this happen without a fight.

Jayna fought with everything she had, but he was so much stronger than she was. On top of that, her right arm throbbed like hell. It was all she could do to lift it. Worse, the more weight Darren piled on top of her, the deeper the shards of glass from the broken mirror dug into her back.

Crap. Why hadn't she thought of it before?

Ignoring the pain in her injured arm, she searched blindly on the floor for a piece of mirror she could use as a weapon. Her fingers closed around one, and she cried out as the sharp glass sliced into her hand. But the feel of her belt coming undone drove the sting away, and she swung her hand up, stabbing at anything she could reach.

Darren was so drunk and enraged he didn't realize

what was happening until she'd slashed his face so hard the glass crunched under her hand. Blood poured down his face and he bellowed like a wounded animal. But instead of throwing himself off her like she'd hoped, he brought back his fist to punch her.

Knowing a blow like that would end her fight, Jayna tightened her fingers around the piece of mirror and swung at the most vulnerable area she could reach—his neck. The long, jagged piece of glass only stopped when the part she'd been holding broke off in her grasp. The rest was buried in the right side of Darren's fat neck four inches deep.

He let her go and reached for his neck. Jayna twisted sideways, kicking him in the chest, then crawled out from under him and scrambled to her feet. She staggered toward the window, stumbling when she heard Darren behind her. Oh God, he was still coming!

She grabbed the porcelain Wonder Woman lamp that had been sitting on her nightstand since her real dad had given it to her fifth on her birthday, spun around, and smashed Darren over the head. The lamp shattered, and Darren slumped to the floor with the pieces.

Jayna looked around. There was a lot of blood on the floor, both hers and Darren's. But she was still standing, and he wasn't.

A sound from the doorway startled her out of her daze, and she lifted her head to see her mom standing staring at her in horror.

"What did you do?" her mother demanded, running to Darren's side and kneeling down beside him.

Jayna didn't try to explain. Her mom wouldn't listen or care. Darren was still breathing, but Jayna had no idea if he was going to stay that way. The cops might believe she'd been defending herself, or they might not. She'd never had much faith in cops. They weren't interested in helping people like her.

This wasn't something she could get out of by spending the night at a friend's house either. She had to get away from there.

Jayna stepped around her mom, who was still blubbering and fussing over the unconscious Darren, and grabbed the charger for her phone. Then she scooped up the small amount of money she had in her sock drawer and headed for the window. Her mom didn't even say anything to her as she climbed out.

Jayna stood on the fire escape, afraid she'd take a header down it if she didn't. But she felt surprisingly steady considering what had just happened. Her hand was barely bleeding and her arm didn't hurt nearly as bad as before.

Maybe it was shock, she mused as she climbed down the fire escape. Or maybe she was simply a whole hell of a lot tougher than she ever thought she could be.

"Damn right you're tough," she muttered, almost believing it as the pain in her arm and hand receded a little more with each step. "You don't need anyone to make it on your own."

Chapter 1

Dallas, Texas, Present Day

EYES GLUED TO HIS BINOCULARS, OFFICER ERIC BECKER surveyed the dimly lit warehouse across from the rooftop he was positioned on. It was four o'clock in the morning, and the place was about as quiet as you could expect a major import/export warehouse located outside the Dallas/Fort Worth International Airport to be.

"Anything yet?" Xander Riggs queried softly through Becker's earpiece.

Becker checked the heavy shadows along the west side of the warehouse before answering his squad leader.

"Nothing yet. But they'll be here. This target is too good to pass up."

"They'd better show," fellow SWAT officer Max Lowry muttered over the internal communications channel. "I have a hundred dollars riding on it."

"Which I'll be more than happy to take off your hands when it turns out Becker is wrong," the team's resident medic-slash-sniper, Alex Trevino, added.

"Cut the chatter and stay alert," Xander growled.

Silence descended over the radio as Becker's teammates went back to watching their assigned sectors. Like him, they were positioned in a loose circle around the main warehouse, either on rooftops or hidden inside trucks or shipping containers. The idea was to let the thieves slip past them and into the warehouse. Then Xander would give the word and they'd move in, trapping the bad guys in their net. Of course, the plan would only work if the thieves made an appearance. But Becker wasn't worried. He'd studied the ring's MO long enough to know they'd show. And soon. It was as quiet as it was going to get down there.

A secure and bonded freight company like World Cargo was open for business 24-7, but there were always lulls in the workload, and the biggest one was right now, after the midnight rush and before the pace picked up again at sunrise. It might have seemed like the warehouse was deserted, but there were four security guards roaming the twelve-foot-high perimeter fence, with another stationed in an armored shack located just inside the gated entrance. Becker couldn't see them from his vantage point, but he knew there were two more guards inside the warehouse. It was risky leaving all the guards in place for this operation, but if they hadn't, the thieves would have known something was up.

Movement out of the corner of Becker's eye caught his attention, and he swung his binoculars to scan the long row of windows that covered the upper level of the warehouse. A moment later, a uniformed security guard walked past. That must have been what he'd seen.

Becker relaxed and swept his binoculars over the rest of his sector as he considered how the death of organized crime boss Walter Hardy had paved the way for these new thieves to move into the city and take over.

Hardy had been a major player in Dallas, but it wasn't until Sergeant Gage Dixon, the commander of the SWAT team, had gone all werewolf on the jackass and ripped out his throat that people really understood what kind of grip Hardy had maintained on almost every criminal enterprise in the city.

Hell, for a few blissful weeks following Hardy's death, violent crime rates had dropped to the lowest levels the city had seen in nearly forty years. Of course, that wasn't the reason Gage had killed the man. He'd ripped Hardy to pieces because the son of a bitch had been dumb enough to kidnap the woman Gage had fallen in love with. Not a smart thing to do. But Hardy's sudden departure from this earth had benefitted the local community in so many ways, Gage's action probably should have counted as a public service.

Unfortunately, nature abhors a vacuum. Within a couple months of Hardy's death, every violent offender with a gun and delusions of grandeur was making a play to take over control of the old man's territory. At first, the scumbags spent most of their time killing each other. Soon enough though, deals started being made, alliances started forming, and it looked like Dallas was heading for a serious turf war.

Then, when it seemed like things couldn't get worse, a group of outsiders showed up and the shit really hit the fan. Within weeks, they'd put a serious dent in the local criminal leadership, wiping out a lot of people in the process. In the last week alone, they'd taken out two jewelry stores, an art gallery, and an electronics store. They were good—and dangerous.

Becker was musing over how easy it had been to create a search algorithm to predict the crew's next target based on the types of places they'd already hit when another shadowy movement through the warehouse's windows caught his attention. He swung his binoculars up, expecting to see the security guard again, but instead, he saw a man dressed head to toe in black and carrying an MP5 submachine gun.

"Shit. They're already inside," he shouted into his mic.

Jumping to his feet, Becker headed for the rappelling rope, coiled and waiting for a quick descent down the backside of the building. He wrapped the rope around the snap link attached to his harness, then tossed the other end over the side.

"How the hell did they get in there without us seeing them?" Xander demanded in his ear.

"They must have come inside with one of the earlier shipments," Becker said as he stepped to the edge of the building and kicked himself backward into space.

The rope slid through his gloved hands as he sailed down from the third-floor roof in a single large bound. He ignored the heat in his hands, waiting until he was only a few feet above the ground before jerking his right hand behind his back and braking hard. His downward momentum immediately stopped. He hit the pavement, then ran toward the warehouse, sliding his M4 off his back at the same time.

"Should we try to warn them?" Khaki Blake, teammate and Xander's significant other, asked across the radio.

Becker could hear the sound of feet pounding on pavement through his earpiece—the rest of the team running for their entry positions.

"Negative," Xander ordered. "The suspects could have the guards' radios."

Becker swore as he raced to the side entrance, where he was supposed to meet up with fellow SWAT officer and explosives expert Landry Cooper. They had no idea how many bad guys were in the warehouse or where they were. If the guards weren't already dead, the suspects now had two hostages they could use as human shields to hide behind on their way out. That made this operation a hell of a lot harder.

He absently heard Xander tell the on-scene commander to keep the rest of the Dallas PD officers at a distance. Xander didn't want their fellow cops running into the building, shooting at everything that moved, including SWAT.

Cooper was already waiting at the heavy metal security door when Becker got there, his gold eyes glinting from behind his ski mask. Becker waited as Cooper punched the code into the cypher lock on the wall, then led the way. They both hesitated as soon as they got inside, waiting for the rest of the squad to signal they were ready to go.

That was when Becker realized there was something really strange going on in the warehouse—so strange that it took him a second to realize what had him pinging all of a sudden.

"Shit," he muttered, finally recognizing the familiar scent in the air. "We might have a problem, team. The guys we're going up against are werewolves. Every one of them."

There was stunned silence on the other end of the radio.

"You sure?" Xander asked.

"He's sure," Cooper answered before Becker could say anything, his North Carolina accent barely discernable. "I smell them too."

Xander's curse was terse over the radio. "Everyone, stay together and watch yourselves."

Becker didn't need to be told twice, and he doubted anyone else did either. The idea of facing criminals who were just as strong, fast, and hard to take down as the SWAT team was more than enough to keep them on their toes.

He and Cooper moved slowly through the warehouse, checking behind every box and pallet as they instinctively covered each other. How the hell had another werewolf pack moved into Dallas without them realizing it?

He was still trying to come up with an answer when gunshots sounded from the far side of the warehouse.

"Contact!" the SWAT team's lead armorer, Trevor McCall, shouted over the radio. "Khaki and I are engaged with two of them, both heavily armed. They're definitely werewolves. I put four rounds into one of them and he's still going."

More gunfire came from somewhere off to the left of Becker, then even more from the right. Bullets ricocheted off the concrete floor and steel shelving units, punching holes in shipping crates and containers, and making it damn near impossible to figure out which direction the bad guys were shooting from.

"I'm pushing the exterior security guards and the rest of the DPD to the outside perimeter," Xander announced. "We can't let regular cops engage with these guys or it'll be a bloodbath. This is all on us."

"Roger that," Becker said.

"Incoming!" Cooper shouted.

Becker turned just in time to see two hulking figures dressed eerily similar to him and Cooper—black garb and tactical vests—and toting automatic weapons, which the bad guys were aiming in their direction.

Becker ducked behind the closest wooden packing crate while Cooper dove for cover behind another as bullets whizzed past them, all six feet five inches of him managing it without getting hit. Using the crate as a shield, Becker stuck the barrel of his M4 out and took aim. He hated the idea of killing fellow werewolves, but he didn't have a choice. This crew would take him and every member of his pack down without hesitation. It was pack against pack, and there was no question about what he had to do.

Becker put two rounds through the thug on the right, just above the top of his tactical vest. The werewolf stumbled back, but then charged forward with a growl, his eyes turning a vivid yellow-gold, his lip curling in a snarl, exposing his fangs.

Becker lifted his weapon a little higher and squeezed the trigger, putting three 5.56mm ball rounds through the werewolf's forehead. That stopped him cold and he immediately went down. On the other side of the aisle, Cooper took out the second werewolf.

That left about a dozen more. They came at him and Cooper from multiple directions at once, using their keen hearing and sense of smell to pinpoint their location. They even attacked from above, climbing on top of shelving units and trying to pin them down in crossfire.

In the two years he'd been with SWAT, Becker had never gone up against anyone who was even close to being a match for him and his pack. These guys were fast and they were strong. But while they fought like berserkers, they didn't fight as a pack. That gave Becker and Cooper the advantage. When they put down yet another werewolf—this one fast and wiry, who'd climbed and hopped around on the shelving units like a frigging monkey—the rest of them turned tail and ran.

On the downside, that meant he and Cooper had to split up. It was dangerous, and Xander would have their asses for it, but it was worth the risk if they could take down this crew.

"I found the two guards," Khaki reported over the radio. "They're alive but unconscious."

Xander said something in reply, but Becker didn't hear what it was because he was too busy trying to figure out the new scent his nose had just picked up. It was unmistakably werewolf, but unlike any werewolf he'd ever smelled before. It reminded him a little of Khaki but sweeter.

He took a breath, then another and another, until he was almost hyperventilating. *Shit.* He could barely hold up his weapon.

Becker shook his head, trying to clear it as he rounded the corner, and came face-to-face with a female were-wolf so beautiful that all he could do was stop and stare. She stared back, her blue eyes as wide as saucers. Her heart beat a hundred miles an hour and there was blood splattered on the tactical vest she wore. Becker's heart lurched at the thought of her being hurt. But one sniff confirmed the blood wasn't hers. It belonged to one of the other werewolves with her.

He opened his mouth to order her to drop the MP5 she had aimed at him, but nothing would come out. It was like she'd robbed him of the ability to speak. But he had to get the weapon away from her. If she pulled the trigger, he'd be dead. Shooting her wasn't an option though, and the idea of arresting her didn't make him feel any better.

Becker didn't consider whether what he was about to do was smart but simply lowered his weapon and took his finger off the trigger, letting his M4 hang loosely against his chest by the strap over his shoulder. Then he slowly lifted both hands as if in surrender.

He'd done it to put her at ease, but her heart pounded even harder. Her eyes darted left and right, her ponytail swinging from side to side. And while she kept her weapon trained on him, at least her finger wasn't wrapped around the trigger now.

Becker pulled up the black ski mask hiding his face, then switched off his mic. When he finally managed to find his voice, he didn't want his teammates listening in.

"Relax and put down the gun," he said, keeping his voice soft and calm even though gunfire echoed in the rest of the warehouse. "We can work this out. No one else has to get hurt."

She didn't say anything or lower her weapon. She didn't run either. That was progress, he supposed.

He was wondering if he should try a different tack when Xander's voice came across loud and clear over the radio in his ear. "They're bolting, so be careful. The few left are going to fight like caged rats."

Becker didn't have to ask if the woman heard what Xander said. She was a werewolf like him, which meant she had the same exceptional hearing. If he needed further confirmation, the look of terror on her face would have been it. He couldn't blame her; her pack had just abandoned her.

Off to the right, the sounds of gunfire increased, and so did the howls. Boots thudded on the concrete floor, heading in their direction.

She looked around again, trying to see every direction at once. Her grip on her weapon tightened, and she swung it at whoever was coming their way.

Oh hell, she's going to start shooting.

Swearing under his breath, Becker closed the distance between them and ripped the MP5 out of her hands, tossing it aside. She bared her fangs in a snarl, but before she could get the sound out, he slapped a hand over her mouth.

"Trust me," he said in her ear.

Wrapping his free arm around her, he picked her up and half carried, half dragged her over to the nearest crate. Ignoring her struggles, he ripped the top off the crate, praying there'd be enough room inside. It was empty except for a rolled up painting.

"Thank you, Lord," he breathed.

Taking his hand away from her mouth, he swung her up in his arms and dumped her inside as gently as he could. She hit the bottom of the crate with an oomph, then immediately sat up.

"What are you doing?" she demanded in a voice so soft and silky it almost brought him to his knees.

He shook off the hold her voice had on him and reached for the top to the crate. "Stay here until it's safe to leave."

Ignoring her startled look, he pushed her down with one hand and pulled the lid into place with the other.

Shit, that was close.

Blowing out a breath, he turned to find Cooper standing there staring at him like he'd lost his ever-loving mind.

Cooper switched off his mic with a flick of his thumb before shoving up his ski mask, a scowl on his face. "What the fuck are you doing?"

Becker's mind whirled like an out-of-control windmill. How the hell could he explain what Cooper had seen?

He couldn't. He only hoped his friend would give him the benefit of the doubt. "Trust me. I have to do this."

Cooper opened his mouth, then closed it again. His dark eyes went to the crate, his jaw flexing. Becker tensed, ready to stop his friend if it looked like he was going to rip off the lid. But instead, Cooper gave him a long, thoughtful look, then turned and walked over to another stack of boxes.

Becker frowned as Cooper picked up one of the cardboard boxes and carried it back over to the crate where the female werewolf was hiding. Cooper ripped open the box and pulled out a big fancy decanter of what looked like whiskey. Taking off the top, he dumped the whole thing over the crate before reaching for another and doing the same thing. Becker couldn't miss the overpowering smell of jasmine and buttercups.

Not whiskey. *Perfume.*

Cooper was covering her scent. Why the hell hadn't he thought of that?

Becker grabbed two more bottles and poured it on the crate. When they were done, Cooper shoved the box of empty perfume bottles out of the way, then glared at Becker.

"You better know what the hell you're doing," he muttered before striding off.

Giving the crate one more quick look, Becker slung his weapon off his shoulder and hurried to catch up to Cooper. They reached the end of the aisle just in time to see Xander finishing off an enemy werewolf.

Xander shook his head. "Damn, these things are

psychotic. It's like they'd rather die than give themselves up." His gaze went to the section of warehouse where Becker and Cooper had been, and made a face. "Jeez, it recks down there. Is it all clear?"

Becker nodded. "No one down there."

"Good," Xander said. "Let's wrap this up then."

Becker waited until his squad leader turned and led the way to the other end of the warehouse before following.

Okay, you beautiful werewolf. I've done my part. The rest is up to you.

Chapter 2

JAYNA SAT WITH HER KNEES TUCKED UP AND HER EAR pressed against the side of the crate, straining to hear if there was anyone still in the warehouse. She normally would have used her sense of smell to determine that, but the two SWAT guys had doused the box in perfume. At first, the scent had been nice, but after breathing it in for the past six hours, she wasn't sure her nose even worked anymore.

She didn't hear anything but waited a few more minutes just to be on the safe side. Even so, she cautiously pushed up the lid and peeked around. When she didn't see anyone, she slid it aside and hopped out, almost stepping in a box of empty perfume bottles. The fancy label caught her eye—Clive Christian. Wow, that was some insanely expensive stuff. Someone was going to be pissed.

But that wasn't her problem. Getting out of the warehouse was.

Jayna slowly made her way toward the nearest exit, checking over her shoulder every few steps and ready to duck behind the nearest crate, container, or barrel. She passed a lot of yellow crime tape on the way, as well as little pieces of numbered plastic markers set out on the floor beside each and every cartridge case. She'd been too worried about staying alive to think about it at the time, but crap, there'd been a lot of shooting.

She was halfway to the door and freedom when she

remembered she was still wearing her tactical vest. If anyone was around, she didn't want them thinking she was a criminal—even if she was. Shrugging out of it, she dropped it in one of the big industrial trash cans she passed. Next, she stripped off her black sweater and threw that on top of the vest, then covered everything with the paper already in the container. Unless someone went digging, they'd never see them.

Hoping a woman in black jeans, a white T-shirt, and boots wouldn't attract too much attention, she headed for the exit. She quickened her step as she passed the bloodstains on the concrete floor, refusing to look at them. She'd seen four omega werewolves go down last night in the firefight with SWAT. Had the other two made it out? She didn't know why she cared. It wasn't like they'd been worried about her. No, they'd worried about their own asses, just like omegas always did.

But she forced those thoughts aside, focusing instead on avoiding anyone who might be walking around the place, so she wouldn't end up dead too.

There were two men and a woman standing a few yards away from the loading dock, and Jayna instinctively ducked behind a shipping container. She thought they were cops at first, but then she caught sight of the letters *CSI* on the back of their jackets. Crime scene techs on a smoke break.

Jayna chewed on her lip, wondering if she should try another exit. But that would mean wandering around the warehouse looking for one and possibly running into the cops if they were still there.

Taking a deep breath, she walked out onto the loading dock and down the steps, then headed for the main

gate as if she belonged there. Since she didn't know if
the security cameras were back on, she kept her head
down and lifted her hand in a casual wave to the security
guy and patrol officer chatting by the guard shack. Other
than staring at her ass as she walked by, neither paid her
any attention. They were here to keep people out, not
keep them in.

The moment she reached the end of the parking lot,
she darted between the warehouses there, then took off
running. Only then did she finally relax. Nobody could
catch her on foot—nobody. Even so, she didn't start
walking again until she'd put a mile between herself
and the warehouse full of crime scene techs and dried
werewolf blood.

She shuddered as she thought of what had happened
last night. If that big, hunky SWAT cop hadn't helped
her, she'd be in a jail cell right now—or dead.

As she walked along one of the smaller streets near the
airport, she reached for her cell so she could call Liam
Kinney, her pack alpha, for a ride when she realized she'd
left the burner phone in the loft. *Damn*. She'd have to take
a cab. She needed to clear her head a little before she went
back to her pack anyway. The last several weeks had been
crappy and the past few hours even worse.

Why had that big SWAT cop saved her life? She'd been
trying to figure it out since he'd tossed her in that crate.

At first, she'd thought he'd helped because he was
a werewolf like her, but that didn't pass the logic test.
If there was a bond, it sure as hell hadn't kept the other
SWAT werewolves from mowing down her so-called
pack mates like they were dead weeds.

No, there was another reason he'd helped her, and

while Jayna didn't have much use for cops, she could make an exception for this guy. Although, to be totally honest, it wasn't simply the fact that he'd saved her life that had her thinking about him so much. There was also the minor issue of being so attracted to him that she'd barely been able to comprehend what he was doing when he'd picked her up and put her in that box.

That wasn't like her. She didn't swoon over guys, regardless of how cute they were.

Maybe her strange reaction was because he was a particularly strong alpha. Maybe he put off some kind of pheromone that made female beta wolves go a little nuts. That made sense, right? The alternative was that she'd fallen in love at first sniff, which was completely crazy.

Not nearly as crazy as an all-alpha werewolf SWAT team. On top of that, she was pretty sure she'd gotten a glimpse at a female alpha.

Liam had told her there was no such thing as a female alpha. He claimed a woman could never be strong enough to control the rage that an alpha lived with every day. He'd also said there weren't any other large werewolf packs in the United States. He insisted that only a strong alpha like him could hold a group of betas together, and that alphas like him were too rare for there to be more than one or two major packs in existence at the same time in the entire world.

Well, she now had it on good authority that he was wrong on both counts. Every one of those SWAT werewolves had been well over six feet and looked stronger than a herd of bulls. And the female alpha was faster and more aggressive than anyone in Jayna's pack ever dreamed of being.

Jayna crossed the street, then cut through the parking lot to where the taxis were lined up in front of the airport terminal. She climbed into the first taxi and gave the cabbie directions to the renovated loft on Canton Street, where she and the rest of the pack were staying, then leaned back and gazed out the window.

While Liam might have been stronger than the other werewolves in her pack, he wouldn't be a match for any of those guys on the SWAT team. Jayna couldn't imagine how Liam would react if he ever came face-to-face with the werewolf who'd picked her up like a rag doll and stuffed her in that box like an oversized Christmas present. He'd probably run the other way.

Jayna mentally cringed, immediately feeling bad for thinking like that. Liam was the one who'd gotten her off the streets after she'd left home…when she'd been cold, hungry, and confused. He'd helped her understand what that night with her stepfather had turned her into, how it wasn't a bad thing, even how to control the anger inside her. With his guidance, she'd come to accept that she wasn't cursed but, instead, was amazing.

Liam had taken her into his pack and made her feel like she belonged. He'd given her friends and a new family, people who understood what she'd been dealing with because they'd dealt with it too. He'd taught her that the pack had her back, and she'd learned what it meant to trust people again. She owed him more than she could ever repay, and the rest of the pack felt the same way. He was like an older brother to all of them.

That was why they were here in Dallas stealing things for a group of Albanian mobsters when everything in her screamed they should get the hell out of Dodge.

It wasn't like they hadn't stolen stuff before. The pack's nomadic lifestyle sometimes made it hard to pay the bills and still put enough food on the table for all of them and their crazy appetites. It had only been little stuff here and there, and it had never involved carrying guns or hurting anyone. But Liam had borrowed money from a man named Armend Frasheri, the head of an Albanian crime family, and the only way Liam could pay him back was to work off his debt. If he didn't, Frasheri would kill him. It was as simple as that. And because Liam had used the borrowed money to support the pack, she and her pack mates felt obligated to go along with the plan.

Of course, they hadn't known at the time that Frasheri was a mobster—or that Liam had told the man and the thugs who worked for him that they were werewolves. But when Liam had introduced them to the crime boss, Jayna had known the pack was in trouble. Because Frasheri wanted them to act as his enforcers, using their werewolf strength to help him take over the city.

When Jayna and the others had hesitated, Liam had promised they'd leave as soon as he paid back the money he owed. That had been almost four weeks ago. And in that time, Liam had not only gotten comfortable in his new role as lead enforcer, but had also brought in omega werewolves to fill out the ranks, though where he'd found them she wasn't exactly sure.

The pack had run into omegas frequently over the years. Werewolves were rare, but they always seemed to find each other. It was like there was some kind of instinct that drew them to each other. And while the pack sure as hell never went out looking for omegas, those same omegas always seemed to come looking for them. Going it alone could be hard on a werewolf, so Jayna understood why one would want to join the pack, but that didn't mean they were stupid enough to let just any omega run with them.

Omegas were loners who were big and strong…almost as strong as alphas. But unlike alphas, omegas couldn't control their emotions or their rage. Something about being without other werewolves for company did strange things to their heads. It was like they were more animal than human, and when they lost it, look the hell out.

Even when they could control themselves, they weren't suited to pack life because they could never put the group ahead of their own wants and desires. But now, without talking it over with any of them, Liam had decided to bring them in, saying he was the pack alpha and would do whatever he felt was right.

Jayna snorted. Liam was doing that a lot more these days, deciding his opinion was the only one that mattered. She didn't care that Liam felt he had the right to do anything he wanted or that Frasheri wanted more enforcers. Omegas couldn't be trusted. She'd known the moment Liam had hired them that things were going to go bad.

She'd found out just how bad last night…over and over again. First, they'd ignored Liam's instructions to focus on the platinum medallions, instead poking around the warehouse like they were shopping at a freaking Sam's Club. Then, when the SWAT pack had shown up, the omegas had refused to fight as a team, abandoning her.

One more piece of proof that omegas couldn't be trusted to do anything but cover their asses—and that Liam had been wrong to allow them into the pack.

Jayna asked the cabbie to let her off two blocks from the loft—not because she was concerned the man would remember her or where she was staying. No, she'd hopped out early so she could delay her return just a little bit longer. It was juvenile, but she really didn't want to go back, and if it wasn't for her pack, she wouldn't have.

She nodded at the people on the street as she walked toward the industrial-style building on Canton Street. With its renovated lofts and bohemian feel, this part of Dallas was way beyond the pack's means, but with Frasheri footing the bill, that wasn't an issue. The Albanian mobster hadn't purchased just a single loft apartment either, but an entire building. Considering there were almost thirty people in addition to Frasheri living there—her pack, the omegas, and the Albanians—they needed it.

Jayna saw the two Albanians standing guard on either side of the building's front door long before they saw her, and the urge to turn around and walk away hit her again. But she kept going. She wouldn't leave her pack mates no matter how much it hurt to stay here.

How the hell had her life gotten so screwed up so fast?

The stocky, dark-haired Albanians blatantly eyed her as she walked up the wide concrete steps to the entrance of the building, but didn't say anything. They'd almost certainly heard about what had gone down last night and were probably curious why she was just now showing up. But they didn't try to stop her. They weren't dumb enough to try that.

Inside the large central atrium, someone came at Jayna so fast they were a blur. The only thing that kept her from shifting and taking a swipe with her claws was the petite, dark-haired girl's scent. Megan Dorsey wrapped Jayna in an embrace so tight she could barely breathe.

"I'm okay, Megan," she said with a strained laugh. "You can stop now."

Despite her words, Jayna didn't care if the other werewolf hugged her so hard she broke a rib. Megan was more than her closest friend in the pack; the twenty-two-year-old girl was her sister in every way that mattered. For about the hundredth time, Jayna said a silent prayer of thanks that Megan hadn't gone on the job at the warehouse with her. Quiet and gentle by nature, she wouldn't have fared well once the shooting started.

Megan finally pulled away and looked up at Jayna, her blue eyes filled with relief. "Where have you been? We were worried to death. I couldn't even call because you forgot to take your phone. Again."

Jayna opened her mouth to answer when the rest of her pack entered the lobby at a full run. All three of them stopped at the sight of her: Moe Jenkins, a muscular African American kid barely out of his teens; Joseph Garner, a twenty-eight-year-old, blond, blue-eyed farm boy from the heart of the Iowa Corn Belt; and Chris Hughes, a self-proclaimed redneck from Biloxi. Jayna's heart squeezed for a moment. As one, the guys rushed over to greet her, and together with Megan, they enveloped her in a big group hug. These four were exactly why she'd come back.

No one looking at them would ever call them a family, and in reality, the five of them couldn't be more different. But they'd all had their own violent episodes that had changed them forever.

The pack had picked up Moe about a year ago in a back alley in L.A. after he'd been beaten nearly to death by a gang who didn't like him walking in their territory at night.

Joseph had been shot while trying to help an elderly couple whose car had broken down on the side of the road. The shooters had been a bunch of teens out taking pot shots at road signs who'd decided shooting a person would be more fun.

Chris had been out celebrating with some old friends from high school when a cop had noticed their car weaving all over the road. His best friend in the world had been driving and tried to outrun the cop. After a long chase, during which Chris had begged his friend to stop, they ended up in a river after flipping the car over a dozen times. Chris had been thrown so far out of the vehicle, the police never even knew he was there, and he lay broken and bleeding for four days until his body had healed itself. He still moved with a noticeable limp thanks to a broken leg that had healed without being set straight.

And then there was Megan, whose story was worse than any of the others.

Yeah, they were a screwed-up collection of somewhat damaged people, but they were Jayna's family, and she loved them completely.

Moe was the one to finally break up the hug fest, pulling back to nudge her. "We've been glued to the TV all morning, waiting for them to say you'd been arrested. When we didn't hear anything, we really started getting worried. Where have you been?"

She was about to answer when a rough growl from across the lobby interrupted her. "That's a damn good question. Where the hell *have* you been?"

Four pairs of eyes flared into bright color as her friends responded to the accusatory tone with a partial shift and turned as one to face the big, curly-haired werewolf who'd come into the lobby.

Brandon West was one of the first omegas Liam had brought into the pack, and he was the biggest asshole of the bunch, but somehow, he'd become the informal leader of the omegas. Worse, these days, it seemed Liam spent more time with this jerk than he did with his real pack.

"What the hell do you care?" Joseph demanded. "You were one of the shitheads who ran out and left her on her own."

Brandon advanced on Joseph, clearly expecting the blond to be intimidated by his greater size and glowing eyes. It didn't work. Joseph stood his ground and bared his fangs in a low snarl.

Brandon stopped short—probably because he knew Jayna and the rest of the pack would stand with Joseph. The same couldn't be said of the few other omegas who'd drifted into the lobby. They didn't have a loyal bone in their bodies.

"I care because I have to wonder how the hell she made it out when all those other werewolves—bigger werewolves—didn't," Brandon said. "How do we know she didn't get grabbed by the cops and decide to make a deal with them?"

Jayna's hackles rose. She might be alive because some SWAT cop had saved her life for reasons she couldn't begin to understand, but those other omegas were dead because they'd been too stupid to listen to her when the raid had started. And only a dumbass omega like Brandon would think for a second that she'd betray her pack to the cops—probably because it was what he'd do.

She was just about to tear into the omega—figuratively, at least—when Brandon stunned her into silence by leaning forward and sniffing her.

"What the hell is that smell?" he muttered.

Jayna's stomach clenched. *Crap. He must smell the SWAT cop all over me.* How could he not? The guy had pulled her against his body and slapped his gloved hand across her mouth. There had to have been a scent transfer, even with the gloves and tactical vest he'd been wearing.

Her mind spun a hundred miles an hour as she tried to come up with an explanation that wouldn't paint her in a horrible light. But nothing came.

Brandon backed up a step, his lip curling. "You smell like you spent the night in a French whorehouse."

Jayna's mind faltered for a second. What the hell was this stupid jerk talking about? Then it hit her... the perfume.

She'd been sitting in the stuff for so long she barely smelled it anymore. But since Brandon had called her attention to it, she realized she did smell like a walking bottle of perfume. Thankfully, the potent fragrance overpowered every other scent that might be on her.

Now that she had a second to catch her breath and calm down, she doubted Brandon could have smelled the SWAT cop on her even if she hadn't been doused in perfume. They hadn't even realized the SWAT team had been made up of werewolves until she'd told Brandon and the others back in the warehouse. That was because omegas couldn't use their noses worth a crap. As they got older, the only werewolf abilities they seemed to

retain were their strength and aggression, and the claws
and fangs that came with them. They let most of their
finer talents simply waste away.

She grabbed at the opportunity offered by the distraction of the perfume and took a step toward the tall
omega. Brandon flinched slightly but didn't retreat.
"It's not a French whorehouse you're smelling, not that
I believe for a second you've ever been in one. What
you're smelling is Clive Christian perfume, and it's
worth almost as much as that platinum we were there to
steal. I got tossed into a whole pallet of it when I fought
with one of those SWAT cops. You remember them—
the big-ass alpha werewolves you and your omega
friends ran from like a bunch of little girls while leaving
the real girl behind to fight them by herself?"

Brandon seemed stunned. "You fought them hand
to hand?"

Jayna took another step closer and let her fangs slide
out as far as they would go. For whatever reason, her
canine teeth were starting to come in longer these days…
almost as long as Liam's. And when she was really fired
up, like now, her incisors seemed to be sharper too.
Megan had told her that made her look damn intimidating to other werewolves, especially omegas.

"That's what real werewolves do once we're out of
ammo but there's still someone in our way," she said.
"Or didn't you think I could because I'm a woman?"

Brandon looked like he wanted to say that's exactly
what he thought, but she knew he didn't have the balls
to try it. The rest of her pack standing right behind
her obviously had something to do with that. But she
noticed him eyeing her fangs and debating just how

tough she had to be if she'd stood up to those SWAT werewolves by herself.

Brandon might have gotten in a lot of fights and had the face of a lifelong bar brawler to prove it, but right then, she knew he was wondering if she was someone he should stay away from. On the other hand, he didn't want to look like a wuss in front of the other omegas—or the Albanians who'd come in while the two of them were squaring off.

Jayna was still waiting to see what Brandon would do when the sound of someone clapping cut through the tension in the room like a knife.

She turned to see Kostandin, Frasheri's trusted underboss—or "Kos" as everyone called him—leaning with his massive shoulder against a doorjamb on the far side of the lobby, his big, scarred hands slapping together in a slow, deliberate show of disdain.

"Perhaps if the rest of you had balls as big as Jayna's, last night's job would not have failed so miserably."

The man's heavily accented words were softly spoken, but he might as well have thrown a hand grenade into the room. The Albanians and omegas who'd been hanging around the edges of the atrium melted away without another word. Her pack members and Brandon were still there, but Jayna could almost taste their desire to be anywhere else. She couldn't blame them. She wanted to be someplace else too.

Even though Kostandin wasn't a werewolf, he still scared the hell out of everyone, and that seemed to include the other Albanians as well. The man was Frasheri's nephew, but the two couldn't have been more different. While Frasheri's every action seemed to be driven by a clinically detached desire to make the family richer and more powerful, Kos seemed to only care about one thing—hurting people.

She tried not to flinch when Kos walked over and put a hand on her shoulder, letting the tips of his long fingers graze her neck slightly as he squeezed possessively. "Good to see you back, she-wolf. I would have been very upset if you had died in that warehouse." He turned to eye Brandon. "More upset than I am at the loss of all those platinum medallions. If Jayna had died, I would have likely been forced to kill those I thought were at fault."

Brandon dropped his eyes to stare at the floor. Around Jayna, her pack was gazing at the marble floor just as intently. *Good*. That meant no one saw the shudder that passed through her body as Kostandin's hand slowly slid down her back and dropped away. The way he looked at her sometimes reminded her of her stepfather.

Jayna had known Kos was a sick bastard the first time she'd looked in those cold, dark eyes of his. Since then, she'd seen him go out of his way to inflict pain on people before he killed them—shooting them in the knees, cutting off fingers, slashing faces with the wicked-looking knife he always carried—all so he could see the fear in his victim's eyes before the end.

She wasn't naive enough to believe that any of the people Kos killed were innocent, not by a long shot. They'd been the worst kind of drug dealers, pimps, and gangbangers, and the Albanian mobster hadn't done anything to them that they probably hadn't done to others. But that knowledge didn't keep her from seeing those dead people every time she closed her eyes. It didn't stop the involuntary shiver that passed through her when she remembered the gleam Kos got in his eyes as he toyed with his prey either.

Beside her, Kostandin regarded her appraisingly, as if he could somehow hear what she was thinking. She frequently caught him looking at her like that. Sometimes it made her think he'd have happily put a collar around her neck so he could keep her as a pet.

Liam chose that moment to come into the lobby, and for the first time in a while, Jayna was glad for his presence, if for no other reason than it momentarily distracted Kos enough for her to put some distance between them. While not quite as tall or muscled as the SWAT werewolf, Liam was bigger than any of the Albanians and a couple of the omegas.

She gently nudged Megan and the guys toward Liam, falling into step with them.

"Jayna, you're back!"

The concern in Liam's voice seemed genuine, but the smile on his face didn't quite reach his hazel eyes. He seemed more concerned with reading the situation, probably trying to see if her disappearance last night would reflect poorly on him.

"Liam." Kostandin's tone stopped her pack leader in his tracks. "I thought you said there weren't any other alpha werewolves in this country."

Liam looked shocked for a moment, but he quickly recovered. "There aren't. I told you, Brandon made a mistake. Those SWAT cops might have been werewolves, but they sure as hell weren't alphas."

Kos didn't answer for a long time, and the silence started to become uncomfortable. Finally, he turned and speared Jayna with a look. "You just said they were alphas. Were you mistaken?"

Liam grumbled something under his breath she couldn't make out. But what was she supposed to do, lie and say that the werewolves who'd taken out the pack omegas had just been big boned?

She lifted her chin. "They were alphas."

Liam opened his mouth to say something, but Kostandin cut him off. "How many alphas?"

Jayna didn't answer right away. She had no idea how many werewolves they'd faced. She tried to remember how many different scents she'd smelled. She'd picked up at least five of them, including the woman. Not that she was even considering saying anything about her. If Liam had a cow about there being other alphas in Dallas, he'd lose his mind if she told him there was a female alpha too.

She opened her mouth to tell Kostandin how many alphas she'd seen when a sudden unexplainable impulse to drop the number by one hit her. Was she actually feeling protective about the SWAT guy who'd saved her life? Did she really think she'd be helping him if the Albanian thought there were less of them than there really were?

That was stupid. If the Albanians thought they were facing an overwhelming number of these SWAT werewolves, maybe they'd say the hell with Dallas, and she and the rest of the pack could be done with them.

"Well?" Kos prompted.

"Seven at least," she said. "Maybe eight."

Her answer earned a gasp from Liam and the rest of her pack. She couldn't blame them. She was having a hard time imagining that many alphas all living together, much less functioning as a team.

Kos frowned. "All alphas? You're sure of that?"

"Yes." She jerked her head in Brandon's direction. "As I'm sure he told you, they were all big, fast, and strong. I got away, but it was more luck than anything."

She was hoping that last little part might convince Kos this was a no-win situation, but he merely nodded thoughtfully, then looked at Liam.

"Start figuring out exactly what we're up against," he ordered. "Find out if there are more alphas than Jayna saw, where they live, and when they're most vulnerable."

Liam's eyes sharpened. "We're going after them?"

Kostandin didn't answer. He didn't have to. All it took was one glimpse of the sick gleam in the Albanian's eyes to know that he intended to kill every member of the other werewolf pack in the most vicious way possible.

Kos walked away with Liam and Brandon following closely behind. As they were leaving the lobby, she heard Brandon asking when they would strike and Kostandin saying something about patience. She could have kept eavesdropping on the conversation and probably heard the rest of their plan, but she resisted. The way her stomach was twisting in knots, she decided she didn't want to know what they were planning to do.

Megan and the guys looked at Jayna as if they expected her to come up with a way out of this for all of them. They'd agreed to this job because of Liam, but none of them had signed up for killing anybody—not cops and especially not other werewolves. But the way this was shaping up, they might not have a choice. Kostandin and his Albanians wouldn't think twice about going after those SWAT werewolves, and Liam seemed to be willing to go along with anything Kos suggested. Even Brandon and his omegas would be happy to help.

Trying to stand against both the Albanians and the omegas? That was a fight their small pack couldn't win. All they could do was go along and hope a chance to get out of this situation presented itself.

Could she really just sit back and let Kostandin and the others go after those SWAT werewolves—especially the one who had saved her life—without doing anything? She didn't want to, but it wasn't like she could warn them. She'd never caught her savior's name, and she sure as hell couldn't call in an anonymous tip to the hunky werewolf with the amazing blue eyes.

What the hell was she going to do?

Chapter 3

"SO WHAT THE HELL ARE YOU GOING TO DO?" COOPER asked Becker the moment they were inside the armory's security cage.

Tuffie, the team's unofficial mascot, had followed them into the building, figuring something must be up if the two of them were slipping off to the most private place on the SWAT compound right in the midst of all the insanity going on. The pit bull mix took up a position by the door like she was standing guard. Becker shook his head. Maybe that was exactly what she *was* doing. Sometimes Becker thought that dog understood more than anyone gave her credit for.

Cooper had been trying to talk to him privately ever since they'd gotten back to the compound this morning, but they hadn't had a chance to slip away until a few minutes ago. When you worked with fifteen other werewolves, all of whom had incredibly good hearing, finding a little privacy could be tough.

Becker wasn't surprised that everyone was losing their minds. It wasn't every day they got into a gun battle with another pack of werewolves. And while Xander's squad had technically won—taking down five of the nearly psychotic werewolves from the mob pack—nobody was in the mood to cheer. Their success had come at a cost. Hale Delaney, along with Max and Alex, had been hit with multiple rounds from the other pack's submachine guns. If they hadn't been werewolves, they'd all be dead. As if that weren't bad enough, Khaki had been bitten. Seriously…bitten. She'd shot one of the enemy werewolves eight times, and the guy had still been able to get his fangs latched on to her shoulder. Khaki would be fine, but Xander was still so pissed that no one could even look at him without earning a snarl.

Becker leaned back against the counter separating the weapons and ammo area from the front of the building. "Do about what?"

Cooper looked at him like he was insane. Even Tuffie's jaw dropped. Hell, maybe he was a little nuts. After nearly half a day to think about it, he still had no idea why he'd behaved the way he had around that female werewolf. Not only had he not arrested her, but he had hidden her in a box so no one else could either. That wasn't exactly normal.

"You're joking, right?" Cooper said. "You know you have to tell Gage and Xander about that female werewolf. You got a good look at her face. If we can ID her, she could lead us to the rest of her pack."

Becker's gut clenched. Some part of him knew it was the right thing to do. Shit, her pack had nearly beaten those poor security guards to death. On top of that, there were at least six other werewolves out there besides her, all probably just as insane and out of control as the ones they'd killed at the warehouse. But he couldn't betray her. He didn't understand why, but he couldn't.

"I can't do that," he said.

"Why the hell not?" Cooper demanded. "She's a criminal. Shit, Becker, she pointed her automatic weapon at you."

"But she didn't pull the trigger," he argued. "She could have, but she didn't. She's not like the others. She's not a criminal."

Cooper snorted. "How can you know that?"

Becker knew his friend was just trying to get him to see reason, which normally would have been a good approach. But as far as this woman was concerned, reason didn't enter into the picture. For the first time in his life, he was making decisions based purely on instinct and emotion. He was usually linear and calculating. This should have been freaking him out, but the funny part was that it felt right.

He ran a hand through his short, dark blond hair and sighed. "I can't tell you how I know…I just do. She's different. You have to believe me when I say that. And whatever you do, you can't tell Gage or anybody else about her."

Cooper pulled a tall metal stool out from behind the counter and sat down. Tuffie left her place by the door and moved closer, as if she really wanted to hear the next part of their conversation.

"Becker, you're asking me to lie to Gage and the rest of the team about something that could get a lot of people killed, so no bullshitting. You need to be completely honest with me on this." Cooper pinned him with a hard look. "Are you doing this because you think a woman you've known all of sixty seconds could be *The One* for you?"

Ever since Gage had met Mac, the rest of the SWAT team had been seeing *The One* in every woman who gave them a casual glance. After Xander met Khaki, it had only gotten worse. It was the number one topic of conversation whenever they had some downtime. Hell, even when they were on incidents. Becker was just as guilty as the other guys when it came to wondering if there was someone special out there for him.

Right now, though, his first impulse was to say *Hell no!* He'd exchanged half a dozen words with her in all of thirty seconds. It's not like he was in love with her or anything like that. He was asking Cooper to lie for him because he thought she was innocent and because… well, she seemed nice.

Shit, that was lame.

The longer he stood there trying to come up with an answer, the longer Cooper's theory had to sink in. Was his friend right? Was the reason he'd reacted so strongly to this beautiful werewolf because they were somehow linked together like Gage and Mac, and Xander and Khaki?

That was crazy. The odds were incredibly stacked against a werewolf ever meeting his one-in-a-billion soul mate. There was no way Becker could have met his in the midst of an armed robbery. That kind of crap didn't happen in the real world.

But it had happened for Gage and Xander. So maybe it had happened for him too.

He pushed at a piece of dirt on the floor with the toe of his boot before finally shrugging. "I don't know. Maybe."

Cooper folded his arms, his dark eyes regarding Becker thoughtfully. "Are you sure you're not just projecting? That you want this woman to be *The One* so badly you're willing to overlook anything that doesn't fit?"

"What the hell does that mean?" Becker demanded. He pushed away from the counter. "Since when did you turn into Dr. Phil?"

Cooper held up his hands. "I'm just saying. I know you've been looking around the next corner for that one-in-a-billion babe for you ever since Gage met Mac. I get it."

Becker didn't say anything. Cooper was right. He hadn't had a serious relationship since he'd gone through his change, and if there was a perfect woman out there for him, he wouldn't turn a blind eye to her—or turn her in to his fellow cops.

"So what if I am eager to find *The One* for me?" he asked. "What kind of dumbass werewolf *wants* to live his life alone?"

Cooper seemed to think about that. "I get what you're saying. But given that you really, really want this woman to be *The One*, are you sure you aren't just seeing what you want to see?"

"No. I'm telling you, there's something about her." Becker eyed his friend. "So…are you going to say anything to Gage?"

Cooper looked to Tuffie for help, but the dog's expression remained happily neutral, as if to say Cooper was on his own with this one.

Cooper muttered something under his breath. "Why am I the one who has to keep everybody's secrets when they're doing something stupid?"

Becker chuckled, remembering how Cooper had kept Xander and Khaki's relationship secret from everybody on the team for a while. "Because you're so good at it."

Cooper shook his head. "Okay, so we don't tell Gage and the rest of the Pack. What do we do then?"

Becker frowned. "Hold on. There is no *we*. I've already gotten you in deep enough by asking you to lie for me."

"If this all goes south, it's not like Gage and Xander will go easier on me because all I did was lie to them," Cooper pointed out. "It's in my best interest to make sure this all works out right. If it doesn't, we'll probably both end up getting punched through a brick wall. So, how can I help?"

Dammit, Cooper could be stubborn. Becker should have told his friend that he didn't want him involved, but the truth was, he could use the help. And as Cooper pointed out, Gage would be pissed anyway. Then again, Gage was always pissed about something.

"The first thing we need to do is get out of here so I can do some digging," he told Cooper. "Think you can come up with an excuse without making anyone suspicious?"

Cooper thought about it for a moment, then grinned. "Yeah. We tell Gage the truth."

Becker gaped. Had Cooper missed the part where he said they couldn't tell anyone about the werewolf babe?

But Cooper was already out the door with Tuffie at his heels, leaving Becker no choice but to catch up.

Cooper's version of the truth was telling Gage that the two of them wanted to check out the warehouse to see if they could find something that would lead to the other pack. Becker had expected it to be harder than that, but Gage hadn't even batted an eye.

Cooper glanced at Becker as they headed to the parking lot. "See how easy things are when you tell the truth?"

Becker just snorted as he walked over to his bike. He could have ridden with Cooper, but since Becker didn't know where the trail might lead, he figured he might need his wheels, so he took his Harley instead. Besides, the ride might help him get his head right where that

female werewolf was concerned. Could she really be
The One? Yes, he'd been immediately attracted to her
and so rattled that he'd barely been able to think, but
shouldn't he have felt something more definitive? Gage
and Xander claimed they'd known they'd met their soul
mates the moment they saw them. Why hadn't he?

Unless being attracted to a woman even though she'd
been pointing a weapon in his face at the time actually
was a sign he'd met *The One*.

Stupid thoughts like that were still bouncing around his
head when they arrived at the warehouse. He pushed them
aside as he parked his bike beside Cooper's Wrangler.

Cooper motioned to the helmet strapped to the backseat as Becker climbed off his Harley. "Why do you
carry that if you never wear it?"

Becker shrugged. "Never know when you're going to
meet a safety-conscious hottie looking for a ride."

"If she was safety conscious, wouldn't she want you
to wear a helmet too?"

"Huh. Never really thought about it that way."

"Yeah, I figured you hadn't," Cooper said drily.
"And as long as you're thinking about it, you might
want to consider that a safety-conscious hottie probably
wouldn't want to ride on a motorcycle anyway. There's
a reason doctors call them 'organ donor vehicles.'"

"I guess I'm just looking for a regular hottie then,"
Becker said. "Forget the safety-conscious part."

Cooper just shook his head and fell into step beside
Becker. The crime scene techs were done processing
the warehouse, but the young patrol officer left on duty
still signed them into the logbook before letting them
go inside.

"Were you guys part of the SWAT team that took down that crew this morning?" the patrolman asked. Then he hurried on enthusiastically, "I got a look inside. It was like a combat zone. Must have been crazy, huh?"

Becker nodded but didn't say anything.

"World Cargo had its insurance people in here a little while ago," the officer continued. "I heard them say the suspects who got away made it out with something like fifty of those platinum medallions. That's a pretty big haul, right?"

Becker headed into the warehouse, leaving Cooper to deal with the overeager patrolman. Guarding an inactive crime scene had to be boring as hell, and any other time, he would have chatted with the guy, but right now, he had some urgent crap to take care of.

He headed straight for the crate where he'd told the female werewolf to hide but stopped midstride when he picked up her scent by a big trash can. He dug through papers and cardboard until he came up with her light-weight tactical vest and black sweater. Smart girl. She'd dumped them so she wouldn't look suspicious. He checked them for anything he could use to track her, but the stuff was clean.

He could have followed her scent out of the ware-house, but he knew that wouldn't lead anywhere but a dead end wherever she'd gotten into a vehicle. No were-wolf's nose was good enough to follow her beyond that.

He continued on to the crate and was just climbing inside to look around when Cooper showed up.

"What are you looking for?" his friend asked. "I'm pretty sure she didn't leave her phone number in there for you."

"Probably not," Becker agreed. "I'm hoping I can find something that might give me a clue about who she is."

Cooper rested his forearm on the edge of the crate. "You know, this would have been a lot easier if you'd remembered to get her name."

"Yeah, well, I was a little distracted at the time."

Becker hunkered down in the tight confines of the box, envisioning the beautiful female werewolf doing the same thing as he breathed in her incredible scent. Despite the perfume permeating the wood, he could still smell her.

"So what was it?" Cooper asked as Becker rummaged through the packing material in the bottom of the crate.

Becker glanced up at his friend. "What do you mean?"

"What was it about her that got to you? Was it her face? Her scent? The way she talked?"

Becker stopped what he was doing to lean back and consider the question. "I'm not sure," he finally admitted. "I've been asking myself the same thing all day and still haven't come up with the answer."

He let his butt slide down until he was sitting in the same cramped space where the female werewolf had sat, except she'd done it with the lid closed and cops wandering around just outside the thin wooden walls. The thought of her being trapped and scared in here suddenly made him want to growl and tear into something—violently. He resisted the urge and instead forced himself to take a deep breath and focus on the question Cooper had asked.

"She was beautiful," he finally said. "You know when people say someone has the face of an angel? Well, that was her. It completely took my breath away. She smelled

amazing too. Like a cherry lollipop. And her voice…
her voice was soft and just a little bit husky. She was
so perfect, I swore my heart was about to explode." He
shook his head. "It was more than all that though. I can't
explain it, but something inside me knew she was special. Something told me I could spend the rest of my life
looking and never find another woman like this one."

Cooper lifted a brow. "Wow, that's pretty…epic."

Becker chuckled. "Yeah, I guess it is. Of course, now
I have to find her, or I'll be the werewolf known for
losing the woman who might just be *The One*."

He was about to hop out of the crate when a little
slip of paper different in color than the rest of the packing material caught his eye. He picked it up to get a
better look.

It was a partial receipt from a Starbucks for a cinnamon dolce latte with a time stamp from three days ago
just before noon. Unfortunately, the part with the credit
card information was missing. There wasn't even a store
number or address. He had no idea which Starbucks the
latte had been purchased at or the name of the person
who had bought it, but he didn't need any of that.

"What's that?" Cooper asked, leaning in for a look.

Becker held up the tiny scrap of paper so his friend
could see it. "This is the clue that's going to help me find
a certain female werewolf."

Cooper frowned. "How do you even know it's hers?"

Becker held the piece of paper under Cooper's nose.
"Of course it's hers. Smell it."

Cooper sniffed, then shrugged. "If you say so. I'll
agree that might be a werewolf's scent on there, maybe
even female, but that doesn't mean it's hers. She could

have sat on it or something. That receipt could lead you to Mario the plumber."

Becker vaulted out of the crate with a laugh. "I don't know why you even bother sniffing anything. Your nose hasn't been right since you were trapped down in that tunnel full of homemade explosives a few months ago. Trust me, this thing smells like cherry lollipops. It's hers."

"Okay, let's assume you're right and that piece of paper belonged to your mystery werewolf girl," Cooper said as they headed for the exit. "There's nothing on it. How's it going to help you find her?"

"That's the easy part," Becker told him as they walked out of the warehouse. He nodded at the poor patrolman still standing at the gate. "All I have to do is get on a computer and start violating about a hundred state and federal laws. I should have an answer by tomorrow."

"I probably don't want to know exactly what you're planning on doing," Cooper said. "That way, I can't be forced to testify against you when the NSA swoops in and arrests your ass."

"Probably a good idea," Becker agreed as he climbed on his bike and cranked it into rumbling life.

Cooper leaned in close to be heard over the engine. "Is there anything I can do to help?"

Becker didn't answer. His best friend was offering to do something illegal if Becker told him it would help find his mystery werewolf. All he had to do was ask.

But just because Cooper would willingly risk everything to help him find this woman didn't mean Becker had the right to ask him. Becker liked to think the female werewolf wasn't like the other werewolves at the warehouse, that she was simply in over her head, but he didn't know that. If he was able to track her down, it might be to discover she wasn't the woman he thought.

If any of this went bad, it probably wouldn't end well for him—or anyone helping him.

He shook his head. "Nah. I just to need some time to find her. Do you think you could cover for me with Gage and Xander? I can't do what I have in mind with those crappy computers we have in the office."

"Yeah, I can do that," Cooper said. "But be careful, okay? People catch you hacking, getting kicked off the SWAT team will be the least of your problems. The feds put people in prison for the crap you're talking about doing."

Becker nodded absently, already busy developing a plan—one that involved him hacking into Starbucks's credit card system to figure out which stores in the greater Dallas/Fort Worth area had sold a cinnamon dolce latte around the time stamp on the receipt. Then he'd slip into the array of traffic cameras around the city to take a peek at the stores in question. All he had to do then was match the face of the werewolf he was looking for with a credit card receipt, and he'd have her.

He was so engrossed in the technical challenge that lay ahead of him—not to mention groaning at the thought of how many hours he'd have to spend looking at grainy video footage—that he barely remembered his friend was still there until Cooper gripped his shoulder.

"I'm serious," Cooper said. "I know you really want to find this woman, but you need to be careful. Even if she is everything you hope she is, that doesn't mean her pack mates are going to be too friendly if they figure out you're the one who killed some of their members."

Becker hadn't given that part of the equation any consideration at all. *Shit*. He'd been so focused on finding her that he hadn't even thought about how he was going to deal with the rest of her pack.

He shrugged. "I'm not that worried about it. Once I get a chance to talk with her face-to-face, I'll be able to convince her to leave her pack and run away with me."

Cooper looked dubious. "Has it ever occurred to you that this woman might not even find you attractive?"

"No."

Grinning, he punched his foot down, shifted the bike into first gear, and tore out of the warehouse parking lot.

Becker's smile faded as he turned onto the road. After the way he'd reacted to the female werewolf, it was difficult not thinking he'd stumbled across the one woman in the universe he was meant to be with. But what if after going through all kinds of hell to track her down, he discovered she didn't feel the same about him? Just because she might be *The One* for him, there was nothing in the legend that ensured he was *The One* for her. For all he knew, she might be in love with someone already—like some maladjusted werewolf from her own pack.

That thought depressed him, but he forced himself to push the nagging doubts aside. It wasn't going to happen that way, he told himself firmly. He was going to find her, and when he did, she was going to feel exactly the same way about him that he felt about her.

It wasn't until that moment that Becker realized how much he'd already invested in the female werewolf. Had Gage and Xander felt this overwhelming pull the moment they'd met their future mates?

He only hoped his situation worked out as well as theirs had. But then again, neither one of them had fallen for a rogue werewolf who was part of a pack trying to take over the city.

Chapter 4

"MAKE SURE YOU TAKE OUT THE TWO GUARDS THE moment you step through the door."

Liam gestured at the hand-drawn sketch of the drug lab that he, Kostandin, and Brandon had been going over for the last hour or so on the far side of the atrium. From the sounds of it, they'd be hitting the place in the next day or two. Jayna prayed they wouldn't take anyone from her pack with them.

It was bad enough to hear Kos so casually talking about taking two people's lives. But hearing her alpha talk about killing two people—people who had never done a damn thing to their pack and likely never would—made her feel ill.

She couldn't sit around and listen to it anymore.

"Where are you going?" Liam asked when she pushed away from the wall and started for the door.

She gritted her teeth at the suspicion in his voice. "To Starbucks," she said over her shoulder, not bothering to ask if he or anyone else wanted anything. That suspicion had been showing up more and more since they'd started working for the Albanians. It was like he knew how much she disapproved of what he was asking the pack to do. For all she knew, maybe an alpha could pick up on stuff like that.

Fortunately, she had a reputation as someone who couldn't sit still for very long. Liam and the rest of her pack had known that for a long time, and the Albanians and omegas had figured it out pretty quick.

She could feel Liam's gaze following her as she crossed the atrium, and she slid him a sidelong glance out of the corner of her eye. That was when she realized that Kos was watching her just as intently—only his gaze was way more disconcerting than Liam's. He might have been thinking sexual thoughts about her, which was skeevy enough for sure, but he also might have been imagining what it would be like to cut off her fingers one by one. With him, there was no way to tell.

Outside, Jayna turned left and headed down the sidewalk. There was a Starbucks about six blocks in that direction where she liked to hang out and people watch while drinking her latte. It was a good place to get away from the crap going on in the loft.

She was a block from the coffee shop when she caught a familiar scent on the breeze. *It can't be.*

Pulse skipping, she whirled around and saw the hunky, blue-eyed SWAT cop from the warehouse casually leaning against the corner of a building watching her.

Crap.

Where the hell had he materialized from? She'd just come from that direction and hadn't seen—or smelled—him.

Jayna darted a glance left and right, expecting to see a million cops descending on her, but all she saw were normal, everyday people going about their business. Even more puzzling, she didn't sense anything bad coming down on her. Ever since going through her change, she'd been able to feel when things were about to go sideways, like they had back in the warehouse. But right now she wasn't getting that sensation, and it worried the hell out of her. Could an alpha like this SWAT cop somehow block her senses?

She looked back at him, expecting to see him coming toward her. She was surprised to find him still standing exactly where he'd been before, looking way too calm and casual for her taste. In a pair of faded jeans, black motorcycle boots, and a pullover hoodie, he looked good. Damn good. He was even grinning.

She had to admit he had a nice smile...for a cop. His scent was also a lot more interesting than she'd remembered. Had he smelled that delicious back in the warehouse?

Jayna took a small step back and almost fell off the curb. She caught herself, resisting the urge to look around to see how many people had seen her. There was no way she was going to take her eyes off him.

The smile slowly slipped from Officer Hunky's face, and he took a step in her direction. Panic gripped her. She really liked it more when he smiled. It didn't make him any less intimidating, but at least she could tell herself that he wasn't measuring her for a prison jumpsuit.

She slowly edged to the right, but he angled to intercept her. She moved faster, still afraid to take her eyes off him. He moved with her, taking a longer stride, and she gulped at how much ground he was able to cover with those muscular legs of his. What the hell? Why was she thinking about how hot he was? He intended to arrest her and send her to prison for the rest of her life!

Maybe he saw the panic in her eyes or smelled it in the air. Whatever it was, he picked up the pace and in three strides nearly cut the distance between them in half.

The hell with this!

Jayna turned and took off running straight down the middle of the one-way road. She had to dodge around a few angry drivers, but it was better than trying to race through the crowd of people on the sidewalk. She crossed over the next street against the light, running even faster.

Boots thumped the pavement behind her, but she wasn't too worried. No way in hell could a guy as big and muscular as Officer Hunky catch her. She'd been a fast runner before going through her change, but now she was a freaking gazelle.

Four blocks later, she darted through an alley, then sprinted down the sidewalk on the other side. She glanced over her shoulder and nearly screamed in surprise. The SWAT cop was only a few yards behind her, running with an easy stride and that same lazy grin on his face. With the wind in her face, she hadn't been able to pick up his scent.

She dug deep and put on every shred of speed she had, not caring who saw. Liam had told her to never run this fast in public, but she doubted Liam had ever been chased by a mountainous werewolf cop who was apparently half-cheetah as well. *Screw the rules*.

The farther she ran, the more industrial the area became and the fewer people there were on the street. As a criminal running from a cop, that shouldn't have bothered her, but as a female beta running from an alpha big enough to eat her, it terrified the crap out of her. If she couldn't get away from him, maybe she should head back into a more crowded area.

She glanced over her shoulder again to see the

blue-eyed SWAT cop in the exact same position he'd been in before.

"You're pretty fast, but I'm faster," he said. "And since I could do this all day, you might as well stop so I can talk to you."

Stop so they could talk? He must think she was stupid.

Jayna should have called his bluff and kept running, but she was so pissed off, she stomped on the brakes, forcing him to dodge to the side to avoid crashing into her. She got some satisfaction from the fact that it took him five feet to bring himself to a full stop, and even then he still almost fell on his ass. But he quickly got it together and spun around to face her. She backpedaled as he came toward her.

He immediately stopped and held up his hands. "I'm not going to hurt you—or arrest you. I just want to talk." He lifted the bottom of his hoodie. "See? No gun."

There might not be a gun, but there was a mesmerizing expanse of muscles there. Thank God he lowered his shirt or she'd still be staring at them.

"Why aren't you turning me over to your cop friends right now?" she demanded.

He shrugged. "To tell the truth, I have absolutely no idea. But let's talk anyway."

The answer was so unexpected—and so honest—that she couldn't help but believe him. She knew it was stupid, yet something told her the big SWAT cop really wasn't there to bust her. But just because she thought he wasn't planning to slap cuffs on her in the next five seconds, that didn't mean she was going to be friendly.

She folded her arms. "Okay. So talk."

He looked around at the surrounding buildings with

their broken windows and boarded-up doors, and she knew he was thinking this was a crappy place to talk. But it wasn't like she could invite him back to the loft with her. That would go over so well with her alpha. And she was sure the Albanians would just be delighted.

This is one of the alpha SWAT cops I mentioned. He wants to chat, so could you give us some privacy?

Officer Hunky turned his blue eyes on her. "My bike is parked just a few blocks from here. I was hoping we could go for a ride and find another coffee shop." When she didn't answer, he added, "Just to talk, Jayna. I promise."

Her heart stopped. "How do you know my name?"

He winced, as if realizing he'd let something out of the bag, then ran a hand through his dark blond hair. "Um, yeah. I know your name—at least the name on the debit card you use to buy your lattes. But no one else knows. Not even my pack."

Again, she didn't know why, but she believed him. Still, it freaked her out that a man she'd known for all of thirty seconds knew her name—and her debit card number. She was about to ask how the hell he knew when he interrupted her with that charming dimpled grin of his.

"By the way, my name is Eric Becker. And I can give you my credit card number if it makes you feel better."

She suddenly found herself forgetting her anger and instead thinking about how nice his name was. He looked like an Eric—big, strong, and handsome. And let's not forget that great smile. Suddenly, Jayna couldn't remember what it was she'd been concerned about just a few moments earlier.

"So, you okay with the coffee shop idea?" he asked.

If she said no, then what? He obviously knew where she lived, so even if she could get away from him, he'd only go to the loft and wait for her to show up.

She nodded, gesturing for him to walk ahead of her, then followed as he turned and led her back in the direction they'd come. She kept her distance, still cautious he might try something, though she wasn't sure what. And as fast as he could move, she wasn't sure she could stop him if he did try something.

She was surprised when he turned in a public parking lot after a few blocks. But the bigger surprise came when they stopped in front of an expensive-looking red-and-black Harley. That's when she remembered him saying something about having a bike. She'd been so freaked over him knowing her name, she must have missed that little detail.

He undid the chin straps on the helmet attached to the small square of leather-covered cushion that constituted a backseat. How did he expect her to sit on that? It would be like balancing her butt on a piece of two-by-four. She was just realizing the small seat probably meant she was going to have to put her arms around him if she wanted to stay on the bike when another thought popped into her head.

"Did you park here knowing I'd run this way or is it just coincidence?"

She hoped it was the latter. If this guy was so good that he could figure out which way she was going to run before she even decided herself, she was completely screwed.

He handed her the helmet, then got on the bike. "A little bit of both actually. I was hoping you wouldn't run, but if you did, I figured it'd be down this way."

"But how did you know I'd stop?" she asked.

He tilted the bike to the side and used his heel to shove up the kickstand, then turned that devastating smile on her. "Honestly, I expected you to get tired and stop well before we got here. But you're in better shape than I gave you credit for, and a hell of a lot faster." He motioned with his chin toward the back of the bike. "Get on. I promise not to bite—unless you ask nicely."

As she eyed the small backseat, she realized she should have probably been insulted by that comment about being in better shape than he thought. But she got the feeling he was trying to give her a compliment. Strangely, she found herself liking the silly idea that he thought she was fast. But just because she appreciated his compliment, that didn't mean she was ready to jump on the bike with him yet.

"How do I know you won't just take me to the nearest police station?" she asked.

He pushed a switch, making the bike rumble and vibrate. She'd never been on a motorcycle before, hadn't even stood this close to one while it was running. It felt powerful.

"I guess you'll just have to trust me," he said. "Besides, if I wanted to arrest you, I would have done it already."

Jayna couldn't argue with that. She put on the helmet, then cinched the chin strap and climbed on the bike.

"Why aren't you wearing a helmet too?" she asked as she tried to figure out how to position her feet on the metal pegs below her and where to put her hands. She finally reached around and twisted her hands into the material of his hoodie, just above his hips. She couldn't help but notice the rippling of his abs and hip flexors as he pushed the heavy bike backward out of the parking space.

He grinned at her over his shoulder. "I only have one helmet and I figure it's more important to protect your pretty face than my ugly mug."

She found herself smiling back at him. It had been a long time since any guy had thrown so many compliments her way, even ones so cheesy. But cheesy or not, she appreciated them.

Eric pulled the bike out onto the road, heading back toward Canton Street and the center of the city. She almost fell off as he sped up, and she had no choice but to lean in closer and wrap her arms more firmly around his waist. Not only did it press her breasts tightly against his muscular back, but it also put her hands really close to a part of his body she refused to let herself think about. She focused on his scent instead. He smelled even better than he had in the warehouse, and it wasn't long before she had to lick her lips to keep from drooling. What was going on? She'd never felt like this around a guy before, not even another werewolf.

After a few minutes of zipping in and out of traffic, she had to admit this motorcycle thing was more fun than she'd expected. Being able to see the road racing by under her feet while the wind whipped across her face and through her hair was pretty cool. It was a lot like the sensation of freedom she felt when she got out in the country and could run as fast as she wanted. It made her feel like she could outrun all the problems waiting for her back at the loft.

She was almost disappointed when the bike slowed and Eric turned into the parking lot of another Starbucks.

They were less than two miles from the loft, but it was far enough off the main road that there wasn't much chance of anyone she knew stumbling on them.

By the time Eric ordered their drinks, she'd gotten most of his scent out of her nose and cleared her head enough to think straight. The ride had been nice, but there were some things she needed to know—now.

"So, Cop. How did you find me?" she asked the moment they sat down at a table in the corner.

He took a sip of his boring black coffee before answering. Why go to a Starbucks and order plain coffee? That was like going to a pizza place and ordering a cheese sandwich.

"Like I said, the name's Eric," he said as he set down his cup. "But my friends call me Becker."

"Okay, how did you find me…Eric?"

He didn't seem bothered by her snarky jab. Instead, he motioned toward her drink. "That."

"My cinnamon dolce latte?"

"I found a partial Starbucks receipt with your scent on it in that crate at the warehouse. It had the name of that drink and a time stamp on it."

She stared at him, trying to understand how he'd gotten from a scrap of paper with a few meaningless bits of data on it to actually sitting in front of her in a single day.

"You had a receipt with a time stamp and you found me just like that?"

He gave her what could only be a sheepish look. "Not exactly. It took a bit more work than that. First, I hacked into the credit card processing company that handles the Starbucks stores in the Dallas area, then dug through hundreds of card swipes until I came up with a list of stores that made a credit sale matching the cost of your drink and the time stamp. Then I slipped into the traffic and online security cameras around each of those stores and spent a few more hours watching grainy surveillance videos until I saw you walking down Canton Street a few minutes after buying your coffee."

She couldn't believe he'd spent all that time tracking her down just so he could talk to her. "But…how did you find out my name?"

He shrugged, looking slightly embarrassed. It was crazy seeing a guy as big as Eric looking like he'd been caught with his hand in the cookie jar.

"Once I confirmed which Starbucks you went to, I was able to dig a little deeper into your credit history. It's not hard to get a name when you do that. Though I had no way of knowing if it was fake or not. Is Jayna Winston your real name?"

She nodded. There was no reason to lie. He could obviously verify her name if he wanted to. He was good with a computer, and she'd never made an effort to hide her identity in the years since leaving Detroit. She hadn't left much of a footprint before joining the pack, and afterward, they didn't hang around any place long enough to leave an indelible mark.

"So you decided to come and hang around Starbucks until I showed up?" she asked.

"Pretty much." He sipped his coffee. "I got to the area a couple hours ago and sniffed around a bit to make sure I was right. All the werewolf scents in the area told me I was, so I backed off and waited for you to make another coffee run. I figured I wouldn't have to wait too long." His mouth quirked. "You seem addicted to your lattes."

"You did all that—hacking into computer systems, watching endless hours of video, hanging around a coffee shop half the morning—just to find me? Why?"

He stopped smiling, his blue eyes suddenly serious. "It seemed like you were in a lot of trouble back in that warehouse. I thought I should find you and try to help."

Since going through her change almost five years ago, Jayna had gotten freaky good at figuring out when people were lying to her, and right now, those instincts were telling her that Eric wasn't being completely honest. But those same instincts told her that she could trust him in spite of that. Whatever he was hiding, it didn't involve arresting her.

"What makes you think I'm in trouble?" She broke off a piece of the coffee cake he'd bought her and nibbled on it. "Maybe I'm the kind of girl who robs warehouses all the time."

His mouth curved into a half smile. "You're a lot of amazing things, Jayna, but you're not that kind of girl. Your heart was thumping a thousand miles an hour when you saw me in that warehouse, even more when you heard over my radio that the other members of your pack had abandoned you."

She snorted. "Trust me, those guys aren't my pack."

"Then why were you running with them?"

Jayna didn't know why she was hesitating, especially after the omegas had left her to fend for herself. She didn't owe them anything.

"It's not by choice," she finally admitted. "They're a group of omegas my alpha brought in to serve as muscle for the Albanian mobsters my real pack and I are stuck working for."

His mouth twitched. "That sounds like something out of a James Bond movie, you know that, right?"

That was way funnier than it should have been given the situation, and she had to bite her lip to keep from laughing. "I've never been a really big fan of James Bond movies."

"Really? I'll have to see what I can do to change your position on them, then." He leaned forward, resting his forearms on the table. "But right now, I'm more interested in what an omega is."

Jayna almost choked on her latte. He was an alpha and he didn't know what an omega was? "You don't know?"

Eric shook his head.

He really didn't. "An omega is a big, strong werewolf like an alpha, but they don't have the natural pack instincts you do. That's why those guys bolted and left me the moment the crap hit the fan at the warehouse. They don't care about anyone but themselves."

"Huh." Eric took a swallow of coffee. "That explains why they didn't fight as a team."

"They're more likely to throw each other to the wolves," she said, then added, "No pun intended. That's why werewolves like me don't like to hang out with them. They don't have any loyalty to anyone."

Eric studied her for a long time, and she wondered if she'd said something wrong. Then he tilted his head to the side, a cute, quizzical look on his face.

"Okay, I'll bite," he said. "What do you mean, werewolves like you?"

She'd met her share of werewolves over the last five

years and none of them had been this clueless. Eric must be even newer to this whole werewolf thing than she'd thought.

"Betas," she said.

She'd hoped for a spark of recognition, but he just sat there with an interested look on his gorgeous face, obviously waiting for her to continue.

"You don't know what a beta is either?" She narrowed her eyes at him. "Exactly how long have you been a werewolf?"

He flushed beneath his tan. "A little over two years, but I was in the police academy for some of that before I joined the Pack, so I'm still learning a lot about werewolves."

Which meant he wasn't much further along than Moe when it came to being a werewolf. But Eric seemed so mature and in charge, she'd assumed he was more experienced. He was an alpha, though, and if half of what Liam had told her about being an alpha was true, Eric had probably spent most of that first year after the change trying to figure out how to control his inner beast. And he had to do it while going through the police academy. When she looked at it that way, he had a good excuse for not knowing what a beta was.

"Sorry," she said. "I thought you'd been a werewolf a lot longer than I have."

He flashed her that megawatt smile. "No big deal. I don't have a problem with you being smarter than I am. I find smart women to be very sexy."

She was the one who blushed this time.

"So…a beta," he continued. "I'm guessing that's halfway between an alpha and an omega?"

She nodded. "Betas aren't as strong and fast as alphas

or omegas. But on the upside, we typically have fewer issues with control than you guys do."

He gave her an appraising look. "You seem pretty fast to me. In fact, you could probably outrun most of my pack. And you look like you're strong too."

Jayna had no idea why his words made her feel so ridiculously good, but they did. "Maybe," she conceded. "I'm a little faster and stronger than the other betas in my pack, but in general, a beta's true strength isn't in their muscles or their agility. It's in their loyalty to each other. Our pack bonds are the strongest of the three types of werewolves because they're the only thing that keeps us safe from rogue omegas. They know that whatever beta they come after, they'll always have to face the whole pack. Betas are linked in a way alphas and omegas never can be."

"Wow. I've never heard of any of that," he said with something close to boyish wonder. "But then again, I didn't know female werewolves even existed until about two months ago when Khaki joined the team. So apparently there's a lot I don't know about werewolves."

Jayna didn't have to ask who Khaki was. There couldn't be two female alpha werewolves running around Dallas. "Yeah, well, if we're being honest, I have to admit I didn't know female alphas existed until I saw your pack mate in the warehouse. That threw me for a loop. I didn't know women could be alphas. I also didn't know alphas could form a pack."

His eyes twinkled. "I guess there's a lot of stuff we can learn from each other."

She studied him over the rim of her cup, trying to figure out if he was playing her. Was he looking to trick her into giving up information about her pack? But every instinct she had told her that wasn't what was going on here. Eric seemed like he was genuinely interested in talking to her. There was only one way to find out if he was toying with her: ask him a question that might pose a threat to his pack and see how he responded.

"How many alphas are in your pack?"

He didn't even hesitate. "Seventeen now that Khaki joined the team. And every one of us would bleed and die for each other."

Jayna's eyes widened. Seventeen alphas all in one place bonding with each other? Liam had said that wasn't even possible. Eric's pack alpha must be one fierce beast to keep all of them in line.

Across from her, Eric leaned in a little closer. "Not counting the omegas, how many members are in your pack?"

She was so distracted by his scent that she almost didn't hear the question. Why did he smell so different— and so much more delicious—than every other werewolf? She wanted to bury her nose in his neck and breathe in even more of him.

Jayna quickly sat back before she did.

She'd promised herself she wouldn't tell him anything that would put her pack in danger, but telling him how many of them there were wouldn't pose a threat. It wasn't like he and his alpha buddies had anything to fear from five betas. Besides, he'd been so open with her. It seemed wrong not to answer him.

"There are four other betas besides me. And our alpha."

"How long have you been with them?"

"Four years," she said. "I changed about a year before that."

She expected him to ask why she'd changed and what she'd done for that year on her own. But instead, he took the conversation in a totally different direction.

"How did you and your pack get mixed up with a gang of Albanian mobsters?"

When Jayna had gotten on the back of his bike, she hadn't intended to tell Eric anything at all, but she'd already revealed how many members were in her pack and now she found herself confiding in him about things she shouldn't be, including how her pack had been forced to steal stuff over the years just to survive.

"None of us liked stealing, but we didn't have much of a choice. No matter how much we worked, we never seemed to have enough to buy food and keep a decent roof over our heads at the same time." She broke off another piece of cake but didn't eat it. "Then a few weeks ago, Liam—that's our alpha—admitted he'd had to borrow money to help us through some rough patches. And it wasn't from a bank."

"I'm guessing this is where the Albanians come in," Eric said.

She nodded. "For some reason, Liam told the Albanians about our pack. When they got their hands on all of his outstanding IOUs, we had no choice but to work for them to pay off that debt. Either that, or they'll kill him."

Eric frowned. "You know if you and your pack stay with these Albanians, you're going to get yourselves killed, right?"

"I know. But there's nothing I can do about it."

Jayna popped the piece of cake in her mouth and chewed in frustration. She could have killed Liam for getting the pack into this mess.

"Why the hell not?" Eric demanded. "If you know this is dangerous, why don't you and the rest of your pack just leave?"

"They won't leave Liam. He's the alpha, and they won't walk away from him."

"And you won't walk away from them."

"I can't," she said softly. "They need me."

Eric didn't say anything for a moment. Then he sighed. "Okay, I get that. What I don't get is why Liam doesn't stand up to the Albanians. I know they threatened his life, but he's your alpha. Where I come from, an alpha does whatever he has to do to protect the Pack."

She stared down at her cup. That's what she thought an alpha was supposed to do too. But how could she admit that to Eric? Worse, how could she tell him she thought Liam had been lying to the pack all along?

When Liam had told them about the Albanians holding his IOUs, she'd thought something had been off. It wasn't until they'd gotten to Dallas and she saw how at ease Liam was with them that she began to suspect he'd lied about everything. She had no proof, but it just seemed like Liam had manipulated the whole pack to get them to work for the Albanians.

"We can still take down the Albanians," Eric was saying. "You just have to make sure you get your pack out of the loft before the raid."

Jayna's hand tightened around her coffee cup as she fought to keep her claws from coming out. She knew she shouldn't have trusted a cop. "Raid? I thought you said you weren't interested in arresting us."

Okay, that was semantics. Actually, he'd said he

wasn't interested in arresting her. He didn't say anything about her pack. But they were a package deal.

If Eric knew how close she was to shifting, he didn't let it show. "I'm not. And as long as you and your pack are far away from the loft when my pack and I go in, no one else needs to know you were involved in the robbery at the warehouse."

She relaxed a little at that. "The Albanians never let all of us leave at the same time. They know that if they always keep one of us there, the rest of us won't ever try to run."

The muscle in Eric's jaw flexed. "Dammit. Tell me about the Albanians, then."

"What do you want to know?"

"How many of them there are, who's in charge, what their routine is like—anything you can think of."

Jayna started with Frasheri, then moved on to Kostandin. Eric's eyes flashed gold when she said Kos was half a chicken nugget away from being a serial killer. She was about to remind Eric where they were, afraid he might shift right there in Starbucks, but his eyes were back to their normal color before she could get the words out. Well, that was unexpected. All she'd done was mention she and her pack mates were wary of Kos, and Eric looked like he wanted to rip the Albanian to shreds. She wished Liam were as protective of their pack.

"Want another?" Eric asked as she drank the last of her latte.

Jayna was tempted to say yes simply so she could hang out with him a little while longer. Despite talking about the Albanians and the mess Liam had gotten them into, she was having fun with Eric, which was something she hadn't done in a really long time. But she'd already been away from the loft too long.

"I can't," she said. "They'll think something is wrong if I'm gone much longer."

Eric looked as bummed as she felt, but didn't say anything. He knew as well as she did why she had to go. She couldn't leave her pack behind, and he wouldn't ask her to.

"Will you be okay getting back?"

Jayna could only nod. That was the first time anyone other than her pack mates had ever shown concern for her. It felt…nice.

She was halfway out of her chair when she remembered something crazy important she needed to tell Eric. She sat back down. He did too.

"Damn, I almost forgot," she said. "Kostandin is planning to take out your pack. He doesn't care that you guys are cops. He wants all of you dead."

She expected Eric to freak out, or at least immediately pull out his cell phone and call his alpha, but he simply nodded and said he'd let them know, like he was used to people trying to kill them all the time.

He stood when she did. "You're going to need to wash off my scent before you go back, or they'll smell me all over you."

"Crap. You're right." She hadn't even thought about that. "How am I going to get it off? I don't think a sponge bath in the bathroom at Starbucks is going to do it."

"You're going to have to take a shower."

That meant getting a hotel room. How the hell was she going to afford that?

Jayna was still wondering if she could somehow wash

in Starbucks when Eric pulled out his wallet, yanked out all the cash he had in it, and held it out to her.

"Buy what you need and get a hotel room. It'd be best if you washed your clothes too, but I'm guessing you don't have time for that, so spray a lot of perfume on them instead."

To say she was stunned would be an understatement. Eric was a cop. He should have been arresting her instead of helping her.

"You might want to take the money now," he said softly. "It's starting to look like I'm offering to pay you for a sexual favor or something."

That got her moving. She quickly reached for the money, shoving it in her pocket with a nod of thanks.

"Be careful," he said. "I don't know what I'm going to do yet, but I promise I'll come up with some way to get you and your pack mates out of this mess. Just try to stay alive long enough for me to do it, okay?"

Jayna nodded, a tiny part of her believing he really could help them. But she quickly dashed that hope. There was no simple way out of a crappy situation like this. That was one thing her life to this point had taught her.

She agreed to be as careful as she could—and to exchange phone numbers with him. She was embarrassed pulling out the cheap prepaid cell phone Liam had given her, but Eric didn't say a word as he entered his name and phone number into the memory. Then she gave him her number and watched as he typed it into his fancy iPhone so fast she could barely see his fingers move.

"Don't call me unless it's important," she said after he put his phone away. "The only people who have this number are my pack mates. If it rings when they're all there, Liam will flip out."

He nodded. "Can we meet again tomorrow? Around this same time? I should have some kind of plan by then."

Even though she had no idea why, Jayna agreed. Meeting him twice in two days was beyond dangerous. She must have been insane. Clandestine dates with a cop who thought he could save her and her pack from a gang of vicious mobsters—what the hell was she thinking?

Eric opened his mouth, then closed it. She thought he was going to ask her to stay. For one crazy moment, she almost wished he would. But then the real world intruded and she remembered she'd been gone from the loft for a long time.

Giving Eric a small smile, she forced herself to turn and walk toward the door, pleased that she was able to keep herself from turning back to see if he was watching her…at least until she reached the door. Then she threw a brief glance his way. He was still standing where she'd left him, gazing at her with those beautiful blue eyes.

Why did that make her so happy?

Chapter 5

IT TOOK EVERY OUNCE OF WEREWOLF STRENGTH Becker possessed not to follow Jayna to make sure she got back to the loft okay. If he had, he would never have been able to leave, and he couldn't help Jayna and her pack if he staked out the loft 24-7. Now, on the ride back to his apartment, all he could think about were the past few hours he'd spent with her. He'd go to his death before he ever told a soul, but it had been the best date he'd ever been on. Maybe that was because he'd never been on one that started with a full-out sprint across downtown Dallas.

Damn, Jayna was fast as hell. He'd really had to push it to keep up with her, which had shocked him. He could outrun anyone in his SWAT pack without even breaking a sweat. And the way she'd gone from flat-out hauling ass to a full stop in two steps was unbelievable. He'd almost snapped his ankles trying to do the same.

But as much as he'd enjoyed racing Jayna, he'd liked the benefits that came with it even more—the view of her ass in those curve-hugging jeans and the pheromones coming off her incredible body. In fact, he was having a hard time figuring out which one of those things had come closest to making him nearly pass out.

While Becker would have liked to spend the rest of the drive to his apartment fantasizing about Jayna, he had more pressing things to think about—like figuring out how to help her and her pack. And he needed to do it fast. The longer they stayed with the Albanians, the more chances there were that it would end badly.

But just because he needed to come up with a solution fast didn't mean he could. Other than finding a place near the loft and trying to keep an eye on Jayna's pack from a distance, he had nothing. As plans went, it was pretty damn useless.

He was still trying to come up with something when he turned into his apartment complex and saw Cooper's Jeep Wrangler in the guest parking spot beside his reserved space. When Becker pulled in beside him, Cooper got out and fixed him with a pissed-off look.

"Why the hell aren't you answering your phone? I haven't heard a word from you in over twenty-four hours and every time I called, it went to voice mail. Where the hell have you been?"

Becker flipped down the kickstand on the bike, then climbed off. "With Jayna—the female werewolf from the warehouse."

Cooper did a double take. "You found her? What'd you find out?"

Becker jerked his head at his apartment building. "I'll tell you about it inside."

He led the way up to his fourth-floor apartment, dropped his keys on the table just inside the door, and headed for the kitchen. He opened the fridge and started to reach for a couple beers but grabbed two bottles of water instead. Cooper was on duty, and while werewolves couldn't get drunk, smelling like beer wasn't a smart thing to do when you were in uniform.

He tossed one of the bottles to Cooper, then cracked open his own. He leaned against the counter and took a long pull before getting his friend up to speed on the situation. Between the Albanian mobster with the serial-killer underboss, the mercenary omegas, a jackass alpha, and Jayna's pack of betas, even Becker's head was spinning by the time he was done, and he already knew the story.

"Oh yeah," he added. "There's one other thing. The sadistic underboss I told you about, Kostandin, is gunning for us. Guess he figures they won't be able to focus on what they want to do in Dallas until we're out of the picture."

Cooper nodded. "I'll make sure the Pack knows. So, Jayna's a beta, huh? And the werewolves who run without a pack are called omegas? Gage should really give a class on some of this stuff because there's obviously a lot we don't know."

No kidding. Then again, maybe Gage didn't know betas existed either. "Yeah, well, she and her pack are in deep crap if we can't come up with a way to help them."

"And there's no way you can convince them to walk away from this asshole Liam?" Cooper asked.

Becker shook his head. "Not a chance. Her pack won't leave, and Jayna won't leave without them."

"Huh." Cooper's mouth edged up. "You got to respect that."

"No, I don't have to respect it," Becker snapped. He swigged the rest of his water and angrily threw the bottle in the recycle bin. "The Albanians are dangerous. She's going to get killed."

Cooper raised a brow, clearly surprised by the

vehemence in Becker's voice, but didn't say anything.
Becker ground his jaw. He rarely got pissed, especially
at his best friend, but he was worried as hell about Jayna.

"So, what did you tell Xander and Gage about why
I didn't show up for work today?" he asked, trying to
steer the conversation in a different direction. When
he'd texted Cooper yesterday to tell him he wouldn't be
in, his friend had said he'd come up with some reason
Gage would buy.

Cooper shook his head. "I told them your sister was
having problems with her pregnancy and you were
spending most of the day on the phone trying to figure
out if you needed to go to Denver."

Becker frowned. As lies went, that was a good one,
except... "My sister isn't pregnant."

"But no one knows that," Cooper said. "And if you
need to disappear for a few days to help get Jayna and her
pack out of the mess they're in, it's the perfect cover."

Becker couldn't argue with that. Now he just had to
figure out how to make it happen.

"So, what's the plan?" Cooper asked.

"I'm not quite sure yet." Becker told him about his
original idea to raid the loft when Jayna's pack wasn't
there and why that wouldn't work. "Other than staking
out the place to make sure they're safe, I got nothing."

Cooper regarded him thoughtfully. "How far would
you go to keep her safe?"

"That's a dumbass question. I'd go as far as I have to."

"I thought you'd say that." Cooper sighed. "Then it's
obvious what you need to do."

Becker frowned again. "It is?"

"Yeah," Cooper said. "If you can't get Jayna out of

the situation, you need to get yourself into it, so you can protect her."

Becker shook his head. "I don't think sitting on the place is going to work. Not only would one of the werewolves pick up my scent sooner or later, but I also wouldn't be close enough to protect Jayna when it really matters. If the Albanians send her out on another job like that warehouse gig, I wouldn't even know it was happening until it was too late."

"Then you need to be closer," Cooper said. "So close you'd be right under the other werewolves' noses…and you can go on those jobs with her."

Becker's heart started to thud as he realized what his friend was getting at. *Shit*. Leave it to Cooper to come up with a plan that verged on suicidal. "You're suggesting that I go in undercover?"

"Yeah." Cooper grinned, as if he thought his plan was foolproof. "You said her alpha is bringing in omegas to fill out the ranks. You can go in as one of them and keep Jayna safe from the inside."

Becker snorted. "That's insane. You remember how shitty my first, last, and only undercover job turned out, right?"

"You weren't a werewolf back then," Cooper pointed out. "And the second one is always easier."

How the hell would Cooper know? He'd never done any undercover work. "That doesn't mean I'm going to be any better at it now."

"You'll be better now because you have to be. The life of the woman you think is your soul mate depends on it."

That thought scared the hell out of Becker so much his hands shook. "There's no way I can go in there.

They'll know I'm a cop the moment they check me out. And I'm pretty sure I can't just make up a name. These Albanians seem a little sharper than that."

Cooper thought about that for a second before he grinned. "Then you need to go in with a new identity, a really good one established a long time ago by professionals."

At first Becker didn't know what Cooper was talking about, but when he figured it out, he couldn't keep the smile off his face. "You think we can break into Gage's safe without him knowing it?"

"We don't have to break in. Gage uses the date when he changed into a werewolf as the combination."

"And how would you know that?" Becker asked.

Cooper chuckled. "Because I'm a very curious were-wolf by nature."

Jayna was torn as she walked the last few blocks to the loft. She dreaded facing Liam and Kos and the crap she knew was coming her way. If she didn't love her pack mates more than anything in the world, she wouldn't have gone back there. Kos was going to be suspicious about why she had been gone so long, and Liam was almost certain to be furious.

It wasn't her fault though. Walking away from that Starbucks had been hard. Well, walking away from the coffee shop hadn't been that difficult. It was leaving Eric that had been tough. She couldn't understand why a guy she barely knew had that kind of effect on her. When she walked out of that coffee shop, she'd felt this crazy sensation…like she was leaving something really important behind. The urge to run back in had been almost overwhelming. But she'd forced herself to keep going. It was going to take a while to shower, and it was going to take even longer if she hung around mooning over the big, blue-eyed were-hunk.

She'd stopped at a pharmacy on the way and picked up a bottle of perfume and the fruitiest shampoo she could find. Then she'd gotten a room at the Holiday Inn Express a few blocks off Canton, drawing a bit more attention than she'd liked when she pulled out the wad of cash Eric had given her and discovered that most of the bills were fifties. *Who the heck walks around with that kind of money in their wallet?*

Jayna expected to see Megan and the guys waiting for her, but they were nowhere in sight. Instead, she found two Albanians and an omega parked on the couch in front of the giant TV, playing video games, while another omega watched. On the other side of the atrium, Liam, Kostandin, and Brandon were still deep in conversation about a job. She heard Brandon ask how they would get in the safe and Kostandin saying something about the daytime manager knowing the combination.

"Don't be afraid to break a few bones to get her to talk," Kos said. "Just make sure you break the ones on her left hand—she still has to open the safe."

She walked over to the omega watching the guys playing video games. Short and stocky, with curly hair, he had a mustache and full beard that could have used a trim. "Where are Megan and the guys?"

He barely glanced at her. "What the hell do I look like, your secretary?"

Jayna didn't realize she'd shifted until she started forward, her canines and claws extended, her right hand poised to rip out the idiot's throat.

The omega's eyes widened in alarm and he quickly backpedaled, raising his hands in an attempt to protect his face and neck. "Shit. Chill out! The girl is upstairs. The three guys are checking out a drug lab that Kos wants to take down in a couple days."

Jayna's rage immediately faded. Her pack mates were okay—or at least as okay as they could be considering the present situation.

Abruptly aware of eyes on her, she glanced around and saw everyone staring at her. The omega she'd been about to shred was looking at her like she had horns as well as fangs and claws. She didn't know why he was so terrified. Sure, she'd lost control for a second, but the guy had to know there was no way a beta her size could take on an omega without her pack. But as he took another step back, she realized he clearly wasn't aware of that fact.

On the other side of the lobby, Liam frowned at her in obvious displeasure—probably pissed she was usurping his pack authority again. Beside him, Kos regarded her with an expression of sick amusement. That pissed her off even more than the look her alpha was throwing her way.

Screw them both, Jayna thought as she turned and headed for the kitchen. She grabbed the first thing she saw on the counter—a box of frosted cinnamon Pop Tarts. She yanked out a pack and ripped it open, then bit into the pastry. It didn't taste nearly as good as the coffee cake Eric had gotten her at Starbucks. That had tasted better than anything in this room ever could, and she had no doubt it was because he'd been sitting across from her.

Jayna was so wrapped up in thoughts of Eric that she didn't notice Kostandin coming in until she turned and almost bounced off his oversized chest. How the hell had he been able to sneak up on her like that? He was the size of a house.

The fact that a guy as creepy as Kos could sneak up on her gave her goose bumps all over, and she took an involuntary step back. She might have scared the hell out of the omega out in the lobby, but it was obvious Kos wasn't intimidated by her in the least.

He closed the distance between them, and before she realized what he was doing, he'd leaned in and sniffed her hair. She pulled back in revulsion even as he chuckled.

"You smell good, she-wolf. Like a peach." He gave her an oily smile. "I like peaches."

Jayna tried to walk past him, but he moved with her, blocking her path and gazing down at her with an unnerving glint in his eyes. She growled, reaching for the rage she'd just unleashed on the omega only a few minutes ago. But that powerful rage—and the were-wolf who'd shown it—now seemed to be AWOL. In its place was a frightened seventeen-year-old girl facing not a sadistic mobster but a sadistic stepfather. For a second, she was so scared she could barely think, much less defend herself.

Then something angry reared up inside her—the same thing that had refused to let Darren rape her so many years ago.

Lifting her hands, she shoved the big Albanian so hard that he stumbled back a few feet. The power and rage she'd felt earlier still wasn't there, but her claws were out and ready to do some damage if Kostandin didn't get the hell out of her way.

But before she could use them, Kos chuckled and moved aside to let her pass. Jayna hesitated, waiting to see if it was some kind of trick. When Kos only lifted a brow, she slowly walked past him and headed for the door, but his voice stopped her cold.

"I know you do not enjoy the things you've had to do lately, things your pack leader has been making you do," he said softly. "I could change that. If you were a bit…nicer to me…you wouldn't have to go out and do those things again."

Jayna whirled around with a growl. "I'd rather take my chances getting shot and killed than spend one second being…*nice*…to you."

For a moment, Kos let his normal, expressionless mask crack a little, and Jayna saw a depth of hatred and evil there that nearly took her breath away. But just as quickly, the look was gone, replaced by the cold, dead stare she was used to. She turned and started for the door only to be stopped once again by a voice that was so emotionless she wasn't sure it was even human.

"Perhaps I will make the same offer to your friend… the little wolf pup. She hates going out there even more than you. Do you think little Megan will be nicer to me?"

Jayna had no problem finding her rage now. Her eyes blazed as her claws and fangs extended even farther than they had in the lobby, and she spun around to advance on Kostandin, ready to tear him to pieces.

He didn't even flinch as he reached behind his back and pulled out a really big handgun. Jayna didn't know much about guns beyond loading and pulling the trigger, but this one looked big enough to do a whole lot of damage, even to a werewolf. And Kos had the barrel pointed calmly at her head.

She stopped, not going any closer but damn sure not backing off either. "You go anywhere near Megan—or any members of my pack—and I'll tear you apart. I swear it."

Kostandin wasn't fazed by her threat. Instead, he kept the automatic pointed at her head for a few more seconds before casually slipping it into the holster behind his back. Then he chuckled again and brushed past her.

He stopped just outside the door and looked back. "*Your* pack, Jayna? Does Liam know you've taken over?"

Jayna didn't offer a reply. That was okay because Kos didn't seem to expect one.

Still trembling with anger, she headed for the stairwell. She had one foot on the steps when Liam's voice stopped her this time. *Dammit*. Was the whole world trying to piss her off today? She turned around to see him jogging to catch up with her. Fifteen years older than her, she used to think of Liam as the big brother she never had. Now, she didn't know what to think of him.

"Where have you been all day?"

Normally, she would have come up with a good lie, trusting in her ability to talk her way out of most tight corners. But after the run-in with Kostandin, she wasn't in the mood to play games with Liam. Right now, she wanted to make sure Megan was okay.

"I was out taking care of something."

His eyes narrowed. "What kind of something?"

Jayna felt her fangs slip out at the suspicion in his voice. She forced them back in and regarded her alpha with what she hoped was a calm expression. "I had to get out of here for a while." She jerked her head toward the lobby. "Away from all…this."

Liam frowned. "Why would you want to get away from this? It's the best thing that's ever happened to us."

If she'd had any doubt that he'd lied about Frasheri forcing them to work for him, she didn't now. "Best thing that ever happened to us? You're kidding, right?"

His face darkened. "Why do you always have to act like this? I've never done anything but try to take care of all of you. Frasheri and Kos are going to look out for us…protect us."

She'd thought Liam had simply looked the other way when it came to all the illegal crap the Albanians were into, but now she realized he really was indifferent to the danger he'd put the pack squarely in the middle of.

"Protect us from whom?" she demanded. "The only people who are likely to hurt us are these new friends of yours. Or haven't you seen the way Kostandin and his buddies look at Megan and me?"

Liam actually looked like he didn't know what she was talking about. Maybe he didn't.

She turned and started up the stairs, done with the stupid conversation. But apparently, Liam wasn't.

"Kos values us too much to risk pissing me off."

Liam made it sound like he and the Albanian were equals. He was even further gone than she'd thought if he didn't know Kos was using him.

She threw a disgusted look over her shoulder as she kept walking. "You keep believing that right up until it's too late."

"What the hell does that mean?" Liam asked.

She stopped and turned to look at him. Liam was standing at the bottom of the steps, an annoyed look on his face.

"When we first came down here, you said your debt would be paid off in a few weeks," she said. "Well, it's been a few weeks and we're still here."

Liam didn't answer right away. "We've got something good going here, Jayna. We'd be crazy to leave. Can't you see that?"

No, thinking Liam might actually come clean with her and admit there was no debt and never had been was crazy. She should have known better.

Jayna didn't say anything as she turned to climb up the stairs again. Fortunately, Liam was smart enough not to follow her. If he had, Jayna knew she wouldn't be able to help what happened.

She walked down the hall to the small, one-bedroom efficiency apartment on the third floor that she and Megan shared and tapped on the door. Even though they both had a key to the place, they had no idea if Kostandin or one of the other Albanians had a second one. So anytime one of them was in the room, they slid a chair under the doorknob to wedge the door closed even after they put the chain on it. It wouldn't stop any of those thugs for long, but it would slow them down.

She heard Megan move the chair aside and undo the door chain. A moment later, the door opened. Megan stepped back so Jayna could enter, then closed the door and locked it again.

"Hey! I was wondering when you'd be back." Megan smiled. "You smell different. New shampoo?"

Jayna opened her mouth to tell her best friend about Eric, but then closed it again. She wanted to trust Megan, wanted to think she wouldn't tell Liam anything Jayna asked her to keep secret. But honestly, Jayna wasn't sure what Megan would do if Liam got in her face and asked her straight out if she knew where Jayna had been. Even if Megan could keep from telling Liam, she still might slip up and tell one of their other pack mates, which was essentially the same thing. The guys, especially Joseph, were still really tight with their pack alpha.

So, feeling like a piece of crap, Jayna smiled back. "Yeah."

Jayna was careful not to look at her friend as she wedged the chair back under the door. By the time she turned around, Megan was sitting cross-legged on her bed, regarding her expectantly.

"What are we going to do?" Megan asked.

Jayna walked over to the other bed and sat down. "About what?" she asked as she took off her boots.

"About these things Liam and Kostandin are making us do. I heard them talking earlier about a job they want us to take lead on. Something involving a jewelry store." Megan sighed. "I don't know anything about security at a jewelry store, but I'm guessing there will be guards—and guns. If things keep going like this, one of us is going to get hurt or worse. At the very least, they're going to ask one of us to kill someone, maybe even one of those alpha werewolves from SWAT. I know that we have to stay here until the rest of the debt is paid off, but I don't want to have anything to do with killing anyone."

Jayna's stomach clenched at the thought of one of her pack mates killing someone, especially one of the alphas from Eric's pack—if that was even possible. She wasn't sure about Liam anymore, but the rest of her pack weren't killers. She knew it in her soul.

She pulled her legs up and wrapped her arms around her knees. "I don't want any of us to have anything to do with that."

Megan chewed on her thumbnail. She always did when she was worried. "Do you think Liam could work something out with the Albanians? Maybe he could pay back the money some other way."

Jayna was so close to telling Megan that Liam had lied about everything, but she couldn't make herself say the words. Liam might have gotten them into this mess, but she wasn't ready to turn her pack against their alpha yet.

"Something tells me the Albanians won't go for that," she finally said.

Megan nibbled on her nail some more. "Maybe we should just leave. There has to be someplace we can go where the Albanians won't be able to find us."

If only it were that easy. "Liam won't leave. And I don't think the guys will go if he doesn't. Are you ready to leave them behind?"

Megan sighed and shook her head. Then she looked at Jayna sharply, her pulse suddenly pounding so fast it seemed to echo in the room. "You won't leave on your own, will you?"

The panic in Megan's voice was so painful to hear, it almost brought tears to Jayna's eyes. Getting up, she walked the three short strides that separated her bed from Megan's and plopped down beside the other girl. She wrapped her arm around Megan's shoulders and hugged her close.

"I'll never leave you," she murmured, resting her cheek against Megan's silky, dark hair. "Never."

Megan immediately relaxed, her heart rate slowly

returning to normal as she wrapped her arms around Jayna. Megan had been through so much and depended on Jayna. Jayna would die before she let the girl down.

"We'll be okay," Jayna whispered. "We'll find a way out of this. I promise."

"I believe you," Megan said. "You're the heart and soul of this pack. If you say we'll be okay, we will."

The burden on Jayna's shoulders suddenly felt like it weighed a thousand pounds. How the heck could she do anything? She was only a beta.

Jayna thought about Eric Becker and how the big alpha had promised to help her and her pack. She almost laughed at the notion that some outsider—a cop to boot—would ever help them. But something told her that Eric was going to come through for them.

She prayed her instincts were right because she needed something miraculous to happen if she was going to get her pack out of this situation alive.

Chapter 6

THE PLAN WAS SIMPLE. WALK INTO GAGE'S OFFICE, get the fake ID out of the safe, drop a leave form on the boss's desk, and be out before anyone came in for PT that morning.

That was why Becker and Cooper got to the compound at oh dark thirty. Luckily, Cooper was right about the combination to the safe being the date Gage had changed into a werewolf, so opening it wasn't a problem. Even finding the high-quality forgeries the SWAT commander had made just in case the Pack ever had to go on the run was easy.

In addition to a license and passport, there were also credit cards. Becker had seen some good fakes when he was with the Secret Service, but this stuff was some of the best he'd ever laid eyes on. The name was even perfect—Eric Bauer. Definitely close enough to his own that he'd instinctively answer to it.

"That was almost too easy." Becker grinned as he dropped his leave form on Gage's desk and followed Cooper out of their boss's office. "Maybe we're in the wrong line of work."

Then the door of the admin building opened and Gage walked in.

Shit.

Gage stared at them—not exactly with suspicion but definitely with curiosity. "What are you guys doing here so early?"

Becker's mind went completely blank. He was going undercover with a group of werewolves who would tear him apart if they even sniffed something wasn't legit. And right now, he couldn't come up with a single excuse that explained why he and Cooper were at the compound so early.

"I, um, had to come in early and drop off a leave form," he finally said, trying to sound casual.

His boss frowned. "You're taking leave? Now?"

"Yeah."

Becker glanced at Cooper to find his friend regarding him patiently. Clearly, there wouldn't be any help coming from that direction. *So what now?* Gage was really good at sniffing out lies, and if he called Becker on this one, his undercover assignment would be over before it started.

"It's my sister. They think they might have to induce labor." He felt like crap for bringing her into this and lying about her being pregnant, but he didn't have a choice. Jayna's life might depend on it. "I know my timing is bad, especially with the other pack in town, but I really think I should be there. It's her first child and all."

Becker held his breath, waiting for Gage to call bullshit on the lie, but his boss didn't. Maybe Becker wasn't such a crappy liar after all. Or maybe Gage knew how close Becker was with his family and thought that any weird vibes he picked up were because Becker was worried about his sister.

"Take all the time you need," Gage said. "And when she has the baby, make sure you take pictures. Mackenzie will want to see the kid. She's crazy about stuff like that."

Becker promised he would, then added, "I'll check in as often as I can."

"That went a hell of a lot better than I thought it would," Cooper said as they walked across the parking lot.

"No thanks to you," Becker muttered. "You could have helped me out when Gage started grilling me."

Cooper snorted. "Trust me, that wasn't grilling. When you walk into that loft, you're going to be grilled. The questions will be coming at you fast and hard. You'd better be ready to talk a good game, or you're toast." When they got to Becker's bike, Cooper stopped to face him. "I'm serious. You up for this?"

All Becker had to do was imagine Jayna in that loft full of killers. He was going in there whether he was up for it or not.

"I'm good," Becker said as he climbed on his bike. "You just be ready when I call you with whatever I uncover. The faster we take down these guys, the faster we can get Jayna's pack out of there."

"I'll be waiting," Cooper said. "Watch your back in there."

Becker reached to start his bike, then stopped. "Almost forgot. Can you stop by and feed my fish every few days? And talk to them too. They get lonely when I'm not home."

Cooper made a face. "Who the hell talks to their fish?"

"Me. You'll feed them, right?"

"Yeah, I'll feed them. But I'm sure as hell not talking to them," Cooper said. "Now get outta here before anyone else shows up and asks what you're doing here so early."

Becker chuckled as he cranked the engine, but his amusement disappeared the moment he rode out of the parking lot. Cooper's warning echoed in his head. Damn straight he'd watch his back—because there'd be no one else around to do it for him.

—∿∿—

The thought that Jayna might not show briefly entered Becker's mind on the ride over to the coffee shop, but he quickly dismissed it. Jayna would be there. If not today, then tomorrow. All he had to do was keep going back to that Starbucks until she did.

He grabbed a cup of coffee and found a table in the corner where he could put his back to the wall and keep an eye on the door. In between, he surfed the net on his phone and skimmed his fake IDs so he'd be familiar with his alter ego. He was so busy trying to memorize the address on his driver's license—some rural trailer park near Waco—that he didn't notice Jayna had walked in and was coming his way until her intoxicating scent nearly knocked him out of his chair.

He looked up to see her backlit by the midmorning sun pouring through the open door, silhouetting her curvy figure and gorgeous mane of dark blond hair. When she caught sight of him looking at her, a smile tilted up the corners of her beautiful lips, and just like that, the tension he hadn't even known was there left his body.

Jayna motioned that she was going to get a drink. A few minutes later, she slipped into the seat opposite him, a venti latte in her hand. She looked pleased to see him—or maybe that was just his imagination.

"I'm glad you could come," he said. "I wasn't sure if you'd be able to get away again so soon."

"Me either. But there weren't many people hanging around the loft this morning." She sipped her latte.

"Besides, you said you might have a plan on how to get my pack out of this mess. I'm willing to take any risk if it helps them."

He gave her a hurt look. "And here I was thinking you were meeting me because of my scintillating conversational skills."

She laughed, and Becker couldn't get over the effect that sound had on him. It was like an extension cord plugged straight into his heart. Damn, he had it bad for this woman.

"Nope," she said. "I'm just here for the latte and the plan."

He grinned. "Well, if that's the case, I guess I should probably tell you I've come up with one."

Jayna leaned forward, bringing that delicious scent of hers even closer. "You did? What is it?"

While she might be eager to hear what he had to say, Becker got the feeling she was a little cautious too. He supposed he couldn't blame her.

"The only way I can help you and your pack is if I'm on the inside—as an omega," he said. "So I'm going back to the loft with you."

She stared at him, speechless. "Are you serious? That's your big plan? You're just going to waltz in and say you heard through the grapevine that some Albanian mobsters are looking to hire werewolves off the street to be enforcers?"

Becker had to admit, the plan didn't sound nearly as good when she put it that way. But it was the only one he had, so they were going to have to make it work. It was either that or go back to his raiding-the-loft idea, and Jayna had already made it clear that wasn't an option.

"You said Liam has been recruiting every omega he can find," Becker pointed out. "Why wouldn't he take me in?"

"Because you don't look like an omega."

"What does an omega look like?"

Jayna frowned. "They're big, strong, and aggressive. And more often than not, they're cocky and arrogant too."

"So far you're describing my entire pack and me to a tee."

She thought about that. "Maybe so, but it still won't work."

"Why not?"

"Because omegas aren't so hot."

Well, damn. Becker grinned as a blush colored her cheeks. "Are you saying I'm too hot to be an omega?"

"No!" she said quickly.

"No, I'm not too hot to be an omega? Or no, I'm not hot at all?"

He couldn't help teasing her despite how serious the situation was. It was too much fun watching her get flustered.

She ignored his question. "Omegas have control issues—everybody knows that. But nobody is going to believe you've ever had a problem staying in control of yourself."

Becker probably should have left that one alone, but he couldn't. It was just too good to pass up. "I've never had a woman complain about my lack of self-control, but I really don't see what that has to do with getting people to believe I'm an omega."

Jayna looked confused for a moment; then she blushed even deeper than she had before. "Stop it, Eric!

I'm serious. Why would you even consider walking into that place of your own free will? It's insanity."

His smile melted away. "Why would I go in there? Because it's the only way I can think of to keep you safe. You've made it clear you won't leave without your pack mates, and they aren't ready to walk away from your so-called alpha. I don't have a choice. If you won't come out, I have to go in."

Jayna regarded him thoughtfully. He hoped she wouldn't ask him again why he was doing this. Because he really didn't think it would be a good idea for him to tell her that he thought she was *The One* for him.

"Okay," she finally said. "I appreciate what you're doing, but I still think you're insane. Just don't expect Liam to welcome you with open arms. I don't care if you do call yourself an omega—one look at you, and he's going to view you as a threat to his leadership of the pack. You scream dominant male. He's going to want you gone—fast."

Okay, he'd concede that was definitely a flaw in the plan he and Cooper had come up with, but maybe not a fatal flaw. He frowned as something struck him.

"I thought you said Liam was paying off a debt to the Albanians," Becker said. "Why would they listen to anything he had to say?"

She wrapped her hands around the cardboard cup as if warming them and didn't answer right away. "I think Liam lied about that. I don't know if he approached the Albanians or they found us, but I have a feeling he's working for them of his own free will. And before you ask, no one else in my pack is aware of that, and I don't want to turn them against Liam unless I'm absolutely

sure I'm right. That's why I didn't say anything about it
to you yesterday."

Okay. That changed things a little bit.

"Regardless of whether Liam is there of his own
free will or not, the Albanians are still calling the shots,
right?" Becker asked.

She nodded. "Definitely. Kostandin makes nearly
every important decision about the pack and how we're
used, and I'm pretty sure he isn't all that impressed
with Liam."

Becker grinned. "I think you've just figured out how
to get me into that loft."

"I did?" Jayna asked with an absolutely adorable look
of confusion.

Who was he kidding? All of her looks were adorable.

"You did." His grin broadened. "We make sure that
you introduce me to Kostandin first. If I impress him,
I'm as good as in."

———

Jayna poked her head in the front door of the lobby
only long enough to confirm that both Frasheri and Kos
were in there before motioning to Eric. This plan of his
was crazy, but it was too late to turn back now. Even as
she took a deep breath and tried to calm her nerves, the
big SWAT werewolf came bouncing up the steps like
he owned the place, backpack slung casually over one
shoulder. How could he be so calm when he was walking
into a building full of criminals and omegas who would
gladly kill him a hundred times over if they even got a
hint he was a cop?

The Albanian guards at the door immediately

reached behind their backs for the guns they kept holstered there.

"Don't be stupid," Eric said with a growl so deep Jayna felt it vibrate in her chest.

She glanced at him and was shocked to see him glaring at the two Albanians with eyes the deepest golden yellow she'd ever seen and fangs so long she wasn't sure how they fit in his mouth. Even as she watched, his jawline broadened slightly, like it was trying to make room for more teeth.

Jayna blinked. Okay, that was freaking scary—but kind of cool too. Purely in a werewolf kind of way, of course.

The two guards took a step back, hearts hammering in their chests. Eric strode past them as if they didn't even exist and swept into the lobby. She took a deep breath, doing her best to project the same calm attitude as she led him across the lobby. Out of the corner of her eye, she saw Megan and Moe stop halfway down the steps, their mouths hanging open. The two omegas sprawled on the couch playing video games looked equally shocked. So did the Albanians playing pool. She'd made no secret of the fact that she didn't like omegas, so everyone probably wondered what she was doing with one. Then again, maybe they were all staring because Eric was so damn big.

She ignored all of them, instead focusing on Frasheri and Kos, who were standing near the big planning table on the far side of the room. The two men eyed her and Eric suspiciously.

Luckily, Liam wasn't around.

Kos gave her a cold look. "Who is your new friend, Jayna?"

"This is Eric Bauer," she said, using the fake surname the SWAT werewolf had given her. "He approached me at the coffee shop, wanting to know if you'd be interested in hiring someone like him."

"Someone like him?" Frasheri prompted.

She turned to the older man. Tall with salt-and-pepper hair and a perpetual tan, Frasheri looked younger than his sixty years. "Eric is an omega. Liam said you've been looking to hire more of them."

"Yes, we are." Frasheri studied her for a moment before turning his gaze on Eric. "I'm a distrustful man by nature, Mr. Bauer, but also curious. Tell me, how did you learn that some of your kind worked for us? Or where to find us, for that matter?"

Jayna darted Eric a quick look, hoping no one noticed the way her pulse spiked.

But Eric shrugged, acting as if he hadn't picked up on the menace in Frasheri's tone at all. "Word of what's been going on in Dallas has been getting around. When I heard rumors you were using enforcers who have been tearing the local thugs and gangbangers to shreds, literally, it wasn't difficult to put two and two together. Finding you once I got here wasn't hard either. All I had to do was go to the one part of town everyone was telling me to stay away from."

Kostandin's eyes narrowed. "What makes you think we'd be interested in having you work for us?"

Eric's mouth twitched, and Jayna was once again struck by how calm he was. She wished she could say the same about herself.

"I know the kind of stuff they do for you." Eric motioned with his head toward the omegas on the other side of the room. "It's nothing I have a problem with, and I can do it better than anyone you already have working for you."

The corners of Frasheri's wide mouth turned up, and it looked like he was about to say something, but just then Liam stormed into the lobby, Brandon at his side. They both looked like they'd smelled something rotten.

Crap.

"Who is this and what the hell is he doing here?"

Liam brushed past the Albanians and omegas to take a confrontational position in front of Eric, his eyes flashing and the tips of his canines showing. He was probably trying to be intimidating, but after seeing Eric's version of scary, Liam didn't carry it off as well. It didn't help that he was a good five inches shorter than Eric and forty pounds lighter.

She was about to answer Liam, but Frasheri spoke first.

"This is Eric Bauer. Jayna met him and thought he would be a good fit for the pack."

Jayna had just enough time to wince before Liam turned to glare at her. Oh yeah, he was pissed.

Liam frowned at Frasheri. "And you're willing to hire him, just like that?"

"I haven't decided yet," Frasheri admitted. "Jayna obviously saw something she liked if she brought him back here. And I can always use more werewolves in my employ."

Liam glanced at Eric, eyes narrowing as if trying to figure out exactly what it was Jayna saw in him. Eric regarded Liam without any outward expression.

"If we're going up against those SWAT werewolves, we're going to need omegas who know what the hell they're doing in a fight," Liam told Frasheri. "How do we know this guy can handle himself? Just because he's big doesn't mean anything—except that he's probably slow and stupid."

"Possibly," Kostandin said. "But it's easy enough to find that out." He motioned with his hand. "Move the chairs and tables aside."

Jayna's heart thumped as she figured out why the Albanian would want a space cleared in the middle of the lobby. He wanted Eric to prove he could fight. Right here, right now.

That shouldn't have worried her. Eric was trained for this kind of stuff. And even if he wasn't, why should she care? It wasn't like he was a member of her pack. But if that was the case, why was she so freaked at the thought of him getting so much as a scratch? She was practically on the verge of hyperventilating.

Her heart wasn't the only one going into overdrive. Liam's was beating pretty hard too. Was it in anticipation or something else? She couldn't tell by the expression on his face, which seemed more annoyed than anything as he looked at Frasheri.

"You don't expect me to fight this idiot do you?" Liam demanded. "I'm an alpha. He's not. What good would it do to see me tear him apart?"

Kos regarded Liam for a long, drawn-out moment before lifting a brow. "Of course not. As you say, what would be gained by having you fight this mere omega?"

"Right," Liam agreed.

Clearly, her pack leader hadn't realized the significance of the question mark at the end of Kostandin's statement. Jayna had the feeling Kos would enjoy seeing

Liam fight Eric. To tell the truth, Jayna wouldn't have minded seeing it herself.

"Perhaps you could select someone more appropriate for Eric to fight," Frasheri suggested. "Someone who wouldn't tear him apart, as you say."

Liam seemed to miss the subtle undertone of Frasheri's words, much as he'd done with Kostandin's. He turned and looked at Brandon. "Would you mind showing this outsider how a pack werewolf handles himself?"

So now Brandon was part of their pack? The thought made Jayna ill. She wasn't shocked by Liam's selection though. If he had a pet among the omegas, it was Brandon. And the lead omega was definitely one of the few werewolves in the room who would be a physical match for Eric.

But then Liam did something that shocked her. He turned to another one of the big omegas who'd been playing pool when she and Eric walked in and motioned him forward. "You too, Caleb." He glanced at Frasheri and Kos. "You want to see how the new omega handles himself, let's see."

Jayna was so focused on Eric tossing his backpack and leather jacket on the floor to face the omegas that she barely noticed Megan and Moe had come to stand beside her.

Brandon and Caleb snarled and launched themselves at Eric without warning, fangs extended and claws out. Jayna expected Eric to get out of the way or leap at one of the werewolves—something. But he only stood there with a slight smile on his face. He hadn't even shifted to protect himself. It was like he was frozen.

Jayna didn't realize she'd moved until Megan

grabbed her arm. Not that she could have done much to help Eric anyway.

Smelling an easy victory, Brandon went in low at Eric's right side, while Caleb attacked from his left.

She cringed. *This is going to be bloody.*

But at the last second, Eric darted to the side and punched Brandon in the chest. The blow stopped the omega's forward momentum cold, knocking him ten feet back across the lobby.

In the same motion, Eric turned and snatched Caleb out of the air. The omega's claws dug into Eric's chest and shoulder before the SWAT cop tossed him across the room, crushing several chairs and a sofa in the process.

Eric spun around to focus on Brandon. Jayna was shocked see that the cop hadn't shifted yet. If it wasn't for the four tracks of blood marring his shirt, she would have thought he was just playing around.

Brandon growled but went at him more cautiously this time. Eric blocked most of the openhanded swipes Brandon threw but didn't go on the offensive himself. Jayna frowned. Why wasn't Eric attacking?

But just then, Brandon overextended himself with one of his swipes, leaving his ribs completely exposed for just a fraction of a second. Eric's fist came up in an upper cut, connecting solidly with Brandon's ribs. There was a thud and a crack, and when Eric tossed Brandon aside this time, the big omega didn't get back up.

Jayna had a ridiculous urge to run over to Eric and hug him. But before she could follow through with that crazy idea, an insane roar echoed in the room. She whipped her head around just in time to see Caleb charging Eric. The omega's claws and fangs were fully extended now, his eyes practically glowing. *Oh crap*. Caleb had completely lost it. A couple cracked ribs wouldn't be enough to end this now.

Jayna wasn't the only one who moved to help this time. Every other werewolf did too. Not that it would do much good. Caleb was already on Eric.

She might have shouted something. It was hard to tell over the snarls and the other people yelling. But Eric and Caleb ignored everyone around them, intent on the struggle that was likely to end with one of them dead.

Caleb didn't even try to take a swing at Eric. The omega was so far gone, he just opened his jaws wide and went in for the kill. Eric's hand shot out, catching Caleb by the throat and flipping the ravaging omega backward, slamming him down violently against the tile floor. Then Eric leaned forward and cut loose with a growl of his own that was so powerful Jayna and every other werewolf in the room stopped in their tracks.

Eric had shifted completely, farther than she'd ever seen a werewolf go before. Besides the long fangs and claws, Eric's shoulders and arms had bunched and spasmed, like they were trying to twist into a completely different shape. Jayna could have sworn his nose and jaw had actually pushed out some. But that was obviously impossible.

As stunned as he was, Caleb struggled to free himself until Eric leaned even closer and put his face right into the omega's, then growled so loudly people two blocks down must have heard it.

Caleb immediately stopped struggling. His fangs and claws disappeared, his hands coming up in surrender. Jayna had never seen anything like it. Eric had forced

Caleb into submission with nothing more than a growl—
although those impressive canines of his might have had
something to do with it. Eric could have easily torn out
Caleb's throat if he'd wanted to.

But Eric didn't lunge forward. Instead, he shifted
back to his normal appearance and reached down to pull
Caleb to his feet. Then he thumped the dazed omega on
the shoulder as if saying, "Good fight, dude."

On the far side of the room, Brandon was only now
climbing to his feet. He threw Eric a venomous glare
as he curled one arm protectively in front of his broken
ribs. Eric would have to watch his back around that jerk.

A few of the omegas and some of the Albanians gathered around Eric, smacking him on the back and laughing, but they moved aside as Kostandin approached. The
Albanian underboss regarded Eric with his sharklike
eyes, then slowly reached behind his back. Jayna immediately tensed, sure he was going to pull out a gun, but
instead, he came out with a big, long knife. She didn't
know whether to be relieved or not. She'd seen Kos use
that knife on a few of his victims. He especially liked
cutting off fingers with it.

Kos tapped the tip of the knife against Eric's chest.
The SWAT werewolf didn't react to the threatening gesture other than to lift his chin a little higher.

"For all your werewolf strength and speed, a knife
through the heart will kill you as quickly as it would any
man," Kos said.

Eric smiled, showing the tips of his fangs. "Maybe.
But for you to get that knife in my heart, you'd have to
be really close. Makes it tougher to knife a man knowing
that if you miss, he's going to rip out your throat."

Kostandin stared at Eric for a moment, his eyes betraying zero emotion. He didn't seem to be any more intimidated by Eric than the werewolf was of him. Considering what Eric had just done, that only confirmed the Albanian was a psychopath.

"I like you," Kos said with a laugh. He slipped the knife into the sheath behind his back, glancing at a fellow Albanian as he walked away. "Find him a room."

Jayna let out the breath she'd been holding. Eric had done it. He'd gotten into the pack.

The need to make sure he really was okay after that fight was suddenly overwhelming, but before she could take a step, Liam caught her arm.

"Stay away from the new omega," he warned, then glanced at Megan and Moe. "All of you. I don't trust him."

Jayna opened her mouth to tell him she didn't need his permission to hang out with Eric or anyone else, but Liam was already heading upstairs to check on Brandon. She turned to Megan and Moe.

"Come on. I'll introduce you to Eric."

Megan exchanged looks with Moe, but they both followed her over to where Eric was talking with Frasheri. The Albanian was studying Eric's fake driver's license.

"If I find anything in your background I don't like, you know I'll kill you, right?" Frasheri said.

Eric seemed unconcerned as he picked up his jacket and slung his pack on his shoulder, but Jayna's stomach clenched as Frasheri strode out of the lobby. Even though Eric had assured her his fake identity would check out, she couldn't help being worried anyway. Suddenly remembering Megan and Moe, she introduced them to Eric. Neither of her pack mates were interested in a meet and greet and clearly couldn't wait to get out of there.

"We're going to grab something to eat," Megan said. "You coming, Jayna?"

"In a little while," she said. "I'm going to show Eric to his room first."

Moe frowned at that while Megan gave Eric a wary look. "Do you want us to come with you?"

Jayna shook her head. "Go get something to eat."

"Are you sure?" Megan asked, and Jayna could see that her best friend was on the verge of panicking.

"I'm sure." She smiled. "I'll be fine."

Megan looked like she wanted to argue, but instead she caught Jayna's hand and pulled her close. "Be careful around him," she whispered in her ear. "He's freaky crazy."

Jayna wanted to assure her pack mates they had nothing to fear from Eric, that he was there to help them out of this mess, but she couldn't. So she simply nodded and gave Megan's hand a squeeze, then told her and Moe that she'd see them later.

One of the Albanians tossed her a set of keys and gave her an apartment number a few doors down from the guys on the fourth floor.

Jayna tried to look casual as she led Eric upstairs. His apartment was almost a mirror image of hers and Megan's.

"Sorry about Megan and Moe," she said as he closed the door behind them. "They think you're just another crazy omega who can't be trusted."

"I figured that." His mouth curved. "Don't worry about it."

Jayna nodded, then frowned, her gaze going to his torn T-shirt. "Let me take a look at those claw marks."

She knew from experience that ragged claw marks could hurt like hell and take a long time to heal.

"You don't have to," he said, but didn't stop her as she pulled his shirt up over his head.

After the fight she'd just seen, Jayna expected to see a bloody mess, but the dozen or so ragged scratches took a backseat to the overall view she got of his truly spectacular upper body. It was hard trying not to stare—Eric was seriously buff. Broad shoulders, thick chest and arm muscles, and abs so ripped she had a crazy desire to nip at them with her fangs.

In addition to all those captivating muscles, there were a couple other things about Eric's body that drew her attention. One was the big wolf head tattoo with the letters SWAT under it that dominated the left side of his chest. Clearly he wouldn't be taking his shirt off anywhere near the Albanians or the omegas—their loss.

The other thing that stood out were the scars. All werewolves had a scar or two, including her pack mates. But Eric had more than a few. There was a big one with what appeared to be stitch marks on either side of it on the right side of his chest. There were two more just above his belly button, both bearing tiny marks on either side, like he'd been cut into, then stitched up again.

Beyond those three big scars, he had half a dozen smaller ones—at least compared to the others—and some of them looked relatively fresh. Compared to all the other damage Eric had obviously sustained in his life, the scratches Caleb and Brandon had given him looked like paper cuts. Still, she wanted to clean them a little.

"Stay put," she said. "I'll be right back."

Taking his shirt, she went into the small kitchen and

got it wet in the sink, then went back over to where Eric was waiting.

"You know you don't have to do that, right?" he said as she carefully cleaned the blood out of each and every scratch.

She glanced up at him. "I haven't seen Caleb or Brandon wash their hands the entire time they've been here. They could be carrying some kind of nasty biological crud under their nails for all you know."

Eric's mouth twitched, but he didn't make a fuss as she continued tending to his wounds. He simply stood there patiently and let her work. She quickly lost herself in the simple task of cleaning the scratches, enjoying the feeling of his warm skin under her fingers. The fact that he smelled so damn good this close up may have had something to do with that. His scent was rather hypnotizing.

She knew she was taking longer to tend his wounds than absolutely necessary. But hey, it had been a long time since she'd enjoyed touching a man's body. It seemed like another life the last time she'd done something like this, and she'd been nothing but a hormonal teenager back then. After what happened the night she'd left home for good, she'd feared she'd lost the ability to enjoy something like this.

Jayna was so caught up in the moment, she almost didn't realize Eric was talking to her. "What?"

Maybe it was the midday sun coming through the window, but for a moment, it seemed like his eyes were glowing a beautiful, golden yellow. Then the color disappeared and he smiled at her.

"I asked if your alpha is always such an ass," he said.

"I think he was really hoping Brandon and Caleb would kill me."

Jayna had to actually shake her head a little to clear it and get herself to focus on anything other than the broad expanse of muscles in front of her.

"Liam wasn't always like that," she said. "When I first joined the pack, I thought he was amazing. He seemed to go out of his way to find betas who needed his help, and he did whatever it took to get them to a better place. But lately, he's changed. Suddenly, it all seems to be about power and money and respect. I don't know where the old Liam went, but the werewolf who took his place is an ass. And yes, I'm guessing he hoped Caleb would go nuts and kill you. It's almost certainly why he picked Caleb in the first place. The guy has major control issues."

Eric didn't say anything for a while. And when he did, it wasn't the disparaging comment about Liam that she expected.

"It must be rough," he said quietly, "seeing the alpha you used to respect disappear like that."

Jayna felt her throat tighten up, surprised at how accurately Eric had pegged exactly how she was feeling. Just thinking about it made tears gather in her eyes. She lowered her head so he couldn't see, busying herself with some of the scratches that trailed down toward his stomach.

"So what's your alpha like?" she asked suddenly, feeling his eyes on her and wanting more than anything to change the subject. She didn't like the idea of Eric seeing her cry or feeling sorry for her. "He must be pretty tough to keep a whole pack full of other alphas in line."

Eric chuckled, and Jayna had the pleasure of watching his abs flex.

"Sergeant Dixon? Yeah, I suppose at first he might come off as tough if you didn't really know him. He's stronger than just about anyone else in the Pack and absolutely fearless under fire. But more than that, he's the man who brought us all together, and he's risked his life for us more times than any of us can count. He's not that much older than the rest of us, but in all the ways that matter, he's more of a father than an alpha. There isn't anything we wouldn't do for him."

Jayna almost felt jealous. At his best, Liam had inspired that kind of devotion in his pack, but that had been a long time ago. Then again, she had to wonder if she and the other betas in her pack would have responded as well to a leader who was so obviously alpha. Maybe Sergeant Dixon was a perfect fit for Eric's pack, but would he have been for hers?

Jayna had cleaned off as much blood as she was going to and set aside Eric's messy shirt, letting her fingers explore his stomach and trail across his muscular chest to his equally well-muscled shoulder. She told herself that she was simply checking to make sure there wasn't any foreign debris in the deeper slashes near the top of his deltoids, but that was bogus. She liked touching him. It made her fingers tingle.

That's when she realized it wasn't just her fingers that were tingling. *Crap*. What the heck was going on? It was like she was sixteen again, getting a chance to make out with the hot guy at school. She licked her lips and surreptitiously glanced at Eric, hoping he hadn't noticed her less-than-casual interest in his muscles.

But apparently he had noticed. That gold flare was back in his eyes, and for a second, they stood there face-to-face, so close that Jayna could feel the warmth of his breath on her cheek.

She licked her lips again, and she saw Eric's sharp eyes follow the path her tongue made with the intensity of a predator. For a moment, she half expected him to lean forward and kiss her. She wasn't sure she would have stopped him. Her lips were tingling now along with the rest of her body. The urge to lean into the kiss she thought was coming was so powerful, it was hard to ignore—and more than a little scary.

Jayna mentally shook herself and took a step back. She'd never liked feeling out of control or scared, even if those feelings were the result of a sexual response stronger than she'd felt in a really long time.

The golden glow immediately dimmed in Eric's eyes. Giving her a small smile, he unzipped his backpack and took out a shirt and dragged it on. Even if she knew it was for the best, it was still hard watching him hide those muscles from sight. She could have gazed at them all day.

"I couldn't help but notice how close you and Megan are," Eric said, casually leaning back against the kitchen counter. "If you didn't look so completely different from each other, I would have guessed you were sisters."

Jayna was surprised by the change in topic, but grateful. It was like Eric had somehow realized she was having a momentary emotional crisis and was trying to help—another point in the big guy's favor.

"In a lot of ways, she is my sister," Jayna admitted. "When we first took Megan into our pack two years ago, she was in pretty bad shape."

"What happened to her? Before she joined your

pack, I mean," Eric said, then added, "If you don't mind me asking."

Jayna didn't answer right away. "Megan's house caught on fire a few days after she turned eighteen. She woke up when she smelled smoke, but by then the whole place was already burning. She tried to get the rest of her family out, but they'd already succumbed to smoke inhalation and she wasn't strong enough to carry them."

"Shit," Eric whispered. "Did any of them make it?"

Jayna shook her head. "No. A firefighter found Megan on the stairs beside her little brother. The guy got them out, but it was too late for her brother. Her parents and her older sister died in the fire too."

"That had to be hard to deal with."

"Yeah," Jayna agreed. "When she woke up in the hospital a few days later and they told her, she didn't handle it well. She blamed herself for being too weak to save them. She threw a chair through her hospital window and jumped out—from six floors up, onto the parking lot pavement."

"Damn," Eric hissed.

"Yeah. Damn." Tears filled Jayna's eyes like they did every time she thought about what had happened to Megan. "Megan should have died immediately, but the fire had brought on her change and the werewolf inside wouldn't let her die. She was hobbling her way onto the freeway when Liam picked up her scent. I don't know how he used to do it, but he could tell there was a werewolf in trouble. Somehow he realized that he couldn't save her though—that I was the only one who could."

Eric frowned. "What do you mean?"

Jayna shrugged. "Megan wanted to die, and she would have kept trying until she found something that worked. So Liam had me stay with her 24-7 for weeks. That was when our bond formed, and with it, she somehow found the will to live again."

Jayna wiped away the tears, remembering those long, dark days, when suddenly Eric was there at her side and his arms were going around her. She didn't stiffen or feel the sense of panic that usually came when a guy got in her space. She just felt warmth.

She relaxed against him, wrapping her arms around him and resting her head on his chest. A few more tears slipped out, but she decided to ignore those in the comfort of the moment.

But on the heels of that warm, comfortable feeling, another sensation crept in, and Jayna's heart started beating faster as her jaws and fingers started tingling—like she was on the verge of shifting. She wasn't stupid. She knew what was happening. She was aroused—so aroused it was almost bringing on an involuntary shift. The intensity of it scared her.

She tried to breathe through it and get herself under control. She'd had sex in the years following Darren's attempted rape—more to convince herself that she was normal than because she wanted it. The sex had been mechanical and meaningless, a way of assuring herself that Darren hadn't broken her.

But she wasn't feeling anything mechanical or meaningless now. Right then, she wanted to have sex with Eric. She wanted it with a hunger that literally had her shaking.

She shouldn't have even been thinking about something like that after telling him Megan's story.

Jayna took a step back. Then another. Eric didn't follow. He simply walked back over to the counter he'd been leaning against before, giving her space to collect herself. Her mind raced to find words that would fill the silence dominating the large, open space around them and the sudden cool gulf that separated her from Eric.

She ran her hand through her long hair. "So, um, what's your plan now that you've gotten yourself into the building?"

It was a lame segue out of the uncomfortable situation, but her mind wasn't working at full efficiency just then.

"It's simple really," Eric said, as if the elephant in the room didn't even exist. "Every time we figure out where the Albanians are planning to strike, we get a tip to my pack mate, Cooper. He'll make sure the info gets to my alpha, who will make life damn hard on Frasheri, Kos, and their pet omegas."

She frowned. "That might work once or twice, but don't you think they'll figure out someone in this building is ratting them out at some point?"

"The fact that there's a gang of mobsters trying to take over control of organized crime in Dallas is about the worst-kept secret in town," Eric said. "Frasheri and Kos have to know every rival gang and thug in the city is watching this place, waiting for them to make another move. We just have to make sure it looks like one of their rivals is tipping off the cops. It shouldn't be too hard since we were waiting for you at the warehouse the other day."

Jayna wondered how SWAT had known they'd hit the warehouse, but she didn't ask.

"How do we make sure that none of my pack gets caught in the crossfire between the cops and the Albanians?"

"I'm going to personally make sure that none of your pack is there when the shooting starts," Eric promised. "You have my word on that."

Coming from anyone else, those words would have been hollow, but Jayna believed them from Eric.

After working out a few more details of their plan to bring the Albanians down, which included Eric giving her Cooper's contact info, Jayna headed back to her room with her head spinning. *What a freaking day.*

Megan yanked open the door the minute she knocked. "Finally! You've been up there showing the new omega his room for an hour. Since when do you hang around with omegas?"

Jayna felt terrible for worrying Megan, but she couldn't tell her who Eric really was. Not yet.

"I don't hang around with them." Jayna locked the door and wedged the chair underneath the knob. "I was just being polite and making sure he got comfortably settled in."

She didn't look at Megan as she walked into the tiny kitchen and grabbed the bag of Doritos sitting on the table. She opened it and reached in for a handful of chips.

"You were just being polite," Megan said. "And I suppose being polite required you to clean his scratches for him?"

Jayna almost choked on a chip. She turned to look at Megan "What?"

Megan pointed at her hand. "There's blood on the back of your hand. Don't even bother denying it belongs to him. His scent is very unique."

Jayna twisted her hand around until she saw the tiny smear. She scrubbed it off with a paper towel. "Um, yeah, I helped him clean up. I thought it'd be a good idea to be friendly to him. We might have to go out on a job together, and it would be nice to have an omega covering our backs and not stabbing us in them."

That line sounded suitably dramatic to her, but Megan didn't look like she was buying it. "Uh-huh. Whatever you say. Will you be helping Brandon and Caleb clean up next?"

Jayna shoved a handful of pointy Doritos in her mouth and crunched loudly.

Megan laughed and waved her hand. "Okay. Go ahead and keep your secrets for now. But if you come up here with Eric's scent all over your clothes again, I'm going to think you've been getting busy with the new guy."

Jayna watched in disbelief as Megan wandered over to her bed and thumbed through an old issue of *Cosmo*. She hadn't even thought about anyone smelling Eric's scent on her. Now that he was going to be living at the loft, it wouldn't be as much of an issue, but she still had to be careful.

But while Megan might be smiling, Jayna knew there were some hurt feelings there too. There had never been secrets between the two of them. Jayna felt crappy about keeping her friend in the dark, but there was simply too much at risk.

There was something Jayna needed to tell Megan

though. She walked over to her own bed and sat down, facing her friend.

"Megan, I have to tell you something, and I need you to promise that you won't breathe a word of what I say to anyone else, not even the guys."

That got Megan's attention. She lowered the magazine and looked at Jayna with alarm. "What's wrong?"

"Nothing," Jayna assured her. "I just need to tell you something."

"Okay," Megan said hesitantly.

Jayna took a deep breath, hoping Megan wouldn't ask a lot of questions she wasn't ready to answer. "If something goes wrong, find Eric. He'll get you and the guys out of here."

Confusion flitted across Megan's face, quickly followed by fear. "What do you mean, 'go wrong'? What do you think is going to happen? And why would Eric help us? He's an omega."

Jayna shook her head, refusing to give in to the instinct begging her to tell Megan everything. "Please don't ask me for details because I can't give them to you right now. But Eric is different. If there's trouble, promise that you'll go to him for help, okay?"

"Okay." Megan bit her lip. "But nothing is going to happen. Right?"

Jayna forced herself to smile. "Of course not. Everything is going to be fine. I just wanted to tell you. In case."

She hoped.

Chapter 7

"HEY, YOU OKAY?" JAYNA ASKED AS SHE GENTLY elbowed him in the ribs.

Becker started. Damn, he'd just about fallen asleep on her shoulder in the back of the big Cadillac Escalade. In the front seat, the two Albanians were quietly talking in their own language while the two omegas occupying the middle row were laughing about something.

He sat up straighter, blinking the sleep—and the early-morning sun—out of his eyes and popping a kink out of his neck. "Sorry about that."

"Don't worry about it. I know you haven't been getting a lot of sleep lately. Speaking of which, you didn't have to come out with me on this one, you know. I could have handled it on my own."

He stretched as much as he could in the tight confines of the rear bench seat of the SUV, careful not to whack Jayna in the head with his elbow. "I know, but I feel better coming with you."

She smiled, her blue eyes teasing. "Okay, but if you fall asleep while we're in there, I'm not going to drag your big butt back to the vehicle. You're too heavy."

He grinned back. "Deal."

Becker wouldn't have cared if he'd had to mainline caffeine to stay awake, there was no way in hell he'd ever have let Jayna go on this job by herself.

Two days ago, he'd been so sure his simple plan was

foolproof. All he had to do was stick close to Jayna and her pack mates and keep them safe, then text Cooper when it looked like the Albanians or the omegas were heading out to do something suitably nefarious.

The only problem was that the Albanians and omegas were up to something nefarious twenty-four hours a day. Worse, almost any time they went out, they took at least one of Jayna's pack mates with them. It was like Kos and Frasheri didn't trust the omegas—or hell, even their own men—to get anything right without one of the pack werewolves being with them. Either that or Kos and Frasheri thought they were some kind of frigging good-luck charms. Then again, maybe the Albanians wanted to ensure that their pack didn't take off. And since Becker was determined to keep them safe, he went out of his way to go on every job they did, even if that meant going without sleep. And for the last two days, that was exactly what he'd done. Liam didn't like it, of course, but Becker ignored the pack alpha and jumped in whichever SUV headed out. So far, all he'd gone on were recon missions, so he hadn't broken the law, and he didn't plan to.

That might be difficult today though, since this morning, they were hitting a small family-owned jewelry store that had recently bought a collection of rough diamonds from a dealer in New York. According to Kos, the store didn't employ a lot of guards, so the big mobster was of the opinion that it should be an easy job. Becker wasn't too sure about that. If they'd just bought a big load of diamonds, they'd likely have extra security on hand. Thank God he'd been able to text Cooper before they'd left. He had a feeling this job was going to go bad.

The two omegas were talking about what they could do with diamonds like the ones they were on their way to steal. Becker ignored them until one of them pulled something shiny out of the pocket of his tactical vest and rolled it back and forth between his fingers.

Well, he'd be damned. The fuckers had skimmed some of the platinum medallions from the warehouse job. He vaguely remembered the officer standing guard the day he and Cooper had gone there saying something about some pieces being stolen, but the other day, he'd heard Kos bemoaning the fact that none of it had made it back to the loft. Clearly, omegas weren't big on the whole loyalty thing. Made him wonder why the Albanians were even willing to trust them.

Becker glanced at Jayna. She was gazing out the window, unaware that he was watching her. The sun highlighted her naturally blond hair, making it look even silkier, and he had to resist the urge to run his fingers through it. Usually he hated being stuffed into tight places, but right then, being squeezed into the seat beside her was pretty close to heaven. Even though he'd been on the go nonstop since he'd infiltrated the pack and hadn't gotten to spend nearly as much time with her as he would have liked, he was still having a good time. For now, being under the same roof was good enough for him.

Yesterday, they'd been able to compare notes in the privacy of his apartment on the information they'd been able to get to Cooper, but unfortunately, there hadn't been a repeat of that magical moment from his first night at the loft, when the sparks had zipped between them. Everything about that moment, from their private conversation to the feel of her warm, soft hands on his skin, made all the risks he was taking seem worthwhile. Controlling himself had been tough though. Being that close to her without kissing her had been pure misery, especially because he'd been able to tell she'd been experiencing the same sensations he was. The delectable change in her scent had been a dead giveaway.

But he'd also sensed something else coming off Jayna—hesitancy verging on downright panic. Something was holding her back when it came to her giving in to the same feelings and emotions that were rushing through his body every time he was around her. Until he figured out what that something was, there was always going to be a wall there. It was frustrating, but he wasn't going to push.

That didn't mean he couldn't daydream though, and sitting with her in the cramped backseat was definitely in the daydreaming category. She smelled so good, it was all he could do not to lean over and lick her like a puppy. He was just wondering if anyone would notice if he scooted closer and buried his face in her long hair when the Escalade turned into an alley, pulled up behind a small building, and stopped.

"The store will not open for another thirty minutes," the Albanian driving the SUV said in thickly accented English. "The old guard will be in the break room, still drinking his coffee."

Becker felt the hair on the back of his neck stand up as the Albanian repeated the instructions Kos had given them earlier. He and Jayna would be responsible for dealing with the guard and herding any other employees into the break room with him. The Albanians would disable the internal video cameras, then stand guard in front of the small jewelry store. The two omegas would be responsible for getting the female manager—the shop owner's daughter—to open the safe and turn over the diamonds. That was the part of the plan that made Becker uneasy. He'd seen the glint in the omegas' eyes when Kos said they could do anything they wanted to the woman as long as she opened the safe. Man, he hoped SWAT got there before the whole thing went down and he had to blow his cover.

"No messing around in there," the Albanian added as he pulled a black ski mask over his face. "Get the diamonds; then get out."

Becker grabbed Jayna's hand and gave it a quick squeeze, then lowered his ski mask and pulled on his gloves. He listened intently as he got out of the SUV and headed for the back door with the others, hoping to hear sirens approaching. If he had heard sirens, he could have convinced the Albanians to give up on the diamonds and get out of there. But no such luck. That didn't mean anything though. If Cooper had gotten the text in time, his SWAT teammates could have been out there, waiting to take them down the second they went in the building. That would be great for the innocent people in the shop—not so great for him and his goal of helping Jayna and her pack.

He wondered for the hundredth time if the plan he and Cooper had cooked up had any chance of working.

But as one of the omegas kicked in the back door and went in with a howl that bordered on maniacal, Becker decided to put all the what-ifs aside. He had enough problems to deal with right now.

Once inside, the Albanians immediately ran down the hallway to the front of the store, while the omegas made a beeline for the manager's office. Becker hesitated, torn between following the two werewolves to make sure they didn't hurt the woman, and sticking to the plan. Jayna gave him a questioning look, clearly worried too. He nodded and jerked his head in the direction of the break room.

He and Jayna rounded up the two female employees and the nice, old security guard in fifteen seconds. The Albanians disabled the security systems and video camera just as fast. Now he had to hope the store manager cooperated.

A woman's scream echoed from the back of the building, followed by the distinctive sound of material being torn.

Shit.

The two women that Jayna had herded into the break room tightened their grips on each other's hands, their faces white. The security guard started to get to his feet, but then took one look at the guns Becker and Jayna were carrying and thought better of it.

One of the Albanians shouted something from the front of the store in his own language, following it up with an order to the omegas to stop wasting time and get the damn safe open.

Becker ground his teeth. He should have simply kidnapped Jayna and her entire pack. Then he could have just walked into the loft and shot every one of these idiots—twice.

"Watch them," he told Jayna, motioning to the security guard and two women. Turning, he left the break room and jogged down the hallway toward the back of the building.

"Get them back on the safe!" the Albanian driver shouted at him from the front room.

Oh yeah, sure. Stop two morons from raping a woman and get them back on task. What the hell was he—a daycare worker for omega werewolves?

Shit. If this was how criminals behaved, it was no wonder he and his SWAT teammates took so many of them down. They were too stupid to live. Then again, maybe this was how Gage felt some days. The SWAT pack could occasionally be a little stupid too. Becker's current predicament was a shining example of that.

The omega standing guard in the hallway outside the manager's office glared at him. "We got this. Go back and babysit the old folks."

What a complete ass, Becker thought as he walked up and punched the guy in the face. The werewolf flew backward and bounced off the wall, bleeding like crazy from a broken nose as he fell to the floor in a dazed heap. He was still moving around though, reminding Becker that it was as hard to knock out an omega as it was to knock out an alpha. He'd have to remember that.

Becker strode into the office to find the store manager on the floor beside her desk, the other omega—the one who liked to play with his platinum medallion—leaning over her menacingly. He'd torn her blouse and was telling her all the horrible things he planned to do to her if she didn't open the safe. The idiot was so intent on threatening her that he didn't realize Becker was there until he yanked the guy to his feet and spun him around, then smashed the back of his head into the nearest hard object he could find—the safe panel. Becker pounded his head into the safe a few times before letting him fall to the floor. The asshole was definitely out cold.

Becker turned and looked at the shop manager. She cringed away from him, terror in her eyes as she tried to hold the tatters of her blouse together. He really wished he could pull up his ski mask. Seeing him like this definitely wasn't helping.

"Do you have an alarm button in this room?" he asked in his softest, least intimidating voice.

The woman stared at him for a moment like he was insane, then motioned under the desk with a shaking hand.

"Would you mind pushing it for me?" he asked.

Now she looked really confused. But she slowly reached under the desk and poked around until a loud alarm started ringing.

"Thanks." Becker bent down to take the platinum medallion out of the omega's vest and slip it into his pocket. "By the way, that diamond merchant you bought from in New York sold you out to a really bad guy. You probably don't want to buy from him anymore." Turning, he jogged out of the room and down the hallway to the front of the store. "Time to leave. Moron hit the alarm."

Jayna was heading his way in a flash, the two Albanians right behind her.

"What about the safe?" the driver asked.

Becker shook his head. "It's a no-go. Our guy smashed the keypad."

The Albanians muttered something in their native language and shook their heads, as if they'd seen this coming. They stepped over the omega who was still rolling around in a daze on the floor in the hallway and raced out the back door. In the distance, sirens echoed in the air. *About damn time*. Becker motioned Jayna out.

"What about him?" she asked, jerking her head at the werewolf still trying to get to his knees.

Becker nudged the omega with his boot, pushing him back down. The guy looked like he really didn't want to bother getting up this time.

"What about him?" Becker said, holding the door open for her.

"You left them to get arrested?" Liam snarled.

Becker returned the other werewolf's glare. When he and Jayna had gotten back without the diamonds and the two omegas, Liam had made it no secret that he was pissed. Frasheri, on the other hand, didn't seem nearly as upset. Instead, he sat at his big desk in front of the huge row of picture windows in his office on the second floor, watching Becker and Liam square off. Even Kos seemed more interested in the power struggle going on than the botched robbery.

"Damn right I did," Becker told Liam. "Any loyalty I felt toward them disappeared the minute I heard they were planning to swipe some of the diamonds for themselves."

Kostandin's eyes narrowed. "Planning to swipe some of the diamonds for themselves?"

"That's bullshit," Liam snapped. "He's making that up to distract you from the fact that he screwed up. Right, Jayna?"

Becker swore silently as Kos and Frasheri looked at Jayna, their eyes questioning. Becker knew she'd back him up, but he still felt like crap for putting her in this position. She didn't seem uncomfortable though. Beside him, her pulse beat in a nice, steady rhythm.

She met Liam's gaze unflinchingly. "Eric's not making anything up."

Becker couldn't resist giving Liam a smug look. "If you need any more proof they were dirty, this should do it."

Pulling the platinum medallion out of his pocket, he tossed it on Frasheri's desk. The silence that descended on the room was deafening. Even Liam seemed speechless for once.

"Where did you get that?" Kos asked.

"One of the omegas flashed it around before we got to the jewelry store," Becker said. "When I went back to see what was taking him and his buddy so long with the safe, I heard them talking about taking a few diamonds for themselves, that no one would notice. Let's just say they should consider themselves lucky to be sitting in a jail cell. If I had my way, those assholes would be in the morgue right now, but the cops showed up."

That part wasn't exactly true, but Frasheri and Kos didn't know that. And from what he'd picked up over the past few days, loyalty was a big thing with the Albanians. They'd never consider Becker or any of the other werewolves part of their inner circle—you had to be a blood relation for that—but they expected anyone who worked for them to be loyal to the family. That included the hired muscle.

Telling Frasheri and Kos that the omegas were traitors fed into the suspicions they probably already had about the unpredictable werewolves. If he played this right, he might be able to drive a wedge between the

Albanians and the omegas, maybe even between them and Liam. If the various factions in the loft were focused on who was betraying them, it'd be a hell of a lot easier to take them out one by one.

"Why would you care that those omegas had been stealing from us?" Kos asked.

Becker shrugged. "Pack doesn't steal from pack. And you're my pack now."

Kos raised an eyebrow at that, then glanced at Frasheri. The older Albanian stared at Becker for a moment before nodding.

"That's it?" Liam demanded, slanting Becker a venomous look. "This a-hole doesn't come back with the diamonds, he gets two of my omegas arrested, and you're fine with that?"

Kostandin gave Liam one of those patented flat-eyed looks of his. "Failure on a job is the price of doing business. But we will not tolerate those who steal from us. And those omegas of yours were stealing from us. Eric has simply done what I would have done in his position. Not only am I fine with it, I require it."

Liam's eyes flashed yellow. "That's—"

But Kos cut him off. "And if I discover you knew what these omegas of yours were doing—"

"I didn't! I swear to you," Liam insisted. "If you weren't so damn worried about me stealing from you, maybe you'd stop and wonder why the cops show up every time a crew has gone out on a job the past couple days."

Becker saw Jayna glance at him, but he didn't look at her. "Maybe someone's been tipping them off."

Frasheri considered that. "Like who?"

Becker shrugged. "A rival crew maybe?"

He and Jayna had talked about suggesting the possibility to Kos and Frasheri but hadn't had a chance to plant the seed yet until now.

"Or maybe you did it," Liam accused.

Becker snorted. "Right. I tipped off the cops and told them we'd be hitting the jewelry store so I could get arrested too. That's brilliant."

Liam opened his mouth to say something, but Kos cut him off.

"We're done here."

This time, Liam left without a fuss, but not before giving Becker and Jayna a look that could have melted the flesh from their bones. Becker couldn't give a damn what the werewolf thought of him, but if that bastard tried to take out his anger on Jayna, Becker would rip off his head and shove it up his ass.

Becker held his hand out toward the door Liam had left open, indicating Jayna should go ahead of him. He gave the Albanians a nod, then followed, closing the door behind them.

Liam was nowhere in sight, but there was an omega and a handful of Albanians hanging around the hallway, so he and Jayna didn't speak until they were in her apartment.

"So, I'm guessing we have a plan B now?" she asked softy.

Becker grinned, glad Jayna had picked up on the seeds he'd planted in Frasheri's office. "Yup. I got the idea when I saw that omega flash the platinum medallion. In between texting Cooper with every tip we can get our hands on, we're going to start doing everything we can to convince Frasheri and Kos that the omegas are a liability—and vice versa. With a little nudging from us, the Albanians and omegas should be at each other's throats in no time."

"And then we can just walk out when the shooting starts." Jayna smiled up at him. "You're pretty devious," she said, then leaned in and put her mouth right next to his ear. "For a cop."

Her whisper was a warm breeze across his skin. With her sweet mouth millimeters from his ear and her intoxicating scent enveloping him—almost causing him to shift—the urge to turn his head and kiss her was damn near impossible to resist. It took every ounce of strength Becker had, but he forced himself to step back.

Not because he didn't trust himself, but because he didn't want to rush her into anything. But before he left, he thought he caught a flash of green in her eyes as she gave him a smile. He was pretty sure that sudden flare of iridescent color had nothing to do with the soft lighting in the apartment and everything to do with her body's response to him.

Chapter 8

JAYNA LEANED OVER ERIC'S BARE, MUSCULAR CHEST, trying not to be sick as she dug a bullet out. It was hard—there was blood everywhere. She'd never done anything like this in her life, and she never wanted to do it again. But when she'd walked into Eric's apartment to find him sitting on the floor with his back to the bed, about to root around in his own chest with a flipping pair of needle-nose pliers while Megan held up a small mirror for him, she knew she had to do *something*. Thank goodness the blood was covering his SWAT tattoo or she'd have to worry about explaining that too.

The mere thought that Eric might actually die freaked her out so much that her canines and claws extended all on their own and she had to pull away for a second to get them to retract. She purposely hadn't let herself think about what was developing between her and Eric. She knew she liked him. She just hadn't realized how much. And now here he was, bleeding out all over the floor. This couldn't be happening.

Eric took her shaking hand in his big one. "Jayna, look at me." She did. "Calm down, okay? I'm not going to die. I just need you to get the bullet out. Once you do, the bleeding will stop and my body will start to heal. I promise. Just relax, and everything will be fine."

Jayna didn't know how that could be possible—he was bleeding so much—but the complete and total conviction in his words made her believe him. She nodded and took a deep breath, letting Eric guide her hand as she slipped the tip of the pliers into the tear in his pec again.

"What the heck happened out there?" she asked, more to distract herself than because she really wanted to know.

"He got shot protecting me," Megan said softly.

That didn't surprise Jayna.

"It was supposed to be easy," Megan added, referring to the recon mission she, Chris, and Eric had gone out on after lunch. "We were just supposed to slip into the Union Pacific secure intermodal terminal and figure out where they park their trucks with all the high-value items. But a security guard saw us and instead of acting cool, the Albanians and omegas started shooting at everything in sight—including each other—and Chris and I ended up getting stuck in the crossfire. I don't understand what's gotten into them. They should have been trying to get away from the security guards, not trying to kill each other."

Jayna had a pretty good idea why the Albanians and omegas weren't exactly besties at the moment, but she pushed those thoughts aside as Eric guided the long jaws of the pliers she held deeper into his chest.

Megan continued her story, something about how Eric had dodged a hail of gunfire twice to get her and Chris to safety.

Jayna stopped listening when she hit something solid and Eric grunted in pain. She froze in panic, sure she'd damaged something critically important in there. "Oh God. I'm sorry."

He shook his head as he helped her manipulate the pliers even deeper. "Keep going."

How can he think so clearly in the middle of something like this?

"I'd be dead if it weren't for Eric," Megan said. "And Chris would probably be in jail."

Jayna felt the tip of the pliers contact something that felt distinctly metallic. She slowly pulled out the pliers, sighing in relief when she saw the smashed-up bullet held securely in its jaws. More blood came out with the bullet, but almost immediately, the flow slowed, and she could tell from the way the tension left Eric's body that the pain had subsided drastically.

"See, I told you I'd be fine," Eric said with a smile that made her stomach start to flutter for a completely different reason. "You did great. You're a natural at this."

Jayna definitely didn't agree with that. But she didn't say anything as she set the pliers on the floor and picked up the towel so she could clean the blood off his chest. Megan leaned forward and kissed Eric on the cheek.

"This is for watching out for Chris," she said, then kissed his cheek again. "And this is for watching out for me."

Eric smiled. "Anytime."

Jayna felt her heart squeeze. A few days ago, Megan had thought Eric was just another crazy omega, but Jayna could tell from the way her pack mates treated him now that they didn't see him that way anymore. In every way that mattered, Eric had become the pack's new alpha. He was the one watching out for them and keeping them safe. The only person who hadn't figured that out was Liam. But then, he'd been so busy bending over backward trying to stay in the Albanians' good graces, he didn't see much of anything anymore.

Liam had come to her yesterday bemoaning the fact that two of "his" omegas had up and left. He thought Kos had chased them off because they were more loyal to Liam than to the Albanian underboss. "It's all falling apart," Liam had said softly, and for a moment, Jayna had almost felt bad for him. Until Liam had told her that he needed Moe and the rest of her pack mates to pick up the slack and go out on even more jobs. "That'll show Kos he needs to keep me around."

That was when Jayna decided she didn't feel bad about Liam losing his pack at all. As Eric had said about his own alpha, a werewolf became a pack leader by showing he cared more about his pack than he did himself. It definitely wasn't how anyone would describe Liam anymore. But it was how they'd describe Eric.

"I'm going back to the room," Megan said, giving Jayna a smile—and a pretty pointed look. "I'll see you later."

Jayna felt her face color. Could Megan be any more obvious? Yesterday, she'd asked Jayna when she was going to make a move on Eric. According to Megan, it was obvious to everyone that Eric had a thing for her. Jayna admitted she had a thing for him too but said it never seemed to be the right time. Megan must have thought now was the right time since Eric was lying half-naked on the floor in a very appreciative mood.

Jayna wasn't so sure about that, but she did want to talk to him about a few things while they had a little privacy. So after Megan left, she told Eric to stay put while she cleaned off the rest of the blood.

"This is becoming a habit," he murmured.

She smiled. "I hope digging bullets out of you doesn't become a habit. I'm a werewolf, not a doctor."

He let out a low, sexy growl as the towel slipped a bit too low. "Okay, tell me you didn't just steal a line from *Star Trek*."

Jayna laughed. "I guess I did. I feel like such a nerd."

He flashed her a grin. "That's okay. I think nerds are sexy."

By the time she got the worst of the mess off, the bleeding had completely stopped and the wound looked measurably better. She was amazed at how fast he healed. None of the werewolves in her pack could have knit up so fast, not even Liam.

She rinsed out the towel, then gently rubbed it over his chest and abs again, in case there were any scratches or cuts she hadn't noticed the first time.

"So, now Megan loves you too, huh?" she said.

Eric's mouth twitched. "Too?"

Jayna smirked right back at him. "I'm talking about Moe. He told me all about what you did at the drug lab the two of you went out to raid with Kos this morning, how you let those gang members go after Kos ordered you to kill them, then burned the place down so no one would know. Moe was pretty worked up, so I didn't get all the details out of him, but I can tell you one thing for sure: as far as he's concerned, you pretty much walk on water."

Eric snorted. "I'm far from that perfect. Those guys I cut loose this morning were hardcore gangbangers. Making meth is the least of their crimes. I told them to get out of town or end up on a slab in the morgue. They chose the first option. I have no way of knowing if they'll leave though. If they show up on the Albanians' radar, I'm screwed. But what else could I do? It wasn't like I could just kill them in cold blood."

Jayna leaned over to wipe up some blood that had gotten on the inside of one of his bulging biceps. The move brought her T-shirt-covered breasts extremely close to his well-muscled chest, and she swore she could feel the heat pouring off him. She cleaned off the blood, then sat back as quickly as she could. While she enjoyed the sensation of being so close to him, she wasn't sure if she liked where that sensation might lead.

There was no denying the attraction between her and Eric, even if the loft wasn't the best place to pursue it. He never pushed, which Jayna appreciated, but she'd have to be blind not to notice the gold that flared in his eyes any time they got close. Even now, after having a bullet dug out of him, she could see the desire burning like molten sunlight.

Her breath hitched, and she had to work to calm her pulse and her breathing, knowing part of Eric's excitement was due to the arousal pheromones that probably poured off her whenever she was this close to him.

"Moe thinks you did the right thing, and so do I," she said. "What did you tell Frasheri when you got back?"

Eric laughed, making his abs tense and flex in the most mesmerizing way. She seriously loved those abs.

"I was going to lie and tell him that Kos was skimming money, but I didn't have to. It turns out Kos told Frasheri we only got fifty grand and a couple bags of meth from the drug lab. All I did was tell Frasheri the truth—that it was more like a hundred grand and fifty baggies of junk."

Jayna's jaw dropped. "You mean that Kos really *is* ripping off his uncle?"

"It looks like it. Frasheri's heart rate went through the roof. A few minutes later, he gave me another one of those big manila envelopes full of cash and asked me to take it to the self-storage locker."

Jayna couldn't believe it. When she and Eric had started Operation Distrust three days ago, they'd had no idea it would work this well. Last night, Frasheri had told Eric that two of his most trusted soldiers had disappeared in the last week and that he believed Kos had killed them. Then Frasheri gave Eric a piece of paper with the address of a nearby self-storage place, the combination to the lock on the door, and a duffel bag full of money and guns to stash there if Kostandin made a move against him. At this rate, war could break out between the two factions by the end of the week. That could be very good for her and her pack.

Jayna was about to say as much to Eric, but as she gazed at him, she forgot about the Albanians. Eric's eyes were molten gold as they burned into hers, and all she could think about was how much she wanted to kiss him right then.

"This is for taking care of Chris, Megan, and the rest of my pack," she whispered as she closed the last few inches between them.

Jayna meant for it to be a simple thank-you kiss, but the moment her lips touched his, her entire body tingled from the contact, and she knew there wasn't going to be anything simple about it. One kiss definitely wasn't going to be enough.

But if she didn't stop to take a breath, she was going to pass out from lack of oxygen. She lifted her head with a soft growl to find Eric regarding her with eyes so gold they almost glowed. He was just as excited as she was. He made no move to pull her close and pick up where they'd left off though. Instead, he caught a tendril of her long hair and curled it around his finger, the corners of his mouth curving up in a smile that was both playful and flirty.

"So, was that a simple thank-you-for-helping-my-pack kiss?" he asked.

"Yeah," she answered, knowing it had been about a whole lot more. "But this next kiss is all for me."

Giving him a smile, she slowly threw her leg over his and straddled his lap, then put her hands on his shoulders and leaned in to cover his mouth with hers. The move was so bold and unlike her, but it felt right too, and she just about lost herself in how amazing kissing Eric was. But as it always did, that little voice in the back of her head that came out whenever she got close to a guy popped up again to tell her she was making a serious mistake. She tried to ignore it, but the voice only got louder until it was practically shouting at her to slow down and get control of herself.

Eric must have picked up on the struggle going on inside her, because this time, he was the one who broke the kiss. "Is everything okay?"

She nodded and gave him a small smile, then leaned in for another kiss, but he stopped her with a frown. She sat back on his thighs and covered her face with her hands. Eric may have been the one guy she could finally open herself up to, and she was going to ruin her chance because she was so screwed up.

Eric's big, strong hands took hold of hers and gently lowered them from her face. "Jayna, what's wrong? If I pushed too hard, I'm sorry. But please, talk to me."

Jayna couldn't look at him, so she stared down at their intertwined hands through eyes welling with tears. "It's not that, I swear. But it's complicated. And a long story."

"Well, with you sitting on me, it's not like I'm going anywhere, so you might as well tell me."

She would have climbed off his lap, but his hands settled on her thighs, keeping her seated firmly right where she was—straddling his hips in a position that made it impossible to ignore how much he enjoyed having her there, even with all the drama going on.

Jayna looked down at her hands. "I went through my change when I was seventeen...the night my stepfather tried to rape me." Eric let out a soft growl but didn't say anything. "Since then, I've had a hard time getting physical with guys, and when I do, it tends not to work out too well for the guy or me because I'm basically a mess."

Jayna held her breath, waiting for him to ease her off his lap and pull away from her, but he didn't. He didn't say anything either. *Oh crap*. This was bad.

She slowly lifted her head, afraid of what she'd see on his face and praying it wouldn't be pity. She'd be off his lap and running with all the speed her werewolf legs possessed if he gave her one second of pity.

But when she met his gaze, there was no pity to be seen. Just understanding.

"Thank you for telling me that. It explains a lot." He gave her a small smile. "But I'm still here. If you feel like telling me the full version of the story, I mean."

She stared at him, speechless. She'd just told him that she was messed up in the head and unlikely to be a good roll in the hay for a really long time to come. Yet here he was, waiting for the rest of the story. And the most amazing part? She was ready to tell him. It was a story that no one but Megan knew in full, and she was ready to tell a guy who wasn't even in her pack, a guy she'd known for less than a week.

So Jayna sat there, straddling his lap, and told him everything, starting with how her real dad had died when she was young, how her mom had turned to drugs first, then crappy guys to get through the day, how Darren had attacked her, and how she'd stabbed him, then walked away without ever looking back. After that, she told him how Liam, Chris, and Joseph had found her practically freezing to death on the streets of Detroit and taken her in. She even told him about sleeping with other guys over the years because she had this crazy notion that if she acted normal, she'd be normal.

"But it never worked," she finished quietly. She had a feeling it would be different with Eric though—if he was patient enough to put up with her while she worked out her issues. She gave him a sheepish look. "Sorry I dumped all that on you at once."

His mouth curved into that smile she loved so much. "You didn't dump anything on me. I'm glad you trust me enough to tell me."

Jayna was glad too, and for the first time in forever, it felt like a weight had been lifted from her shoulders. It felt good.

"Did you ever go back to find out what happened to your mom?" Eric asked. "Or see if your stepfather lived?"

She shook her head. "My face never showed up on any wanted posters, so he must have been okay. As for my mom, well, I didn't think there was any reason to bother. The pack became my family, and I moved on."

Even though Jayna was pretty sure she'd killed the mood after a conversation like that, she couldn't stop from leaning in to press a tender kiss to Eric's lips.

"Thank you," she said. "For listening."

He grinned. "Anytime."

It occurred to her that she should probably get off his lap, but she didn't want to. Despite everything, Eric was still excited. His hard cock, trapped between them as she sat astride his thighs, told her that in no uncertain terms. That hardness felt good…and scary at the same time. She might have slept with guys, but none of them had ever made her feel anything like this.

She looked at him from beneath her lashes. "Maybe we could try and see how things work out with us? I think it would be different with you."

He cupped her face in his hand. "I think it would be different too. But I'd rather find the right place and time to ease into this slowly. I don't like the idea of Kos or Liam or Frasheri walking in here when we're in the middle of something good. So why don't we leave this pot on to simmer for a while?"

She hadn't even thought about someone walking in on them. Eric was right. But that didn't mean she wasn't disappointed.

Eric weaved his fingers into her long hair and pulled her close to give her a long, lingering kiss that left her wanting more. And soon.

If she didn't leave now, she might not have the strength to.

She reluctantly got to her feet, then offered him a hand. He took it and walked with her to the door.

"I'll see you later?" she asked.

He grinned, his blue eyes twinkling. "Count on it."

Jayna went up on her toes to give him another kiss, then slipped out of his room and hurried downstairs. Megan must have heard her coming because her friend opened the door before Jayna could even knock.

"Well?" Megan asked with a grin that would make the Cheshire cat proud. "Did you have fun?"

Jayna laughed. Considering that Megan wasn't much more experienced with guys than Jayna, she was certainly interested in her and Eric hooking up.

"Yes, I had fun," Jayna said. "But all we did was talk."

Megan frowned. "You mean you two didn't...you know?"

Jayna shook her head. "No. We got close, but we both decided the loft isn't exactly the best place to..." She smiled. "You know."

Megan considered that. "Then maybe you and Eric should get out of here for a couple hours and go somewhere you can have privacy."

As much as Jayna loved that idea, she couldn't. "There's no way I'm leaving you and the guys alone for that long."

"That's silly," Megan protested. "We'll be fine. And if we need you, we'll call you and Eric."

Jayna didn't answer as she walked over to the small fridge in the apartment's kitchenette and took out two bottles of water. She handed one to Megan. Her friend took the bottle but didn't open it.

"Jayna, Eric's a really great guy. My mom always said that great guys don't come around that often, and that if you find one, you should hang on to him. And you deserve a great guy like him." Megan smiled. "I'm not saying you have to do anything if you don't want to, but at least get away for a few hours together. If anyone asks, we'll say you went out for coffee or something."

Jayna chewed on her lip. Spending time with Eric away from the loft and all the drama would be nice. Like Megan said, it would only be for a few hours.

Chapter 9

BECKER OPENED THE DOOR TO HIS APARTMENT, PRAYING the place didn't smell like dead fish. Cooper was a good friend—the best—but he wasn't exactly with it when it came to taking care of Becker's fish.

Thankfully, the apartment smelled fine. He tossed his keys on their usual table, closing the door behind him and Jayna.

"Mind if I use your bathroom?" she asked.

"Sure. Down the hall, second door on the right."

Becker watched her go, his eyes locking on the sexy sway of her hips in the yoga pants she wore. He stifled a groan. He'd always had a thing for women in yoga pants, but Jayna took it to a whole new level.

He swore under his breath as she disappeared into the bathroom, berating himself for even going there. Getting away from the loft was about being able to relax together for a few hours, nothing more. He wasn't going to assume they'd have sex.

While he waited for Jayna, he went over to check on his fish and was relieved to see they were fine. They immediately came over to the glass, clearly happy to see him too. Since he didn't know when Cooper had fed them last, he only gave them a few flakes of food. They gobbled them hungrily, swishing their tails in thanks.

As he watched his girls swim around, he thought back to the conversation he and Jayna had had the day before. When she'd told him what her stepfather had done, he'd seriously come close to calling Cooper right then to get an address on the guy. The urge to hunt him down and beat the shit out of him had been overpowering. But he'd forced himself to check his anger. Jayna had moved on from that horrible night, and he needed to respect that.

But he'd sworn that if he was ever fortunate enough to run into that ass wipe, he was going to finish what she'd started.

Down the hall, the bathroom door opened, distracting him from his thoughts of revenge.

"Wow," Jayna said, coming to stand beside him. "That tank is beautiful. Though I have to admit, I never really pegged you as the fish type."

He chuckled. "I could sit and watch them swim for hours. They're actually the perfect pets for me. If I'm a little late because of the job, I don't have to worry about them making a mess on the carpet."

Jayna touched her finger to the glass tank and gently traced it back and forth in time with the motions of the three saltwater fish. "Do they have names?"

"The red one with the silver markings is Lady Liadrin, the dark blue one is Queen Azshara, and the black one with the long, wavy fins is Lady Vashj."

She glanced at him. "Those are the strangest names for fish I've ever heard. What's wrong with Dory?"

He moved closer to her, breathing in her scent as she went back to watching the fish swim among the colorful coral and lush plants. "They're all female characters from World of Warcraft. It's a video game."

"Yeah, I know what World of Warcraft is." She

turned to him with a smile. "Wouldn't have pegged you for a gamer either."

He grinned. "I like to think of myself as a man with varied and complex tastes. Come on. I'll give you a grand tour of the place."

His apartment wasn't that big, so maybe *grand* wasn't the right word, but Jayna seemed eager to look around.

The moment they walked into the kitchen, she locked in on the two big bowls on the floor in the corner. "I thought I smelled a dog." She looked around. "Where is he?"

"I share custody with the rest of the Pack," he said. Then, when she gave him a confused look, added, "We picked up Tuffie a few months ago after she and her owner got shot by some psycho. Her owner didn't make it, so we took her in. We all take turns bringing her home with us."

Jayna smiled and looked wistfully at the bowls. "That's so cool. I always wanted a dog when I was a kid. But with my screwed-up home life, getting a dog was out of the question."

Becker never thought of himself as a softie, but his chest tightened up at her words. "Then I'll make sure you get to meet Tuffie. In fact, we'll make it a priority." He put his arm around her shoulders and pressed a kiss to her temple. "Come on, I'll show you the rest of the place."

They wandered from the kitchen to the second bedroom, which was set up as his computer-room-slash-home-office. Jayna stopped in the doorway and stared at the four computers with their huge, oversized monitors.

"What the heck do you do with all these, spy on the NSA?"

He laughed. "Nah. I used to do work like that, but

these days, I just play around on them. Kind of like a hobby, I guess."

"A hobby, huh?" She lifted a brow. "Like hacking into Starbucks's computers and the city's video cameras so you could find me?"

"Exactly." He grinned. "Some guys like to work on cars or do woodworking. I search for beautiful women who might want to bite me."

She blushed. "I never intended to bite you. Shoot you, yes. But never bite you. At least not the first time we met. The desire to bite you came much later."

Becker had a sudden image of Jayna nipping at his neck with those sexy canines of hers, a thought that immediately made his cock stiffen. He decided he'd better do something intelligent before he gave in to his animal urges and pulled her into his arms. He led her back toward the living room, intending to show her his killer TV and video game setup, but she stopped halfway there.

"What's in here?" she asked, motioning her head toward the closed door.

"My bedroom," he said, heading toward the living room again. "Nothing interesting in there."

Not unless you counted his king-size bed. And while it wasn't all that interesting on its own, he was already picturing her lying back on it, gloriously naked with her silky hair fanned out on the pillows. That image made his cock even harder.

He cleared his throat. "You want to try your hand at a few video games? I promise to take it easy on you."

"I should be offended that you're assuming I suck at video games." Jayna plopped down on his big, comfy couch, then kicked off her flip-flops and sat cross-legged. "But since I don't play them very much, you're probably right."

Becker made a quick detour into the kitchen to grab two bottles of water from the fridge, then powered up his game console and television.

"You sure the TV is big enough?" she teased as she sipped some water. "I'm not sure we'll be able to see it clearly from here."

He selected a simple race car game he thought would be good to start with. "It's the biggest one I could get through the door."

Her lips twitched. "Compensating for something, are we?"

He chuckled as he handed her a controller. "Yeah. Small apartment doors."

Becker had spent a lot of time playing video games with the guys from the team, but as he and Jayna spent the next hour or so goofing off on his couch, he realized he'd never had more fun, even if Jayna was horrible at video games. She must have come to that conclusion too, and decided she needed to level the playing field by blowing softly in his ear and gently nipping at his neck in an effort to get him to mess up. Becker didn't mind and didn't have a problem returning the favor. Jayna let out a soft growl that did crazy things to his body, and he replied with a growl of his own when she tossed her controller on the coffee table and climbed into his lap to kiss him. He slapped the pause button on his controller and kissed her right back. This was much more fun than a video game any day.

He put his hands on her waist, trying to settle her

into a position that wouldn't bring her sweetly curved ass into constant contact with his hard-on, but it was futile. She buried her fingers in his hair with a moan and wiggled around until she was right back where she'd been before.

He groaned low in his throat, his hands sliding down to the curve of her hips. He could feel the heat from her body through his jeans and it was driving him insane. He should stop now before things went too far. But it was obvious that Jayna was enjoying herself as much as he was. If her rapid breathing, elevated pulse, and the slightly extended claws digging into his shirt hadn't told him that, the scent of arousal pouring off her did.

She was definitely having fun.

That didn't mean he wasn't a little shocked when she grabbed the bottom of his shirt and started pulling it up like she was unwrapping a Christmas present.

"Whoa." Becker dragged his mouth away to look at her. "You sure about this?"

She sat back, her lips curving into a shy smile. "I'm sure. But only if you're okay with it."

How the heck was he supposed to respond to that? She wanted to have sex with him. Of course he was okay with it. He just hadn't expected it. "I'm okay with anything you're comfortable with."

Jayna smiled and reached for the bottom of his T-shirt again. He helped her get it over his head, then leaned back. She lightly ran her partially extended claws over his chest, tentatively at first, then with more confidence. Did she have any idea how good that felt? Since she kept doing it, he suspected she did.

Her blue eyes swirled with green as they roamed

over his bare chest. He'd never had a woman look at him so hungrily before, and it was seriously turning him on. As if picking up on his arousal, her eyes shifted completely, turning a vivid green, and Becker's pulse spiked as the tips of her canines appeared and slipped down over her lower lip. The scent that came with unleashing her inner werewolf was mind-numbingly good and made it hard for him to think of anything other than making love to her. But while she was comfortable with what they were doing, that didn't mean she was ready to take things further.

"You okay?" he asked softly, wanting to make sure she wasn't going to do something she'd regret later.

Jayna giggled. Okay, that had to be the sexiest sound he'd ever heard.

"I'm good." She ran her tongue lazily over her fangs. "How about you? You okay?"

"Me? No problems here." He probably would have been able to pull off a more convincing lie if she wasn't pressing right against his straining hard-on.

She smiled, her fangs a flash of white against her strawberry-pink lips. "Good. I wouldn't want to make you uncomfortable or anything."

"*Uncomfortable* definitely isn't the word I would use right now."

"It isn't the word I would use either," she said. "In fact, I'm feeling very comfortable with you right now."

Now it was his turn to grin. "Good. I want you to always be very comfortable with me."

Jayna leaned forward and kissed him again. As her tongue slipped into his mouth, he couldn't stop the low growl that slipped out, nor could he keep one hand from sliding down to caress her ass. He immediately moved it back up to her hips, but she was already pulling away to give him a curious look. Eyes locked with his, she grabbed his hand in hers, then slowly and deliberately put it back on her ass.

"Would it be a bad thing if I admit that I like your hand there?" she asked.

Her expression was both sexy and vulnerable at the same time, and his chest tightened.

"That wouldn't be a bad thing at all," he said huskily. "Like I said, I'm good with anything you're comfortable with."

She smiled and went back to kissing him. He buried his free hand in her hair, tipping her head to the side and tangling his tongue with hers. He slid his other hand from her ass, along her thigh, and back again, giving her bottom a gentle squeeze. Jayna let out a sexy sound of approval as she trailed kisses along his jaw and down his neck. She pressed her lips to his chest, exploring his pecs with her tongue. When she gently nipped him with her fangs, he thought for sure he was going to lose his hold over his inner werewolf.

Okay, that was enough of that. He tightened his hold on her hair, urging her head up. As she sat back on his thighs, Becker closed his eyes and got himself together. He couldn't believe how fast Jayna could make him lose control. She was like his kryptonite.

When he finally got his heart rate somewhere back under a hundred, he opened his eyes to see her regarding him with an amused expression. She must have decided he was okay, because she leaned forward again. For a second, he thought she was going in for another round of teasing with her fangs, but instead she trailed her claws across his chest.

He stifled a groan. *Dammit, you're an alpha. Act like it, would you?*

She traced the tip of one claw over the barely discernable scar from the bullet wound he'd gotten yesterday. "I can't believe how fast this healed."

It took a second for him to change gears, and by the time he had, she'd already moved on to the wolf head tattoo inked over his heart. "This is really cool. Did you get it when you became a werewolf?"

Becker didn't answer right away because she was busy destroying his concentration by running one of her claws around the outside of said tattoo. He bit his tongue—literally—and finally managed an intelligent answer.

"I got it when I joined the SWAT pack. We all have them. To anyone who sees it, the acronym stands for Special Weapons and Tactics, but we call it Special Wolf Alpha Team."

She smiled. "Clever. So how did you become a werewolf anyway?"

The sudden change in subject nearly gave him whiplash, and he had to wonder if Jayna was doing it because she'd realized how close he'd been to losing control.

"It happened when I was with the Secret Service—"

"Whoa, wait a second," she interrupted, her eyes wide. "You worked in the same Secret Service that protects the president?"

He chuckled. "Yeah, that Secret Service. But I never served on a protective detail. I went through all the training necessary to be a special agent, but once the higher-ups in the Denver field office realized how much I knew about computers and electronics, I ended up spending all my time doing network security, white-hat work, and advanced computer surveillance, crap like that. It wasn't exactly what I thought I was signing up for, but it's likely why I was hired in the first place. It's damn hard to get into the Secret Service without one hell of a résumé. Besides, it's what I was good at."

"So you were a computer geek?"

A smile tugged playfully at the corners of her lips as she said the words, making him stifle another groan. Damn, every time she smiled at him, he swore she released some kind of pheromone into the air that practically made him drunk.

He blocked out the endorphin rush her smile gave him and focused on her question. "Yeah, I was a computer geek. But my supervisor knew I wanted to get some field time, so he loaned me out to an anticounterfeiting team. The ring of counterfeiters they were after used these really expensive computers and printers to make their fake money, and I was there to make sense of the computer-based chatter going back and forth on the wiretaps. But when the counterfeiters started talking about bringing in a new computer guy, I went from IT expert to undercover operative overnight."

Jayna regarded him thoughtfully. "I'm going to say this in the nicest possible way, but wasn't that kind of a big jump, considering your lack of field experience?"

He grimaced. "I'd like to say that it wasn't. I certainly didn't think so at the time. I had the training, and the counterfeiters were supposed to be just college kids. The leader of the task force thought I was ready for the field and so did I."

"What went wrong?"

Becker remembered it like it was yesterday. He'd been so eager to get into the field and do some *real work* that he'd never even thought about slowing down and making sure he didn't go half-cocked into a dangerous situation. Not much had changed in that regard, he guessed.

"At first, nothing," he said. "I got into the counterfeiting ring easy enough, which only convinced us more than ever that we were dealing with amateurs. After that, the plan was simple: figure out where they were stockpiling the counterfeit money; then get them to incriminate themselves on tape. But then I met the people the college kids worked for and realized we'd seriously underestimated the guys. The people in charge were mob connected, and they made me in two seconds flat."

"Oh crap," she breathed.

"Yeah, no kidding." Becker shook his head. "One second I'm sitting there talking about the high-quality printers, and the next I have half a dozen weapons pointed at me. I didn't even have a chance to shout out the code word for a compromised operation before they started shooting. I managed to take down three of them before I passed out from blood loss. Next thing I knew, I was waking up in the hospital."

"As a werewolf," she said.

"Yeah. I didn't realize that's what I was until I met Sergeant Dixon, though."

"Why didn't you stay with the Secret Service?"

"We got the bad guys, but the agency took a lot of heat over the body count—and the injured newbie. Even though I took full responsibility for things going bad, the task force leader was the one who paid with his job." Becker sighed. "I was pissed that I'd gotten made, pissed that I'd gotten shot, pissed that I'd gotten the guy who'd given me a chance fired, and really pissed that no one even thought I had enough experience to warrant listening to me when I tried to take the blame. I said some things I probably shouldn't have and was told to sit at my computer and be quiet. But I couldn't see myself doing that anymore, not after everything that had happened. I was still trying to figure out what I wanted to do when Gage—Sergeant Dixon—showed up and offered me a job with SWAT." He shrugged. "After that, it didn't take me too long to get comfortable with being a werewolf. Who doesn't want to be faster and stronger, right?" His mouth twitched. "I can't turn into a full wolf yet, but I'm working on it."

She blinked in confusion. "What do you mean, a full wolf?"

"You know, a wolf, with fur and stuff."

She stared at him for a long time. "We can do that?"

He nodded. "About half the guys in my pack can."

"Wow," she breathed. "That's kind of cool. I had no idea werewolves could do anything like that."

He chuckled. "Finally something I know more about when it comes to being a werewolf than you do."

Jayna laughed with him. "Well, as strange as it sounds, I guess I should be happy you were shot and turned into one, or I wouldn't be here with you right now."

Becker grinned back. "Being here with you makes getting shot worth it."

She caught her lower lip between her teeth. "Does that mean I can go back to doing what I was doing before your heart started racing? Because I was really enjoying myself."

He wanted to say yes more than anything. But then he'd be right back where he'd been—on the edge of losing it.

"I'm not so sure that's a good idea," he said. "I like to think that I have better control over myself than most of the guys in my pack, but I'd be lying if I didn't tell you how difficult it is to keep it together when you start doing certain things."

Her lips curved. "Maybe I wouldn't mind you losing it…just a little."

His heart started thumping again, and his cock hardened painfully. "But maybe that might lead to places you don't want to go."

Her smile disappeared, replaced by a serious little pucker between her brows. "I know you're trying to be careful around me, and I appreciate that. But when I told you about my past, it wasn't so you'd run around treating me like some kind of porcelain doll that has to be handled with kid gloves. When I said I had problems getting physical with guys in the past, a lot of that was because I didn't feel a connection with them. They were just guys. That's not the way I'm feeling with you, not even close. So, if you don't mind, I'd like you to forget what I told you about my issues for the time being and let this go exactly where I want it to go—to your bedroom, where we might discover there's something interesting in there after all."

Becker gazed into her green eyes for a long time, trying to make sure he wasn't misjudging what was going on here. But she never looked away, never gave a hint that she wasn't one hundred percent sure of her decision.

He slowly slipped his hand into her long hair, then carefully pulled her close and kissed her. God, she tasted so damn sweet.

He carefully let his canines slip out ever so slightly. Jayna's moan almost made him lose his tenuous grip on his inner werewolf, but he determinedly tamed the beast. This first time with her had to go perfectly, or there'd never be another.

Jayna broke the kiss, her eyes glowing. "Ready to show me that boring bedroom of yours now?"

This time, Becker didn't even pause to think. He just slid his hands down to her ass, got a good grip, then carried her down the hallway and into his bedroom.

When Jayna decided to take Megan's advice and get away from the loft for a while, she hadn't really thought much about what she and Eric would do. She'd figured they'd hang out, maybe catch a movie or grab something to eat and just talk. She'd assumed there might be some kissing involved. Last night had been way too much fun to take that activity off the table. But the idea that the kissing would progress to anything else had never entered her mind until she climbed on his lap. She'd only done it because it was easier to kiss him that way, but when her bottom brushed against his erection, her inner werewolf took over.

At first, her intense arousal scared her. She knew Eric was just as crazy turned on as she was, but he was still in control enough to slow things down. Whether it was pulling off his shirt or checking to see if she was okay with his hand on her ass, he took the time to make sure they weren't moving too fast. She simply couldn't put into words what that meant to her.

She'd never been with a guy who was willing to let his own pleasure take a backseat to hers. Even when she made his pulse kick into another gear by leaning forward to kiss and nip at his delicious chest muscles, he hadn't thought about himself and what made him feel good, but had put on the brakes to make sure she was okay.

It wasn't until they were talking about how he became a werewolf that she realized they were going to sleep together before they left his apartment. That realization had made her feel amazingly happy—because she wasn't doing it as an experiment to see if she was "normal." She wasn't even doing it because Eric had been so good to her pack. For the first time since she was a teen, she was going to make love with a guy simply because he was smoking hot and perfect for her.

So when his heart started racing again and the scent of his arousal grew so strong she was practically drooling from it, she refused to let him talk her out of going further. She almost cheered when he slipped his hands under her ass and carried her into his bedroom.

Jayna was so focused on Eric's kisses, she barely noticed they'd reached the bed until he carefully set her on her feet beside it. She stood there gazing up at him, mesmerized by the heat in his eyes and the scent streaming off his body. She wanted him so badly that her knees actually felt weak.

She reached down for the hem of her tank top, more than ready to feel her bare breasts pressing up against his warm skin, but Eric got there first.

"Hey, that's my job," he said, flashing her a grin.

Jayna lifted her arms to help him, laughing as he tossed her top halfway across the room. She reached back and unsnapped her bra, then let it fall to the floor. Eric growled and pulled her close, and she got exactly what she'd been wishing for as her tender nipples pressed against the warm skin of his torso. She buried her face in his neck, wrapping her arms around him and basking in the sensation of being this close to him. It felt so perfect and right, it was scary.

Jayna could have stayed like that all night, but the desire to be totally naked in his arms, to feel their legs intertwined, was too strong to ignore for long. She lifted her head and gazed up at him, wondering what she should do next. She may have slept with other guys before, but that didn't mean she considered herself experienced at this. Because of that, she wasn't sure Eric was going to enjoy this moment as much as she was, and she really wanted him to.

She opened her mouth to tell him just that, to say she was sorry in advance if she wasn't as confident and experienced as he was used to. But his finger came down softly on her lips.

"Shh," he whispered. "Don't think so much. Just go with your instincts."

Then he was urging her back, onto his big, comfy bed, his hands at her waist, pulling her tight yoga pants down. She reached for her panties as he was busy tossing aside her pants, but he stopped her with a look. "That's my job, remember?"

She laughed, holding up her hands in surrender. "You taking off my clothes is something I'm going to have to get used to, isn't it?"

His mouth quirked. "Yeah, it is. It's an alpha thing, completely out of my control."

"Sure it is." She leaned back on her elbows and motioned to the tiny piece of black material that was the only thing left between her and complete nakedness. "Well, are you going to take these off?"

Eyes flaring gold, he reached down and wrapped a big hand around her left ankle, lifting her leg high. "I will…when I get there."

Before she could ask what that meant, Eric began kissing his way down the inside of her leg with maddening slowness. She gasped as he trailed a path along her skin with his tongue, then growled as he gently nipped the inside of her thigh with his canines. She buried her fingers in his hair, trying to tug him higher, desperate to feel his mouth on her pussy.

Thank God, Eric didn't make her wait, because she wasn't sure she could have handled it. When he slid his hands under her bottom, she lifted her hips, eager to help him get her panties off. She hadn't realized how excited she was until he pulled the tiny scrap of material down her legs, and she was absolutely soaking wet.

Eric tossed her panties over his shoulder, then gently spread her legs. He held her gaze as he lowered his head, his eyes like molten gold. Jayna tried to prepare herself for how good it would feel, but when he began to lazily trace up and down her folds with his tongue, she knew she hadn't been even close to ready. Not for something that felt this exquisite.

She clutched at the sheets, her breath coming in quick bursts, her hips rotating like they had a mind of their own as his tongue worked its magic. There was no way she could be ready to orgasm this soon—but as Eric's tongue swirled lightly over that most sensitive part of her anatomy, she felt her whole body start to tingle, and she knew her climax was going to be huge.

Jayna undulated her hips faster, digging her claws into the sheets. Eric's grip tightened on her ass, holding her in place as he licked her. That show of dominance was enough to set her off like a rocket. She threw back her head and howled as she exploded. She'd never come that hard before—or that long. Her orgasm kept going and going. And when it was over, even the slow spiral down from heaven afterward was better than the best climax she'd ever experienced before.

She pushed herself up on her elbows to look at him. "I'm not sure there are words to describe how amazing that was."

Eric grinned. "Amazing works for me."

He climbed off the bed and unbuckled his belt. Jayna's pulse quickened as he popped the buttons on his jeans. When he shoved them down, all she could do was stare. God, he looked good naked. She'd seen his bare chest and shoulders plenty of times, but it was nice to see that he had long, muscular legs to match.

And then there was his cock. She hadn't been with a lot of guys, so she hadn't seen a lot, but she had a feeling Eric's was special, which was fitting, she supposed, since he was a very special werewolf.

She would have reached out and wrapped her hand around him, but he was already rummaging in the nightstand for something. After a few moments, he finally came up with a foil-wrapped condom. She was absurdly happy that he had to dig around so long before finding the thing. It meant he didn't use them very often. Silly, she knew, but still.

He tore open the packet, his hands shaking a little. Jayna blinked. Was he actually nervous? But when he lifted his head and gave her a heated look, she realized he was shaking with anticipation, not nerves. She was eager too, and watching him roll on the condom was only making her more impatient. She was practically bouncing on the bed by the time he climbed in with her.

Jayna didn't have to think about what to do next, or where to put her arms, her legs, or any other body part, like she usually had to do with a guy. She and Eric fit together perfectly.

Her legs parted for him and he settled between them, kissing his way up from her belly button, stopping only to suckle tenderly on each nipple before hungrily claiming her mouth. She wrapped her legs around his waist, moaning when she felt his erection nudge the opening of her pussy. She was more than ready to take him inside her, but instead, Eric teased her with the head of his shaft, gliding up and down her folds until she thought she might go insane from the torture.

"Please," she begged hoarsely.

He lifted his head to gaze at her. "Are you sure about this?"

She slid one hand up his chest to cup his jaw, her thumb caressing the stubble there. "More sure than I've been about anything in my life."

It was true. Everything else in her life was crazy right then, but sleeping with Eric? That wasn't crazy at all.

Gold eyes locked with hers, and he entered her ever so slowly. It was incredible and yet frustrating at the same time because Jayna didn't want him to go slow. She wanted all of him, and she wanted him now. She moaned and reached around to dig her fingers into his muscular ass, encouraging him to go deeper.

But he wouldn't do it. Instead, he made love to her like she was the most delicate and precious thing in the world. And while her inner werewolf wanted it hard and fast, the human part of her loved how tender he was. When he finally plunged into her all the way, it made her world spin upside down. Then he began to thrust, and it got even better.

There was no holding back, even if she'd wanted to, and no containing her werewolf either. It was like Eric was making her whole body come, and the desire and unabashed awe on his face as he did was almost as powerful as her climax. Then his eyes flared bright and his fangs elongated, and he began to thrust long and deep, and Jayna knew he was coming too. She wrapped her arms around him, her growls of release combining with his to become one.

Jayna had never imagined that sex could ever be this perfect with anyone. And for a long time after they'd both floated back to earth, she held him close, dreaming of a world that could always be like this.

Chapter 10

JAYNA AND ERIC HAD JUST FINISHED UP ROUND TWO when the doorbell rang. A little stab of fear went through her. What if it was one of the werewolves from Eric's pack? Worse, what if the Albanians had figured out who Eric really was and discovered where he lived?

Eric gave her a quick kiss. "It's probably just one of my neighbors."

Then why did he look so worried?

Jayna sat up and hugged her knees to her chest, silently watching as Eric pulled on his jeans, then yanked his T-shirt over his head. She was worrying for nothing. It was crazy to think the Albanians would have figured out who Eric was and where he lived. If they had, they certainly wouldn't have rung the doorbell.

One of Eric's pack mates would though.

And she was sitting here naked.

She was just about to jump out of bed and get dressed when Eric opened the door and stuck his head in.

He grinned. "It's Cooper. He stopped by to feed the fish and saw my bike outside. You want to meet him?"

"Um…"

Jayna hesitated. Texting Cooper with information was one thing; meeting him in person was another. He was a cop. What if he wasn't quite as accepting of her as Eric was? But Eric wouldn't ask her to meet Cooper if he didn't trust his friend. If he'd been willing to help Eric with this crazy scheme, he must be pretty awesome.

"Okay," she finally said. "I'll get dressed and be right out."

Before going into the living room to meet his friend, Jayna pulled on her clothes and ran her hand through her hair, then took a quick glance in the mirror over the dresser to make sure she didn't look like she'd just spent the past couple hours rolling around in bed with Eric.

Cooper had his back to her but turned when Eric stopped midsentence to smile at her. He was tall and muscular, like Eric, and almost as good-looking. It made her wonder if the Dallas SWAT team only hired were-wolves based on looks and buff bodies.

"Cooper, this is Jayna Winston," Eric said. "Jayna, meet Landry Cooper, my best friend and the only cop crazy enough to help me with this insane plan."

Cooper smiled and held out his hand. "It's nice to finally meet the werewolf on the other end of all those texts I've been getting."

Jayna returned his smile as she shook his hand. While Cooper had that unique werewolf smell, he didn't have a trace of that delectable scent she'd come to associate with Eric. So much for her theory that Eric smelled the way he did because he was such a strong alpha.

"It's nice to finally meet the werewolf I've been texting," she said.

Cooper glanced at Eric. "From what Becker has been telling me, getting your pack out of trouble is worth the pain in the ass all of this has been."

Eric grimaced. "Have Gage and Xander been giving you grief?"

Cooper's mouth twitched. "They're a little pissed that I have a confidential informant inside the werewolf crew and won't tell them who it is. It's nothing I can't handle though."

"You tell anyone else on the team?" Eric asked.

Cooper shook his head. "Nah. All the guys would back you up on this, and Khaki too. But if someone's going to get in hot water, I don't want it to be them."

Jayna understood why Cooper would risk getting into trouble to help Eric because she'd have done the same for any of her own pack mates. "Well, thank you, Cooper. My pack and I appreciate it." She brushed Eric's fingers with hers. "I'm going to get cleaned up a little. I'll be right back."

He nodded and went back to his conversation, but as she walked toward the bedroom, she could feel his gaze on her. She smiled, liking the way it felt.

"Damn," Cooper said. "She's beautiful."

Becker knew that already, but after watching her walk back into his bedroom, he could understand why Cooper might point out the obvious. And if any other guy had said the same thing, he might have been jealous. But Cooper was like a brother.

"Oh yeah," Becker agreed. "If there was ever a woman made to wear yoga pants, it's her."

Cooper shook his head. "What is it with you and those damn yoga pants? I mean, she definitely looks good in them, but sometimes I think you have a psychological condition when it comes to your obsession with the things."

"Maybe. But did you know that twenty percent of women can orgasm while doing yoga?"

"How the hell would I know that? More importantly, how the hell do you?"

"I read it in *Cosmo* a while ago."

Cooper opened his mouth to say something, but then closed it. Finally he just shook his head. "I'm not going to ask because I don't want to know."

Becker laughed. "Probably not. You want to hang around? We can order pizza or something."

Cooper shook his head. "Nah. I only stopped by to feed your fish. I'm going home to get some sleep. I haven't gotten more than an hour or two a night since you went undercover. I need to find a bed before I crash and burn."

Becker could sympathize with that.

"So Jayna's *The One* for you, huh?" Cooper asked.

"Definitely." Becker grinned. "I thought she might be that first day I saw her in the warehouse, but now I'm sure."

Cooper shook his head. "It's crazy that you stumbled over the one werewolf you're supposed to be mated to for the rest of your life in the middle of a robbery. Makes you think there really is some cosmic force out there." He got to his feet. "Okay, I'm gonna get out of here."

Becker walked him to the door.

"Have you figured out how this is all going to end?" Cooper asked, turning to look at him. "At some point, the Albanians or this pack alpha you told me about are going to figure out you're the one tipping off the cops. We can't keep doing this much longer."

"We won't have to," Becker said. "Jayna and I have the Albanians and omegas distrusting each other. In a few days, their whole organization will collapse from the inside. We just need to keep the pressure on until then."

"Be careful." Cooper opened the door. "Tell Jayna it was nice meeting her."

"I will," Becker promised.

"Cooper left already?" Jayna asked as Becker closed the door.

He turned to give her a smile. "Yeah. He was beat. You want something to drink?"

"Sure."

Becker grabbed a couple bottles of water from the fridge, then joined her on the couch.

"I overheard you and Cooper talking before," she said. "What did he mean when he asked you if I was 'the one' for you? He seemed to imply it was more than just your standard romantic attraction."

Becker stared at her, the bottle of water halfway to his mouth. He thought she knew more about being a werewolf than he did. "You don't know about *The One*?"

"The one what?"

He stared down at the bottle of water, trying to get his thoughts straight. "This is going to be complicated, but according to werewolf legend, there's supposed to be one true mate out there in the world for every werewolf. When they meet, there's this automatic connection between them." He grinned. "Kind of like how we felt that spark the first time we met."

Jayna looked dubious. "You make it sound like we're magically meant to be together."

"Is it so hard to believe that people as unique and special as werewolves are meant to find that one perfect person who accepts us for what we are?"

"Yes, it is that hard to believe," she said. "I prefer to think that the way I feel about you is purely because of the person you are, not because of any werewolf magic."

Becker tried not to let his disappointment show. After what had happened to Jayna, it wasn't surprising she didn't believe in magic and happily ever after.

Jayna must have picked up on his mood because her expression softened and she leaned in to kiss him. He slipped a hand in her hair and kissed her back, telling himself that it didn't matter why she felt the things she did for him, as long as she felt them. He had her, and that was all that mattered.

"Do you think we need to head back to the loft yet or can we stay here a while longer?" she asked, her blue eyes turning green.

They'd already been gone a few hours, but...

"I think we have a little bit of time." He grinned. "Do you have something in mind you want to do?"

She nodded with just a hint of that shyness he found so damn cute. "I was thinking we could make out again before we go. Just a quickie, you know?"

"Yeah, I do know," he growled. "Though I don't think there'll be anything quick about it."

Jayna hugged Eric tightly as they rode through the dark streets toward the loft. Today would go down as one of the best days ever—and not just because she adored making love with him, although that was definitely incredible. She simply loved being with him. Even if she wasn't too sure about the whole magical werewolf-connection thing, it didn't mean she couldn't recognize there was something special going on between them. To her, though, it was simply good, old-fashioned chemistry.

It was well past eight o'clock by the time they got back to the loft, and she immediately headed for the stairs to check on Megan. Eric trotted up behind her, but they barely made it halfway before they ran into Liam coming down with Moe and Joseph right behind him. Liam had a pissed-off look on his face.

"Where the hell have you been and why weren't you answering your phone?" he demanded.

The hair on the back of Jayna's neck stood up. "What's wrong?" She glanced at Moe and Joseph. They both looked nervous as hell. "Where are Megan and Chris?"

Liam opened his mouth to answer, but Joseph was faster.

"Kostandin sent them out on a job."

"What kind of job?" Eric asked.

Joseph started to answer, but Liam silenced him with a glare. "Kos sent them after one of the SWAT werewolves, along with half a dozen Albanian soldiers."

It took a moment for Liam's words to sink in, and when they finally did, Jayna couldn't breathe. She almost reached for Eric's hand to steady herself but caught herself at the last minute and grabbed the railing instead. While she was off having sex with Eric, two of her pack mates had been sent out to take down an alpha who was way out of their league. Oh God, what had she done?

"How could you send Megan and Chris after one of those SWAT werewolves?" she demanded, her fangs and claws coming out. "She's not strong enough and neither is Chris."

Liam opened his mouth to say something, but this time Eric was the one who cut him off.

"Where did they go, and when did they leave?"

For a moment, Jayna thought Liam would refuse to tell them just out of spite. But the look on Eric's face must have changed his mind.

"The cop lives over in Lochwood, on Skillman Street. They left thirty minutes ago."

Jayna saw Eric's face go pale, but before she could even think of asking him why—which would have been hard to do in front of Liam and the others—he turned and raced toward the main entrance. She followed, ignoring Liam's shouts that it was too late to make any difference.

Eric was already on his bike and about to pull away when she jumped in front of him.

"You need to move," he hissed, the edges of his eyes glowing as he fought for control. "They went after Cooper."

Dammit. She put her hands on the handlebars and refused to budge. "And Megan and Chris are with them. I'm coming with you."

Eric looked like he wanted to argue, but instead he swore and motioned for her to get on the bike. She ran around and climbed on behind him, holding on tightly as he cranked the gas and tore off through town. She thought they'd been driving fast before, but now he was probably doing a hundred as he weaved in and out of traffic.

They were still several blocks away when Jayna heard gunfire. Her heart stopped. Liam had been right. They were too late.

Eric twisted the throttle and rode even faster.

Three big, black Escalades were pulled across the entrance to an apartment complex, blocking it. There was an olive green Jeep Wrangler parked just on the other side of the Escalades, as if the driver had turned into the lot just in front of the Albanians. She saw Cooper hiding behind the partial protection of the Jeep, blood running down his arms and chest from at least two gunshots.

Jayna flinched as she realized how badly wounded he must have been to be bleeding that much. But his attackers had paid the price to do that to him. Two Albanians were lying on the ground unmoving, and a third was leaning against the rear tire of one of the SUVs, both hands pressed to his head as he tried to stop the bleeding from a wound there.

She searched frantically for Megan and Chris. Her breath hitched as she saw Megan pressing her hand frantically against a wound in Chris's side while he popped off shots in Cooper's direction.

Jayna's heart twisted. She didn't want Chris to shoot Cooper, but she also didn't want her friends to get hurt either. And Megan seemed so worried about Chris that she wasn't even protecting herself. She was practically standing out in the open as she tried to tend to Chris. If Cooper wanted to hit her, she'd be dead.

Fortunately, Cooper was focused on the remaining three Albanians, who were shooting at him. Eric slammed on the brakes and slid the bike to a stop just outside the perimeter established by the three SUVs as another Albanian went down.

Jayna immediately jumped off the Harley so she

could pull Megan and Chris out of the line of fire while Eric launched himself at the last two Albanians with a speed and grace that she and her pack mates could never hope to achieve.

But instead of tearing into the Albanians trying to kill his best friend, he bent and scooped up a shotgun beside one of the dead men. Pumping a shell into the chamber, he leaped over the SUV in front of him and hit the ground on the far side, then, just as quickly, cleared the hood of Cooper's Jeep.

The move caught her by surprise, and all she could do was gape as Eric aimed the shotgun at Cooper's chest and fired. Cooper's shocked look was the last thing she saw before he flew back and out of sight behind the Jeep. Eric advanced on him, pumped the shotgun, then pointed it at his best friend. Even though the Jeep was in the way, she could tell from the angle of the weapon that he was aiming at Cooper's head.

Jayna was moving toward them before she even realized what she was doing. But the boom of the shotgun going off stopped her cold. Under the Jeep, Cooper's legs jerked once, then went still.

Her heart slammed against her ribs. Eric had just shot his pack mate in the head. He had killed one of his own to protect hers.

Eric turned and strode back over to where she still stood immobilized. In the distance, sirens echoed in the night, coming closer.

"Cops are on the way," he said in a flat, emotionless voice. "Let's go."

"Not until I see what that dog looks like," one of the Albanians said.

Eric stepped in front of the Albanian, his eyes flaring gold as he lifted the shotgun and put the end of the barrel against the man's forehead.

"I can show you what it looks like—from the inside."

Jayna never would have imagined Eric could sound so cold and emotionless, but then again, he'd just killed his best friend. Her legs almost gave out as she slowly helped Megan get Chris to his feet and over to one of the SUVs. She didn't want to believe Eric could have done something like that, even if he'd done it for her. She didn't want to be the reason he'd killed anyone, especially Cooper. Her eyes burned with tears as she remembered the way the other werewolf had told her he'd do anything to help Eric.

The Albanian squaring off against Eric muttered something in his own language, then turned and quickly helped his wounded friends get in the other Escalade. A few moments later, two of the SUVs sped away, leaving her alone with Eric and the dead Albanians.

Eric didn't look at her as he walked over to his bike and climbed on. She glanced in Cooper's direction, torn between needing to know and not wanting to know. But the engine of the Harley rumbled to life and she had no choice but to climb on the back. As Eric squealed away, she looked over her shoulder, trying to get a glimpse of something—anything—to convince her that she hadn't seen what she thought she had.

All she could see were flashing blue lights as the cops converged on the scene. Then Eric turned a corner, and her view was obscured. Not that it mattered. Her mind had no problem replaying those last few moments over and over, as if it wanted to make sure she never forgot.

Chapter 11

BEFORE THE SUN WAS EVEN UP THE NEXT MORNING, Becker headed for Jayna's room. The way Jayna looked at him last night outside Cooper's apartment complex had torn out his heart. He needed to get her to understand why he'd done what he had. But between the Albanians and omegas congratulating him, Kos and Frasheri wanting details about what happened, then digging two bullets out of Chris's stomach, privacy had been in short supply last night. While the beta werewolf was healing, he wasn't doing it very fast, so he hadn't felt right about asking Jayna to leave his side.

After he explained things to her, he had to go to the SWAT compound so he could talk to Gage and Xander before the shit hit the fan—more than it already had at least. And last night wasn't something you could explain over the phone or in a text.

Becker was only a few doors down from the apartment that Jayna and Megan shared when Kostandin's voice stopped him.

"Where are you going at this time of the morning?"

Becker had been so focused on what he was going to say to Jayna that he hadn't even realized the mob underboss was coming down the hall. Becker walked past Jayna's door as if he'd been heading for the stairs all along.

"To the SWAT compound," he said. "See how

they're reacting to the death of one of their own, maybe try to figure out which one we should go after next."

Kos grinned. An evil, nasty grin. "You do that, and when you get back, we need to talk about your place in this organization. I think it's time to make a few changes in the wolf pack's leadership, don't you?"

Becker's stomach twisted as he jogged down the steps. Kostandin might not have said it, but a change in leadership likely meant the Albanian intended to kill Liam. Becker didn't think much of the other werewolf, but he sure as hell didn't want him dead. Right now, though, he had bigger issues—like how to explain this whole thing to his own alpha.

He was still rehearsing his speech when he pulled into the parking lot at the compound twenty minutes later. He heard Gage's shouts coming from the admin building as soon as he cut the Harley's engine. A low, deep rumbling growl followed.

Shit. Gage was really pissed.

Becker leaned his bike on the kickstand, then strode over and walked into the building. Gage and Cooper were standing nose to nose, fangs extended and eyes glowing. Mike and Xander were doing their best to get between them, but if things turned ugly, it was going to take a lot more than those two to keep them from fighting.

On the bright side, Cooper looked better than he had last night after Becker had shot him in the chest at point-blank range with that shotgun. He hadn't wanted to shoot Cooper, but at the time, he hadn't been able to come up with a better way to stop the Albanians from killing Cooper while maintaining his cover. Becker knew it wouldn't really hurt Cooper. Knock him on his ass, be painful as hell, for sure, but nothing permanent. The shotgun blast only a foot to the side of his head might have been a bit much, but his friend had immediately picked up on what he was trying to do and played dead like Becker had hoped. Thank God he'd been able to keep that Albanian from walking around the side of Cooper's Jeep to check out the damage, because that would have screwed up everything.

"You're going to tell me who the hell your informant is," Gage growled. "And you're going to do it right the fuck now!"

Gage's jaw broadened to make room for his fangs. There was nobody in the Pack who possessed more control over their werewolf nature than their commander. If he was shifting that far, he was doing it because he was planning on ripping a huge chunk out of Cooper's hide.

Cooper didn't back down though. "I told you, I can't do that. My source is confidential."

"Not from me," Gage snarled, his hands flexing as if he was imagining how good it would feel to wrap his fingers around Cooper's neck and choke the living crap out of him.

Xander stepped in front of Cooper and put his hand on Gage's chest. "Gage—"

But Gage shoved Xander aside. "What the hell is wrong with you?" he demanded of Cooper. "Those Albanian bastards almost killed you."

Becker swore silently. If he didn't do something quick, Gage was going to explode.

"It wasn't the Albanians." *Here goes nothing.* "It was me."

The whole pack turned to face him as one, a mix of

confusion and disbelief on their faces. Off to the side, Tuffie was regarding him with an expression that said this was not the time for full disclosure. Becker dismissed the pooch's concern, but it was impossible to ignore the looks on his pack mates' faces.

Gage's fangs retracted slightly, but his eyes still glowed gold. "What are you talking about? And why the hell are you even here? I thought you were in Denver with your sister."

Becker met his alpha's gaze levelly. "That stuff about my sister? That wasn't quite true. Actually, it was bullshit. I've been staying in a loft on Canton Street with the Albanians and the other werewolf pack."

Gage's eyes narrowed and the temperature in the room dropped by ten degrees. "You've been doing *what*?"

"I sort of went undercover and infiltrated their operation."

Becker braced himself for Gage's wrath, knowing it was going to be epic. Gage strode across the room and wrapped one hand around his throat, slamming him against the wall with a feral growl.

Shit, that hurt.

"What could possibly have convinced you that lying to me about where you were, conducting an unauthorized undercover operation on your own, and shooting Cooper were good ideas?"

Gage may have been his alpha, but Becker refused to be intimidated. "It wasn't really a *what* as much as a *who*, as in a female werewolf that I sort of let escape from that import/export warehouse earlier in the week."

"A female werewolf you *let* escape?" Gage snarled.

It sounded worse when his boss said it. Becker opened his mouth to explain, but Cooper cut him off.

"You didn't really *let* her escape. Considering you hid her in a crate so she wouldn't be found, I'd say you *helped* her escape."

Guess that was Cooper's way of getting back at him for shooting him in the chest.

Gage glared at Cooper, then turned the full force of those gold eyes on Becker again.

He was so fucked.

———

The sound of voices in the hallway woke Jayna up. Recognizing Eric's deep timbre, she jumped out of bed and padded over to the door in her tank top and shorts. She'd tried to talk to Eric privately several times last night but simply hadn't been able to find the right words or the right time. Now, maybe she had.

But then she heard Kostandin's voice, and her hand froze on the doorknob. Eric was saying something about going to the SWAT compound and figuring out which officer to target next. The words brought the events of last night rushing back, and her hand tightened on the knob as she heard Eric and Kos walk away. She rested her forehead against the door with a sigh, trying to make sense of everything that had happened over the past twenty-four hours.

The time she'd spent at Eric's apartment yesterday had been amazing. She'd never dreamed that sex could be so powerful and moving. Just thinking about it made her want to chase after Eric right that minute and ask him to take her back over to his place for more of the same.

But it went beyond how good they were in bed. Eric made her feel safer and happier than she'd been in a very long time, and last night, she could have easily imagined spending the rest of her life with him.

Then he'd shot and killed his best friend. She knew he'd done it to save Megan and Chris, but that didn't make it any better. She'd never wanted any of Eric's pack to die, especially Cooper. The SWAT werewolf's violent death was part of the reason she'd avoided talking to Eric last night. How the hell did you tell the man you were starting to feel so much for that you could never accept what he had done even if he'd done it for you?

But what if she hadn't seen what she thought she saw last night? What if Eric and Cooper had faked the whole scene? It sounded crazy, but the more she thought about it, the more it made sense. By making it look like he'd killed Cooper, Eric had been able to save Megan and Chris without blowing his cover with the Albanians.

It might be hard to believe, but it felt right. And for the first time since last night, Jayna felt like she could breathe again.

"Jayna?"

She turned to see Megan sitting up in bed, blinking at her sleepily.

"Is something wrong?" Megan asked.

"No, nothing's wrong. In fact, everything is just fine." Jayna smiled and walked over to sit on the edge of Megan's bed. "But there is something I need to tell you, something I should have told you from the very beginning."

Megan sat up straighter, her eyes suddenly alert. "You're running away with Eric, aren't you?"

"What?" Jayna frowned. "No, I'm not running away with him."

Megan relaxed slightly but still watched her warily. Jayna reached out and took one of her hands, giving it a squeeze.

"Remember when I said you could trust Eric?"

Megan nodded.

"What I didn't tell you was that you could trust him because he's a cop. Specifically, one of the werewolves on the SWAT team."

Megan's eyes widened. "What? You said he was an omega you met at Starbucks!"

"Shh," Jayna warned, throwing a quick glance over her shoulder. "I couldn't very well say he was a cop. And I did meet him at Starbucks. Well, outside it anyway. Eric was at the warehouse that night with the SWAT team. He helped me hide instead of arresting me, then tracked me down using a receipt from Starbucks that fell out of my pocket. He was waiting outside when I left the loft the next day."

Megan's nose wrinkled in confusion. "That doesn't explain what he's doing here."

"He's trying to help us get out of this crappy situation we're in."

Megan twirled the end of her hair, considering that. "But he killed one of those SWAT werewolves last night."

"I don't think he did," Jayna said. "I think he and the other werewolf just made it look like that."

"That makes sense, I guess." Megan twirled her hair some more. "But I have a question."

"Okay."

"Is Eric in love with you?"

Jayna opened her mouth to deny it but closed it again. Would Eric go to all this trouble if he didn't love her?

"He thinks he is," she finally said. "He believes in a legend that says there's a perfect soul mate out there for every werewolf, and they're destined to be together. He called it *The One*."

"And he thinks you're his *One*?" Megan asked.

Jayna nodded. "I know it's silly, but he really believes it."

Megan gave her a small smile. "After everything we've been through when we became werewolves, you don't think it's possible God would give us someone who could love us for what we are?"

Sometimes, Jayna forgot how idealistic Megan was. Other times, she wished she could be that idealistic herself. "It's because of what happened to us when we became werewolves that I don't believe in it."

Megan let out a sigh. "Forget the legend then. How do you feel about him?"

Jayna looked down at her hands but didn't answer. How could she describe what she felt for Eric when she wasn't sure herself?

"I don't know," she finally admitted. "I know that I love being with him. And I know that he makes me happy. And I know that I felt like we had some sort of connection the moment I saw him in that warehouse."

Megan grinned. "A connection, huh? Sounds like maybe that werewolf-soul-mate thing might be true after all."

Jayna didn't say anything.

"So what's Eric's plan for getting us out of this mess?" Megan asked, changing the subject.

Jayna explained how she and Eric had been trying to undermine the gang from the inside. "It's working, but it may take more time than we have. I think he's with his pack right now, figuring out how to end this sooner rather

than later." Knowing he was at the SWAT compound
planning to take down the Albanians should have scared
the hell out of her, but it didn't. "He promised to protect
us and get us out of here safely, and I believe him."

"All of us?" Megan asked.

"All of us," Jayna confirmed, then added, "Well,
maybe not Liam. He's in really deep with Kostandin
and Frasheri."

Megan frowned but didn't seem surprised. "We
should tell the guys what you just told me."

Jayna nodded, but Megan had already hopped out of
bed and was changing out of her pajamas. Jayna did the
same, exchanging her shorts for a pair of yoga pants;
then, she and Megan headed for the apartment the guys
shared on the fourth floor.

Joseph and Moe were in the small kitchenette, nursing
energy drinks, while Chris was lying on one of the three
air mattresses set up in the middle of what was supposed
to be the living room. He was resting so quietly Jayna
thought he was asleep, but when she and Megan walked
in, he opened his eyes and smiled at them.

Jayna smiled back as she sat down on one of the other
mattresses. "You doing okay?"

He nodded as Megan knelt beside him to check the
bandage. "Yeah. My stomach still hurts like hell, but it's
getting better by the hour. I'll be good as new by tonight."

Jayna hoped so. Before getting involved with the
Albanians, all of them had been injured to some degree
and had always healed, but none of them had ever been
wounded this seriously.

"Is Eric around?" Chris asked. "I wanted to thank
him for patching me up."

"He went out for a while." Jayna glanced at Joseph and Moe. "Actually Eric's the reason Megan and I are here."

Moe frowned as he and Joseph came over to sit down on the other air mattress. "Is he okay?"

"He's fine."

Jayna hesitated, trying to figure out how to explain everything. But there was no easy way to ease into the situation, so she took the same direct approach she'd used with Megan—minus the part about her and Eric sleeping together, of course.

The guys exchanged looks but didn't say anything for a long time. It was Moe who finally broke the silence.

"Do you trust him?"

Jayna nodded.

"And you really think he can find a way to get us out of this mess?" Chris asked.

The realization that Megan and the guys were willing to trust Eric because she did almost brought tears to Jayna's eyes.

"Yes," she finally managed. "But there's more to this than simply getting away from the Albanians. Leaving them could mean leaving Liam too."

She braced herself, expecting the guys to rush to their alpha's defense.

"Liam left us the moment he tricked us into coming here. This was never about him owing money to these people; it was about him getting power and control over a larger pack," Joseph said.

Jayna hadn't thought the guys knew about Liam's betrayal, but obviously they'd figured it out too.

"If you lead us, we'll follow," Moe added.

Jayna did a double take. What were they talking

about? She wasn't an alpha. But when she pointed that out, Megan smiled.

"We might have followed Liam, but like I told you before, you've been the heart and soul of this pack for a long time," she said.

Jayna didn't know what to say to that. She didn't understand how they could expect her to be in charge. She wasn't any stronger than the rest of them. She opened her mouth to tell them that when Moe stiffened.

"There are a whole bunch of omegas coming," he said.

Jayna tensed. The omegas never came down to this end of the hall. If they were coming now, it was because they had a reason.

Moe and Joseph were up in a flash and going for the two MP5s leaning against the wall. Chris pulled his from under the edge of his mattress but stayed where he was. Jayna got to her feet, instinctively putting herself between the locked door and her pack.

The doorknob rattled, then a fist thumped the door so hard it shook in the frame. Jayna made no move to open it, and neither did anyone else.

"I know you're all in there, so you might as well open the door," Liam shouted.

His voice reverberated in the partially renovated hallway, and Jayna could feel the anger there. She knew Liam had been pissed at Eric and her for what happened last night, but this was about something else. She just wasn't sure what.

"Jayna, I have omegas with me," Liam said. "If you don't put down your weapons and open the door, I can't be responsible for what they do."

Crap. That was a threat if she ever heard one. Jayna

glanced over her shoulder. Megan and the guys were looking at her in wide-eyed panic.

"I know Eric is a cop, Jayna," Liam called.

Jayna's stomach dropped, and she jerked her head back around to stare at the door. How had they figured it out? Had they followed Eric to the SWAT compound and seen him go inside? Her blood went cold at the thought.

"A cop?" She tried to sound shocked but wasn't quite sure she pulled it off. Thank God, Liam couldn't see her face. "Are you sure?"

"Don't play dumb with me, Jayna," Liam said. "I know you and the rest of the pack have been helping him."

Double crap.

She opened her mouth to deny it, but Liam interrupted her.

"I ran into those gangbangers from that meth lab Eric burned to the ground, and they didn't look all that crispy. But how could they when he let them get away? Isn't that right, Moe?"

Jayna glanced at Moe. His hand tightened reflexively on his weapon, but he didn't answer.

"I know that Eric tricked you and the rest of the pack, Jayna, and I forgive you," Liam said, his voice softening. "Open the door, so we can talk about this."

Jayna didn't buy that for a second. Once she opened the door, Liam could do anything he wanted, including gunning them down where they stood. But what else could she do? Liam had them cornered.

Jayna glanced at the door to the balcony, then at Chris. It was a long way down to the grassy lawn outside. She, Megan, Joseph, and Moe could make the jump easily, but Chris was still too injured to even consider it.

But if they didn't open the door, Liam would just break it down.

Megan and the guys were looking at her expectantly. God, she wished Eric were there. But he wasn't. He was only a phone call away though.

But her phone was in her room charging, along with Megan's. And none of the guys had phones.

Dammit!

"Jayna, if you don't open this door and come out, we're coming in," Liam yelled.

"Okay. Just a minute," she shouted back, then took Megan's hand and dragged her toward the balcony. "Keep Liam talking," she told the guys.

If this worked, she'd be able to get word to Eric. If it didn't, at least she'd be able to get Megan out safely.

"What...?" Megan began, but the words drifted off as Jayna opened the sliding glass door. Megan's eyes widened. "No way. I'm not going out there. I'm not leaving you guys!"

Jayna tugged on her hand, pulling her onto the balcony. "You're not leaving us. You're going for help. Chris can't jump, and Moe and Joseph will never leave without him. If I go, Liam will lose his mind when he comes through that door. It has to be you. If you don't go, we're not going to make it out of this."

"But—"

Jayna took Megan's other hand and gave them both a squeeze. "Eric is at the SWAT compound. You have to go there and tell him what's going on."

Tears welled in Megan's eyes, spilling over onto her cheeks as she shook her head. "I can't do this. You know I can't."

Since the day Megan jumped out of that hospital window and survived the bone-shattering impact, she'd been terrified of heights. She felt sick if she even looked out a high window, and driving over a tall bridge was against pack rules unless she was sleeping. Asking her to jump from a fourth-story balcony was the very worst thing Jayna could ask her to do. But she was asking her to do it anyway.

"I know you're scared, but I need you to do this," Jayna implored. "For me and for the pack."

More tears rolled down Megan's face. "But what if I hurt myself so bad that I can't go get Eric?"

Jayna released one of Megan's hands to cup her cheek. "Do you trust me?"

Megan didn't hesitate. "You're the only person I trust."

"Then you need to believe me when I say you'll be okay. You won't get hurt, and you're going to get to Eric in time. I wouldn't let you do this if I didn't believe that with every fiber of my soul."

Megan swallowed hard, sniffed once, then nodded. Pulling Jayna close, she hugged her tightly, then walked over to the railing and clambered over it. Jayna followed her to the railing.

"Find a cab and tell the driver you need to go to the SWAT compound. They'll either know where it is or will be able to find out. You have money on you, right?"

Megan nodded as she carefully positioned her feet on the edge of the balcony outside the railing. Jayna brushed her friend's hair back and kissed her cheek.

"I'll try to keep Liam talking as long as I can, but you need to hurry," she said.

Megan nodded, then took a deep breath and jumped.

Jayna leaned out to look over the balcony, wincing as Megan hit the grass below and rolled several times before coming to a stop. She breathed a sigh of relief when Megan jumped to her feet and gave her a smile, then ran toward the main street.

Jayna waited until Megan disappeared from sight, then turned and went back inside the small apartment. Giving the guys a nod she hoped was reassuring, she walked over to the door and turned the knob.

Chapter 12

IT TOOK XANDER, MIKE, AND BROOKS TO PULL GAGE away from Becker's throat.

"Half your squad almost died in that warehouse. One of those werewolves bit Khaki for God's sake!" Gage roared, trying to shake off Xander's hold on his arm. "And you deliberately hid one of them from us? What the hell were you thinking?"

Becker felt his canines elongate and knew his claws weren't far behind. "I'd tell you why I did it if you'd give me a fucking chance to say something without you trying to rip my head off!"

Gage's nostrils flared and Becker braced for impact, sure his alpha was going to come at him again regardless of how many guys were trying to hold him back. But then Gage took a deep breath and retracted his fangs and claws.

"Okay. I'm listening," he said. His eyes still flared gold though. "Let's hear the reason you think will justify putting a criminal before your pack."

The barb stung like hell.

"Jayna isn't a criminal," Becker growled. "She didn't even want to be in that warehouse. But her alpha has aligned their pack with the Albanians and she didn't know how to say no to him."

Becker knew he was pressing his luck, but he also knew he had to take advantage of the time Gage was giving him to explain everything.

"I know it was stupid to go in undercover, but once I tracked her down and realized how much danger she and the other members of her pack were in, I didn't have a choice." He took a breath. "This is probably a good time to also tell you that I gave Jayna my word that she and her pack wouldn't be arrested."

Gage's mouth tightened. "That isn't your call to make."

Becker took a step toward his boss, baring his fangs. The hell with playing nice. If Gage wanted to fight, bring it on.

"Jayna and her pack didn't do anything wrong. They're betas that have an asshole for an alpha who cares more about money and power than he does about his own pack," he said. "If it were Mackenzie, you'd have done the same thing."

Gage's fangs and claws were back, but he didn't say anything.

"What's a beta?" Max asked from beside Cooper.

Becker glanced at his pack mate to see Max looking at him in confusion. Well, at least someone else on the team was as clueless about werewolves as he was.

"It's a werewolf who isn't as strong as an alpha and has an almost overwhelming need to be part of a pack," Gage said tersely, then, giving Becker a pointed look, added, "Typically, they also aren't as reckless as alphas."

"Speaking of werewolves," Khaki interrupted, "one just walked into the compound."

Jayna.

Becker swore under his breath and raced for the door. He was so focused on getting outside before his teammates that it took him a moment to realize the scent coming from the other side of the door didn't belong to

Jayna but to Megan. His stomach lurched. If Megan was here, something bad had gone down, he could feel it.

He ran outside to find Megan standing in the middle of the compound as if trying to decide what to do next. There was a gaping hole in the chain-link fence where she'd torn her way in. The scratches on her bare arms and the blood spotting her shirt proved it hadn't been an easy task for the beta.

Her big, dark eyes darted from him to each of his teammates as they surrounded her. They were obviously scaring the hell out of her, but she stood her ground.

Becker strode forward to put himself between the small werewolf and the rest of the SWAT pack. Cooper broke through the ranks and moved to stand with him.

She glanced at Cooper, then ducked her head. "Glad to see you aren't dead. Sorry about shooting at you last night."

Cooper's mouth twitched. "Don't worry about it. Happens all the time."

Becker appreciated Cooper's support, but there were fifteen other SWAT werewolves aligned against them. But then Khaki walked over to stand beside Cooper.

She glanced at Becker. "Is this Jayna?"

"No, this is Megan. She's Jayna's pack sister," he said, then rushed on before Khaki or anyone else could ask more questions. "What are you doing here, Megan? Where's Jayna?"

"Jayna's in trouble. So are the guys," Megan said, nervously eyeing his pack again. "Liam's figured out that you're a cop, and he knows Jayna and the rest of us have been helping you. When I left, Jayna was trapped with the guys in their apartment, and Liam was threatening to send in his omegas if they didn't come out. I'm really scared for them. I think he's going to kill them."

Shit. This was exactly what he'd been afraid of. If Liam thought Jayna and the guys had betrayed him, there was no telling what he'd do. "I'll get them out of there, Megan. I promise." He glanced at Cooper. "I could use some backup. You in?"

"I'm in," Cooper said. "You get the weapons. I'll grab the tactical gear."

Becker nodded and turned to head for the armory, but Gage caught his arm. "Where the hell do you two think you're going?"

Becker bared his canines with a snarl. He didn't have time for this. "Jayna's in trouble. I'm going to get her out."

"On your own?"

"Looks like it." Becker glared at his boss. "I realize I'm a newbie in this pack and the fact that the woman I love is in danger doesn't concern you as much as when Mac was in trouble, but I'm going to go rescue her. If you want to stop me, you better be ready to kill me."

Gage didn't flinch. Instead, he stared at Becker like he was contemplating whether to take him up on the challenge.

"Are you saying you're willing to walk away from the Pack for this woman?" Gage asked.

"Yes." Becker didn't even have to think about it. "I'll do whatever I have to do to protect Jayna."

Gage slanted Cooper a hard look. "That go for you too?"

"Damn right," Cooper said. "I'm sure as hell not letting him go alone."

"He's not going alone," Xander said, stepping up to stand beside Khaki. "We're coming too."

Becker would have thanked Xander and Khaki, but

he didn't think their support would change Gage's mind. But then one after another, the rest of the Pack fell into place behind Becker, leaving Gage by himself on the imaginary line their alpha had drawn in the dirt. Even Tuffie walked over to stand with them.

Gage pinned Becker with a look. "I guess I don't need to ask whether you think Jayna is *The One* for you, do I?"

Becker shook his head.

Gage sighed. "This team was a whole hell of a lot easier to run before any of us had ever heard about *The One*. You know that, right?"

"Maybe." Becker grinned. "But it wasn't nearly as interesting."

"No, it wasn't." Gage looked around. "Okay, let's get loaded up and get out of here."

"Where's Megan?" Liam asked.

Jayna tried to look casual as she shrugged. Well, as casual as she could with Caleb, Brandon, and half a dozen other omegas pointing automatic weapons at her, Moe, Joseph, and Chris.

"She left an hour ago to pick up breakfast at McDonald's," Jayna said. "She'll be back soon."

Liam looked around the room, his hazel eyes suspicious, but after sniffing the air a few times, he jerked his head at the door. "Downstairs. Now!"

"Chris still hasn't healed," Jayna said. "He's in no shape to be running up and down stairs."

That wasn't a lie, and it might buy them some time until Eric got there. She wasn't sure what he'd do when he did, but she'd feel a lot better with him here.

Liam didn't even look at Chris. "Frasheri wants all of you downstairs. What part of that don't you understand?"

Jayna bit her tongue to keep from telling her alpha—make that former alpha—to shove it. Pissing Liam off more than he already was wouldn't help. Moe and Joseph must have thought so too, because they carefully helped Chris to his feet, then positioned themselves on either side of their injured pack mate, supporting him as he slowly shuffled toward the door.

Brandon brought up the rear as they made their way down the stairs, a smirk on his ugly face. Clearly, the bully was enjoying the view from the top.

Jayna ignored the urge to kick Brandon in the groin and grab his gun as Liam led them into Frasheri's ridiculously large office on the second floor. The Albanian was sitting at his monster of a desk, leaning back in his chair, watching them intently. Jayna's stomach clenched at the sight of the big handgun on the desk in front of him, and at the two Albanian guards behind him, their backs to the huge plate glass window that covered half the wall. The window gave a beautiful view of the loft's inner courtyard area, but at that moment, Jayna couldn't appreciate it. She was too worried about what was going to happen to her and her pack.

The omegas shoved Moe, Joseph, and Chris down on the leather couch against one wall while Liam took Jayna's arm and sat her in the lone arm chair positioned in front of the desk, so she was uncomfortably close to the gun there but still far enough away that she'd never be able to lunge for it before Frasheri could grab it.

Jayna gripped the arms of the chair, her nails extending just enough to dig into the polished wood. *Just stay calm and keep them talking*, she told herself. According to Eric, the SWAT compound was fifteen minutes away by car. That meant she had to figure out a way to stall for at least thirty. Her life and the lives of her pack mates depended on it.

"Liam tells me that Eric's a cop," Frasheri said. "Is that true, Jayna?"

Okay, she hadn't expected that. She'd expected the Albanian mobster to order his men to kill her and her pack immediately, then get as far away from Dallas as he could.

So why wasn't he?

Because he didn't want to believe Liam—not only because Liam was Kostandin's right-hand man, but because Frasheri had already invested so much of his trust in Eric. And Eric knew where Frasheri was hiding his stash of money and weapons.

But if she tried to deny it, Liam would only prove her wrong. So she wouldn't deny it. Instead, she'd use it to her advantage.

Jayna lifted her chin and met Frasheri's eyes. "Yes, Eric is a cop. He's one of the SWAT werewolves."

Frasheri swore, the vein at his temple pulsing, his hands curling into fists. From the corner of her eye, Jayna saw Joseph and the other guys looking at her in shock.

"He was a cop right up to the moment he decided to save my life that night in the warehouse," she added quickly. "When his alpha found out, he fired Eric from the team and kicked him out of his pack. That's why he came here."

Liam snorted. "Oh, please. You don't really expect us to believe that, do you?"

Frasheri held up his hand, cutting Liam off. "What do you mean, he saved your life?"

Jayna shrugged, trying hard to project that total sense of calm confidence Eric seemed to wear like a jacket. "I thought I was about to die, or get arrested if I was lucky. But then Eric came around a corner and instead of shooting me or arresting me, he hid me in a packing crate."

"Bullshit," Brandon muttered.

Jayna had an insane desire to stick her tongue out at the omega but settled for glaring at him. "How do you think I got that expensive perfume all over me? He smashed the bottles on top of the crate to cover my scent from his pack mates."

Frasheri stared at her for a long time. "Why would a cop do that?"

Liam came around from behind her so he could look her in the eye when she answered the question, no doubt so he could determine if she was lying. She knew he wasn't that good at detecting lies, but in this case, she didn't have to take the risk—not when it was easy to tell the truth.

"Because he's not just a cop—he's a werewolf. And werewolves will do anything when they meet *The One* for them."

Frasheri let out a short laugh. "You're kidding, right? You're telling me that Eric took one look at you and decided to chuck his whole career because you're hot?"

"It has nothing to do with looks," she said. "It's deeper than that. You've heard about wolves in the wild mating for life, right? Well, it's like that for werewolves too. Some of our kind say that there's only one mate out there for us. When we meet *The One*, we know it right away, and nothing can come between us."

"That's crap," Liam snapped. "I've never heard anything like that."

"I have," Caleb said slowly as if unsure whether he wanted to get involved in the conversation. "I never thought it was true, but I've heard a lot of older werewolves I've met talk about it. It's kind of like an urban legend."

Frasheri's gaze traveled from Caleb to linger on Liam before coming to rest on her. "So you're saying this is some kind of werewolf love at first sight? So strong that Eric immediately turned against his own pack to be with you?"

She nodded.

Liam snorted. "Jayna, you are so frigging naive. I guess it never occurred to you that Eric might just be playing you to get inside the pack so he could arrest us?"

Jayna narrowed her eyes at Liam. "Right. It was all an elaborate ploy to get inside so he could arrest us. Did you forget that Eric went out and killed one of the members of his own pack last night? Then again, maybe you did forget since you should have been the one there putting a bullet in that SWAT werewolf's head instead of letting Eric do it."

Liam jerked as if she'd slapped him. "What the hell are you trying to say?"

There had been a time when Jayna would have refrained from saying anything hurtful to Liam, but that time had long passed. Right then, she barely felt the normal alpha-beta connection that had always been there. It was like it had never existed at all.

"I'm saying that you stopped being our alpha a long time ago. First, you bring us into this arrangement without talking to us. Then, you bring in the omegas." Brandon growled at that, but she ignored him. "And if that isn't bad enough, you start sending us on jobs that could get us killed while you stay behind where it's safe."

Liam had the good grace to look a little chagrined. But then his lip curled. "I had to stay back here and coordinate pack operations."

Even Caleb and some of the other omegas snorted at that.

"Right," she scoffed. "Because that's what we need from an alpha. Not someone who will take a bullet for another member of the pack, like Eric did for Megan. Not someone who will dig a bullet out of another member of the pack, like he did for Chris. Hell, not even someone who will lead us in a fight when we're in over our head, like he did last night. No, we need someone who will stay inside where it's comfy, cozy, and safe, coordinating the next job."

Liam's eyes flared, a growl of rage rumbling in his throat. Jayna's claws extended all the way, along with her fangs, as he took a step toward her. She tensed, ready to launch herself at him.

The sound of guns coming out and safeties clicking off echoed in the room, reminding Jayna where they were and what they were doing there. She froze.

But Frasheri had his weapon pointed at Liam, not her. The omegas had theirs pointed at Frasheri. And the Albanians had theirs pointed at the omegas. All it would take is one little sneeze to start everyone shooting.

Jayna glanced at the guys still sitting on the couch. They were tense but alert. Both Moe and Joseph had one arm draped over Chris's shoulders. If things went from bad to worse, she knew they'd get Chris out of here.

She turned back to see that Liam's fangs had retracted. But his eyes still swirled with gold.

"I won't bother to ask if you and the other members of your pack consider Eric your alpha now. I think that's obvious," Frasheri said, his gun still pointed at Liam's head. "But I do have one question."

Jayna's breath caught in her throat. Crap, what had she missed?

"You said that Eric is so attracted to you he was willing to turn his back on his career and his pack, but you haven't said anything about whether you feel the same."

She frowned. Why the hell would Frasheri ask her something like that?

She knew the easy answer would be to say she felt the same about Eric. But she couldn't. She knew she was extremely attracted to Eric, more than she'd ever been to any other man. She wasn't quite so sure of anything beyond that though. While Eric might have bought into the whole *The One* thing, she was still on the fence about it.

But as the silence stretched on, she knew she had to say something. She couldn't make anything up either, on the off chance that Liam might pick up on the lie. On the other hand, she needed to say something that would satisfy Frasheri, or that big gun in his hand was likely to be pointed at her next.

"When I'm alone with Eric, I feel happy for the first time in…well…ever," she said softly.

Her answer must have satisfied Frasheri because he didn't turn his weapon her way. Liam, however, was staring daggers in her direction.

Frasheri seemed to be considering what to say next when the door opened and Kostandin strode in with two of his own soldiers. Kos regarded the scene, his mouth twitching as he took in the weapons.

"I leave for a few hours and I miss all the fun," he said. "Who wants to fill me in?"

Liam swung his gaze to Kos. "I discovered that Eric is one of those damn SWAT werewolves. The asshole's been playing us the whole time."

"Son of a bitch," Kos muttered. He glanced at his uncle. "So why is everyone sitting around in here instead of hunting that traitor down?"

"Because Jayna has him believing Eric abandoned his pack for her," Liam said. "That he's in love with her or some shit like that."

The look Kos gave Jayna made her skin crawl, and she had to fight the urge to squirm in her chair.

"I can certainly understand why a man might throw everything away for a chance to be with a woman like our she-wolf," he said.

Liam snorted. "That doesn't explain why Eric let those drug dealers you told him to kill walk away."

Kostandin's head jerked up. "What did you say?"

"He didn't kill those drug dealers like you ordered." Liam turned to her. "Maybe Jayna can tell us why."

Jayna felt the full force of Liam's gaze. *Crap*. What the hell was she going to say to explain why Eric had done that?

She threw a quick look in Frasheri's direction to see where he came out on this. But instead of regarding her, he was locked in a staring contest with his nephew. That's when she remembered how much the two Albanians distrusted each other.

Did she dare exploit that?

"Well, Jayna?" Liam prompted.

"Eric said he let them go because Mr. Frasheri told him to," she said as innocently as she could manage. "Something about them working for us."

Frasheri jerked his head back to look at her so fast she thought he might hurt himself. He stared at her in confusion, his bushy brows coming together to meet in the middle.

Kos pulled out a big handgun and pointed it at his uncle. "You piece of shit. I knew you were trying to fuck me over."

Frasheri opened his mouth to say something, but Kos pulled the trigger before he got the chance. Jayna wasn't sure if the bullet found its target because the whole room erupted in gunfire. Frasheri's and Kostandin's men began shooting at each other while the omegas shot at anyone and everyone, including each other.

Jayna leaped out of the chair, scrambling on her hands and knees over to where Joseph, Moe, and Chris had taken cover behind the couch. She didn't make it more than a few feet before the sound of the shattering glass made her whole body lock up.

She threw herself flat, covering her head with her arms as something exploded. The blast was so loud, she couldn't even think, much less figure out which way the couch was. She carefully lifted her head to get her bearings, but thick smoke swirled in the air, making it hard to see who was moving around her, who was shooting whom, and most importantly, who was winning.

Then someone grabbed her by the hair, yanking her to her feet and dragging her from the room. Her heart thumped as she caught Brandon's scent. She growled and lashed out with her claws. They dug into something, but it didn't seem to bother the big omega. A moment later, she figured out why. Instead of flesh, she'd shredded his heavy leather jacket.

Dammit!

Within seconds, Brandon had her out the door and was dragging her down the hall.

That's when she caught a whiff of another scent, this one sweet and delicious.

Eric.

She fought the grip Brandon now had on her neck, trying anything to get away and ignoring the pain as he tightened his hold in her hair. But she couldn't break loose, not without breaking her neck.

Time for a new plan—one that involved screaming her head off.

"Eric!"

Chapter 13

BECKER'S HEART BEAT A MILLION TIMES A MINUTE AS HE and Cooper slowly rappelled down the exterior of the loft and moved into position on either side of the big row of windows that stretched almost all the way across Frasheri's office. The glass was double paned, making it hard to hear exactly what Jayna was saying inside. But he didn't care. She was alive, and that was all that mattered.

He lifted the slack portion of the descent rope and brought it up to wrap around the snap link on his harness, locking himself in place, then checked the tie-off point twice before glancing at Cooper to make sure his friend was doing the same. The last thing he wanted was to be so worried about saving Jayna that he screwed up a basic rappelling maneuver and ended up sliding down the rope in an uncontrolled fall at the wrong time.

He edged a little closer to the window, staying out of sight of whoever was inside but near enough that he could pick up Jayna's words. She was saying something about him digging a bullet out of Chris. It was obvious she was stalling for time. Pride surged up inside him.

That's right, babe, keep them talking just a little longer. Give us time to get everyone in place.

It had taken him and the rest of the SWAT team barely ten minutes to get to the loft on Canton Street. He'd been tense as hell the whole way. Every time he thought about Jayna, he had a horrible vision of her lying there hurt—or worse. He kept telling himself she was fine, that he'd know if something had happened to her, that he'd feel it in his soul. But that hadn't stopped him from looking at his watch every two seconds and growling at Alex to drive faster.

As soon as they'd pinpointed Jayna's location on the second floor, Gage had sent him and Cooper up to the roof. Now, they were just waiting for Gage and the rest of the team to get into place to take down the other Albanians and omegas scattered throughout the building.

There was only one problem—no one else on the team knew what Jayna's pack mates looked like. If one of them aimed a weapon at anyone in the SWAT pack, they were going to get shot. It was up to Becker to get Joseph, Moe, and Chris out of there. And save Jayna.

Becker shifted a little, so he could see where Jayna's pack mates were or if they were even in the room at all, when he caught sight of Kostandin barging into the room.

Shit.

Becker immediately pulled back, worried the Albanian would see him. But the brief glimpse he'd gotten of the inside of that room had scared the shit out of him. There were at least nine bad guys in there, and every one of them had a weapon pointed at someone.

"Gage, we have a situation," he whispered into his mic. "I don't know what's going on, but we have a Mexican standoff up here. There are weapons pointing everywhere. Cooper and I might need to go in early."

"Roger that," Gage said. "I need another minute to get the last of the team into place, so hold if you can, but go if you have to. We'll improvise from there."

Becker was about to confirm receipt of the instructions, but the sound of gunfire stopped him.

"We're going in!" he shouted at the same time he kicked away from the wall and swung toward the window. A movement to his right told him that Cooper was doing the exact same thing.

When he reached the apex of his swing, he lifted his M4 and put a three-round burst through the window. Pieces of shattered glass were still falling as he and Cooper swung into the room. Becker yanked the quick release on his rappelling harness and dropped to the floor. There was a light thud beside him as Cooper did the same. The second their feet touched down, they both tossed stun grenades, immediately followed by smoke grenades. Becker ducked, covering his eyes from the brilliant flash; then he was up and wading into the smoke-filled room, searching for Jayna and her pack, slugging whoever got in his way.

His nose led him to an overturned chair in front of Frasheri's desk, then across the room to the flipped over couch. Behind it, he found Chris flat on his back and in pain, with Moe and Joseph kneeling over him holding pistols and shooting anyone who tried to get near them. Relief crossed their faces when they saw Becker.

"Where's Jayna?" he shouted.

Panic flashed in Moe's eyes as he frantically looked around. "She was here just a second ago."

Shit.

"Cooper," he said into his mic. "I'm going to find Jayna. Her pack is over by the couch near the wall. Three males—one African American, two white, one injured."

The words were barely out of his mouth when he heard

Jayna shouting his name. Becker ordered Moe, Joseph, and Chris to stay put, then raced for the door, slowing only long enough to rip the MP5 away from the Albanian blocking his way and smacking the man aside with it. He charged down the hallway in the direction he'd heard Jayna's voice.

Becker growled as he caught sight of Brandon dragging Jayna into a room at the far end of the hall. He'd never felt the urge to just plain tear someone apart before, but seeing the omega manhandling Jayna made him want to do that and more. He should have killed Brandon that first day he'd shown up here.

Becker ran through the doorway, skidding to a halt to avoid falling through the huge opening where the floor should have been. Thanks to the construction crew, sections of the floor and walls were gone, revealing rebar, plumbing pipes, electrical conduits, and AC vents. That should have made disappearing difficult, but parts of the floor were piled high with junk, toolboxes, and other construction materials, all of which provided excellent places to hide.

Becker was so focused on tracking them by scent, he didn't see Brandon appear from behind a tool chest with Jayna in front of him as a shield until the omega began shooting at him.

Getting shot didn't bother Becker, but the sight of Brandon's claws wrapped around Jayna's throat so tightly that blood ran down his fingers sent him into a rage like he'd never felt before. He dropped his M4, letting it hang by its strap across his chest, and rushed the omega with a snarl that shook the dust off the walls as he leaped from rebar to rebar. He felt one round, then another smack into his tactical vest. He ignored them, just like he ignored the one that drilled straight through his unprotected right shoulder. The pain didn't even register. It only pissed him off more.

Becker hadn't been a werewolf very long, but unlike some of the guys on the team, he'd never really had a problem with controlling his anger or the random shifting that came with it. But at that moment, he gave in to the instinct to let go and become the animal inside. He'd always been fast, but as his body twisted and rippled into a form that was nearly as much wolf as man, he was practically flying across the floor.

Brandon's eyes flared and he issued a growl of his own as he tossed Jayna aside like a rag doll. Becker's heart tore apart as the woman he loved bounced off a steel support column to land in a crumpled heap. He wanted to race to her side, but that would have left him open to even more bullets. One fatal shot and there'd be nothing to stop Brandon from shooting Jayna too.

Brandon raised his weapon for a head shot as Becker hurtled a tool bin and slammed into the omega like a two-hundred-and-twenty-five-pound truck. Bone crunched— both his and Brandon's—as his momentum drove the omega backward through the air and into the concrete wall. But as violent as the impact had been, Brandon shook it off and came at Becker, eyes like that of a berserker and fangs ready to rip and tear anything they could.

Becker bared his teeth with a deep, menacing growl, more than ready to fight.

Jayna wanted nothing more than to lie there on the floor and hide in the comforting darkness enveloping her, offering a respite from the pain emanating from every part of her body. But the growls and snarls somewhere on the edge of her consciousness wouldn't let her drift off. Eric was fighting Brandon to protect her, and it sounded like he was fighting for his life. She wouldn't let him do that alone.

Gritting her teeth against the pain, she rolled over and pushed to her knees, fighting the darkness threatening to pull her down again. But even when her vision cleared, it was hard to understand what she was seeing because Eric and Brandon were little more than blurs of ripping claws and flashing fangs.

She flinched and looked away as Brandon shredded Eric's tactical vest with his vicious claws, drawing more blood. That was when she saw the handgun on a section of the floor that was still intact. She lunged for it, but Brandon must have seen the move because he gave Eric a shove and headed her way with a snarl.

She rolled onto her hip, ready to defend herself when Eric slammed into Brandon and sent him flying. The omega's claws missed her throat by inches.

Jayna whirled around, expecting them to hit the ground rolling and keep right on fighting, but they both just lay there. Her heart thudded so loudly it echoed in her ears. Why weren't they moving?

After what seemed like forever, Eric finally rolled away from Brandon, onto his back. Jayna cringed at the rusted piece of rebar poking out of Brandon's chest. It must have been sticking up from the floor and impaled the omega.

Eric pressed a hand to his ragged tactical vest, his fangs and claws retracting. Blood seeped between his fingers, running down his hand.

Oh God. The rebar that had pierced Brandon's heart had stabbed Eric too.

Jayna didn't remember moving, but the next thing she knew, she was kneeling by Eric's side, gently pulling his hand away to see how bad the wound was. She ignored the bloody slashes that crisscrossed his face and arms, barely even looking at the bullet wound in his shoulder, more concerned about the ragged laceration caused by the rebar.

Her hands shook so badly, she could barely see what she was doing, and she couldn't understand why. She'd seen him injured before, when she'd dug a bullet out of his chest. But right now, her heart was pounding like nothing she'd ever experienced. She was on the edge of losing it.

She was still trying to control her trembling hands when Eric gently took both of them in his much larger, calloused ones.

"I'm okay, Jayna. It will heal." He released one hand to tenderly run his fingers over her neck. "That bastard scratched you."

The careful way he touched her neck, his fingers tracing Brandon's claw marks as he said the words, it was like they pained him more than the wound in his chest. She was going to cry—she knew it.

"I'm sorry I didn't get to you in time to stop this," he said brokenly.

While his voice was just as soft, there was fire in his eyes, and she pressed a shaking finger to his lips. The thought that he blamed himself for the minor scratches on her neck was ridiculous and precious at the same time. No one outside her pack had ever cared about her until now. But his concern for her went beyond that of a pack mate. As her heartbeat slowly began to return to normal now that his arms were around her, Jayna admitted that maybe her feelings for him went further than she'd thought.

Eric started to say something else, but she shushed him. "I got scratched, that's all. And like you said, it will heal. You got here in time. That's all that matters."

Leaning forward, she kissed him on the mouth. Eric cupped her face, kissing her back. She gasped a little, startled by how fast the fire kindled in her body at the touch of his lips. There was no way in hell she should have been thinking those thoughts at a time like this, not when Eric had just been shot and stabbed. And definitely not when she should be worrying about her pack mates.

Oh God. She hadn't even thought to ask about Megan. Was she okay? Had she been arrested?

Jayna pulled back so suddenly Eric almost fell over. His eyes flew open in surprise, revealing beautiful gold irises. She pushed that distracting observation aside and focused on her first priority—her pack.

"Where's Megan? Is she all right?"

Eric blinked, obviously caught off guard by the question. But then he grinned. "She's okay. She's waiting for you downstairs in our operations vehicle."

Jayna opened her mouth to ask if Megan was in trouble with the law—if all of them were—but then a cough from the doorway interrupted her. She looked over to see Cooper standing there with that same lopsided grin he'd had on his face at Eric's apartment. She smiled back, happy that she'd been right about Eric not killing his best friend. She'd never doubted it for a second—okay, maybe for a second.

"Speaking of the operations van, maybe it's time we get you two down there," Cooper said as he walked over to them. "This place will be crawling with uniformed officers and crime scene techs before long." He looked down at Brandon and grimaced, then turned back to Eric. "What, you couldn't just shoot him?"

Eric stood up and did that manly handshake thing that involved grabbing the other guy's shoulder and squeezing the hell out of it while trying to crush the hand you were shaking at the same time. Eric didn't even complain when Cooper put pressure on the shoulder that had the bullet hole through it. Jayna thought the men in her pack were strange—the ones in Eric's pack were even more bizarre.

Eric shrugged as he reached down and gently helped Jayna to her feet. She couldn't help but wince as she straightened up. Crap, she must have really done some damage bouncing off that column. Eric immediately had an arm around her waist, that concerned look on his face again—the one that made her heart beat funny.

"You okay?" he asked.

She nodded, giving him a small smile. "Just a little sore."

Eric frowned but didn't press. He glanced at Cooper. "How'd it go down there?"

"Most of the omegas didn't go down easy—the animals lost their frigging minds. But a good portion of the Albanians and even some of the more rational omegas gave themselves up once they realized they were outgunned." Cooper pointed at the radio earpiece hanging in tatters against Becker's tactical vest. "You would have already known that if you'd left your earpiece in."

Eric ignored the comment, turning back to her. "You want me to carry you down the stairs?"

Jayna was touched. While the idea of her big, alpha werewolf carrying her out of there held a certain romantic appeal, how would it look for him to carry her when he was bleeding all over the place and all she had were some bumps and bruises?

"I'm okay. I'll just walk slowly." She smiled at him. "But thanks."

He nodded, keeping his arm around her as he guided her toward the door. In the distance, Jayna could hear what sounded like hundreds of sirens approaching the loft. "Eric told me that Megan's okay, but what about Moe, Chris, and Joseph? They haven't been arrested or..."

She couldn't bring herself to say the words.

"They're all fine," Cooper said. "They're down in the operations vehicle with Megan. One of our medics is looking at Chris."

The huge weight on her chest lifted and she could finally breathe again. She didn't know what the future held for her or her pack, but at least they were out from under the Albanians and safe for now.

"What about Liam, our pack alpha?" she asked when they reached the top of the steps. "Is he...?"

"It got a little crazy in that office, especially when everyone started bolting for the exits," Cooper said. "I don't know who was killed, who was arrested, and who escaped."

Eric frowned. "Some of them got away?"

Cooper nodded. "Yeah. I don't know who though. I was a little busy at the time."

Jayna got a sinking feeling in her stomach, her instincts telling her that Liam had been one of the people who'd gotten away. A small part of her was glad. He'd been important to her at one point in her life. But she also remembered how angry Liam had been when he'd realized he was no longer pack alpha and that Eric had taken over. Liam had looked like he was ready to kill. If he was still out there, she hoped he'd leave Dallas and get as far away as he could. She just wasn't sure he would.

—◦◦◦—

It took all the restraint Becker possessed to keep from scooping up Jayna in his arms and carrying her down the stairs. She was moving so gingerly that it hurt to watch her try to get down to the first floor.

He and Cooper took their time leading Jayna through the building and out to the operations vehicle in the parking lot behind the loft. Becker was just thinking he might have to pick her up to get her into the renovated RV, but the moment he opened the door, all her aches and pains disappeared. She must have picked up the scent of her pack mates because she practically leaped through the door.

He climbed in just in time to see Jayna pulling Megan into her arms, hugging the smaller werewolf to her as she moved over to join Moe and Joseph by Chris's side. The beta was stretched out on his back on the floor near the bank of TVs there. Alex and the team's other medic, Trey Duncan, were leaning over the injured werewolf with forceps, bloody hands, and a frigging needle and thread.

"Oh God, Chris. What happened?" Jayna asked as she knelt down beside the werewolf.

Chris gritted his teeth as Trey slid the needle through the ab muscles on either side of the ragged laceration the bullet had made in his stomach the previous night. It was bleeding heavily and didn't look nearly as healed as it should have.

"He tore open the half-healed wound in his stomach fighting those damn Albanians," Joseph said. "The stupid idiot wouldn't stay still no matter how many times we told him to."

Becker knelt down beside Jayna, taking hold of her hand and giving it a squeeze. "Is he going to be okay?" he asked Trey.

"He should have healed already," Trey muttered distractedly as he looped a knot in the thread, then pulled the edges of the wound closed. "He said this happened over twenty-four hours ago, so I don't understand why the wound hasn't closed already. The internal injuries are doing fine, but this muscle tissue should have knitted closed sometime last night. I don't know why it hasn't."

Tears filled Jayna's eyes, but before Becker could say anything to reassure her, Gage spoke.

"He's a beta. That's why the wound hasn't healed. Betas can't handle the amount of damage alphas can, so it takes longer for them to heal. He'll recover much faster now that Trey and Alex have closed up those torn muscles, provided he stays off his feet for a while."

Jayna looked over her shoulder at Gage, as if trying to figure out how much she wanted to trust his words. Apparently, whatever she saw on his face must have satisfied her because she visibly relaxed as she turned back to rest a hand on Chris's forehead.

"He'll stay off his feet," she said firmly. "I can promise you that."

When Alex and Trey were done, they moved away from Chris and out the door, letting Jayna and her pack have unfettered access to their friend. As one, they leaned in to wrap him in their arms. The image was pretty damn moving, even for a werewolf used to living in a pack. If Becker hadn't been sure before, he was now: betas simply possessed a stronger and more dependent bond than the one that existed in his SWAT pack. His pack was tight, but hers was tighter.

Part of him worried what that meant for his relationship with their new leader—and he had no doubt that Jayna was their pack leader now. That fact had become more and more obvious over the past few days, but it was official now. Her pack had chosen her over Liam.

He got to his feet and walked over to where Gage was standing by the open door. He knew the morning's events had been traumatic for all of them, and he got the feeling that being together as a pack was what they needed.

Gage was watching the other pack intently. "So, that's her, huh? The reason you did all of this?"

Becker glanced at Jayna. She was hugging both Moe and Joseph at the same time while Megan kneeled beside them with a big smile on her face. The whole attitude of her pack had changed now that Liam was gone. Whereas everyone had been tense and scared before, now, with Jayna, they were all smiles and laughter. Becker could certainly understand why—Jayna made him feel like that every time he was with her too.

"Yeah, that's her," he said.

"Guess I can understand why you went to such

extreme lengths to be with her then," Gage said. "She seems pretty special."

Gage didn't know the half of it. "She is." He turned to his boss. "Cooper said some of the werewolves and Albanians got away. I need to figure out who."

His alpha nodded. "Go ahead. I'll look after them until you get back."

The loft had turned into a complete zoo in the few minutes he'd been inside the operations vehicle. There were at least twenty patrol cars parked in the lot and along the street, all with their blue lights flashing. Throw in the various ambulances with their red lights and the unmarked cars with flashing headlights and dashboard lights, and the place was lit up like a freaking circus. The sidewalks on the far side of the street from the loft were already filling up with reporters and news vans. Oh yeah, it was turning into a madhouse.

Becker immediately headed up to the second floor, making his way around uniformed cops dragging the Albanians away in cuffs and paramedics pushing the injured and dead away on gurneys. He checked a few body bags as he went, but none of them held Liam or Kostandin. Unfortunately, when he picked up their scents, he realized they'd both slipped out of the loft—together. Worse, they had at least a half-dozen Albanians with them, maybe more. He followed the scent trail out of the building and down the block, where they disappeared. Obviously, they'd gotten into a vehicle and were long gone.

When Becker got back to the operations vehicle, Jayna was talking to Gage, the anxiety back on her beautiful face. Her pack was still gathered in the rear of the

RV, but they looked just as concerned as she did. Becker walked over to stand beside her.

"Frasheri isn't getting out of prison for a long time, I can promise you that," Gage said.

"That doesn't mean anything if we're in there with him," Jayna said. "You still haven't said if you're going to arrest us or not."

Becker held his breath. He found Jayna's hand, interlocking his fingers with hers. It was his way of letting her know he was on her side—and her pack's.

Gage's mouth curved slightly. "If I were going to arrest you and your pack, you wouldn't be in the back of my operations vehicle. You'd already be in jail."

Some of the tension left Jayna's shoulders, but the rest of her pack didn't seem as convinced.

"Why are you letting us go?" Moe asked.

"Because Becker said that none of you actually ever committed any serious crimes. That's good enough for me," Gage said.

"What if Frasheri tells the DA about us, hoping to make a deal?" Megan asked. "Or Caleb?"

"The DA is interested in putting away mob bosses like Frasheri, not people who worked for him," Becker said. "Frasheri is probably scared shitless of you testifying against him."

"And as for Caleb, ratting you out wouldn't be in his best interest," Gage added. "All he has to do is say he was the muscle Frasheri brought in to follow orders. I doubt there'll be any way to pin him to any specific crime. He keeps his head down, he'll be out of prison in less than two years." He glanced at Becker. "Did you come up with anything out there?"

"It looks like Liam and Kostandin got away, along with a few of the Albanians," Becker said. "I tracked their scent for a block before it disappeared."

Gage swore. Becker silently did the same. He didn't like the idea of Jayna's former alpha being anywhere but in prison. She and her pack looked just as alarmed.

Chris pushed himself up on an elbow. Beads of sweat dotted his forehead from the effort and he bit back a grimace. "Liam's going to come for us. We've got to get out of Dallas before he does."

Megan and Joseph both put a hand on Chris's shoulder, gently pushing him back down.

"Hey, that medic guy said you're supposed to take it easy, not get on the first bus out of here," Joseph said. "That means none of us are leaving either. At least not until you've healed up."

"Joseph's right," Megan said. "Besides, just because Liam got away, that doesn't mean he's going to come after us." She looked at Jayna. "Right?"

Becker could practically see Jayna's shoulders bow under the sudden weight of so much responsibility. He knew without having to ask where her mind was headed. She was wondering if she should take her pack and get as far away from Dallas, Frasheri, Liam, and Kostandin as they could.

"Megan's right, Jayna," Becker said. "Liam and Kos are no doubt long gone from here."

If Liam did come after Jayna and her pack though, going on the run was more dangerous than staying in Dallas, where he and the rest of his SWAT team could protect them. But if they were hell-bent on leaving, he'd go with them.

"Jayna?" Moe prompted when she didn't answer.

She looked back and forth from her pack to Becker, anguish clear in her eyes. He wanted to pull her into his arms and tell her that he'd make everything better, but she had a pack that depended on her. They needed her to figure out what to do, not him.

"I don't know if Liam will come after us or not, but Chris is in no shape to go anywhere right now," she finally said. "We should have enough money between us to lie low at a motel for a few days until we figure something out."

"Or you could stay with me," Becker suggested.

It wasn't a question, but it wasn't a command either. Jayna might be new to this alpha thing, but he wasn't going to impose his will on her, ever. That didn't mean he couldn't still be persuasive as hell. Right now, all he was trying to do was show her that she and her pack didn't have to go it alone. She had him now, and his pack would help hers.

Jayna gave him a skeptical look. "All five of us? I don't think we'd fit."

He shrugged. "We can make it work."

"I'm not sure about that, Becker. I've seen how small your apartment is," Gage said. "But I think I might know a place where Jayna and her pack can stay without falling over each other every time they turn around." He looked at Jayna. "If you're okay with that?"

She exchanged looks with her pack mates, then gave Gage a nod.

Relief coursed through Becker's body. Jayna and her pack would be hanging around Dallas long enough for him to convince them to stay permanently.

Chapter 14

"You want something to eat?" Eric asked, tossing his keys on the table inside the door of his apartment.

Jayna started to say no, then stopped. She'd eaten a huge breakfast just a few hours ago, so she shouldn't be hungry, but she was famished again. She'd been eating like a bear since yesterday. Eric and Cooper said it was because she needed the extra energy to heal the damage her body had sustained during the fight with Brandon. She supposed that made sense, considering Trey had told her she'd broken four ribs and fractured several bones in her back bouncing off that column. What didn't make sense was how fast she'd healed. As a beta, it should have taken days to recover, but she was feeling almost back to normal already.

Eric must have taken her silence for consent and jerked his head at the couch as he headed toward the kitchen. "I'll dig us up something to eat. You can turn on the TV if you want."

She curled up on his big, comfy couch, but ignored the TV remote. She didn't feel like watching television, and she definitely had no interest in what the news channels were saying about yesterday's shoot-out at the loft. So instead, she leaned back into the cushions, trying furiously to figure out what she should do with the pack she had become responsible for overnight.

She barely felt capable of taking care of herself on most days, much less four other werewolves. For one horrible minute back in the SWAT operations vehicle yesterday, she'd almost considered walking away from Eric. She hadn't wanted to do it, but being responsible for the rest of her pack meant she had to put other people's needs ahead of her own, especially if it meant keeping them safe from Liam.

But fortunately, Sergeant Dixon, the very large and very intimidating alpha of Eric's pack, had come up with a solution—staying with his future in-laws, Ethan and Kathryn Stone. Jayna still couldn't believe the couple had opened up their beautiful home to people they didn't know, but they had, and for that, she was extremely grateful.

She and Eric had talked about her pack staying at the compound instead, but quickly decided against it. Living in close proximity to seventeen extremely alpha werewolves would have made her pack jumpy as hell. And if Liam and Kos were still in Dallas, there was no way they'd find them down near College Station.

Jayna didn't realize she'd zoned out until Eric walked into the living room carrying two plates piled high with sandwiches. He set them on the coffee table, then went back to the kitchen to grab a monster-sized bag of Doritos and two sodas. She was about to tell him that a single sandwich would have been enough, but then her stomach growled and she decided that maybe she could eat the entire plate of sandwiches.

They didn't talk much as they ate, but that just gave Jayna more time to worry. Was Chris resting like he was supposed to? Were Megan, Moe, and Joseph sticking close to the Stones' place like she'd asked them to? Did she have to worry about Liam or Kos finding them?

God, had her former alpha agonized over everything like this? Something told her he probably hadn't.

Eric must have picked up on her anxiety because he frowned as he reached into the bag for another handful of Doritos. "Still worried about your pack?"

"My pack? Do you have any idea how ridiculous that sounds? I'm not even an alpha."

"Aren't you?"

"No," she said quickly. "I'm a beta like the rest of them."

"I wouldn't be too sure of that. You're eating like an alpha. You're healing like an alpha. Your claws and fangs are longer and sharper than anyone else's in your pack, and all of them naturally turn to you for answers when anything goes wrong." He grinned. "Sounds like an alpha to me."

Jayna placed her empty plate on the coffee table, then stared hard at it as she considered that. "But if I'm an alpha, why don't I know what to do? They're worried and scared, and they're looking to me to tell them what we should do next, and I don't know what to tell them."

Eric set his plate on the table beside hers, then moved closer and put his arm around her shoulders. She leaned her weight into him, resting her head on his muscular chest and letting herself be weak for just a little while.

"You're going to figure this out," he said softly, kissing the top of her head and pulling her even closer. "We're going to figure this out. We just need to find a place for you and your pack to live and work you'll enjoy doing."

"I don't know if that will be enough," she said softly. "We've never lived in one place more than three or four months, less if there was trouble of any kind. And even though Moe is new to the pack, running from problems is already what he's used to doing. It's what all of us are used to doing."

"But it doesn't have to be that way this time. You can stop running and let me help. We can make this work. We just have to try."

Jayna closed her eyes for a moment, listening to the strong beat of his heart under her cheek. She wanted to believe him, but she was terrified at the thought of what would happen if he was wrong.

"But what if we can't?" she asked. "What if we can't find jobs or a place to live? What if the guys don't want to stay here? You just said it. I'm supposed to be their alpha now. I'm supposed to take care of them. What if I have to leave…for them?"

He gently pulled her away from his chest so he could look at her. "If we can't find something for your pack in Dallas, something that really works for them, or if they're not happy here, then I'll leave with you."

Jayna was speechless. She knew Eric cared for her, but she hadn't realized just how deep those feelings really were until now.

"You'd really leave your pack to be with me?" she finally managed.

Saying the words out loud made the whole idea seem even more ridiculous. Why on earth would a guy like Eric give up a job he obviously loved, a fantastic apartment, and a pack that was amazing to live like a nomad with a screwed-up werewolf like her and her band of equally screwed-up pack mates?

"Of course I would," he said as if he was surprised

she was even asking. "I don't know how many different ways I can say this for you to believe it, but you're the person I want to spend the rest of my life with. And if that means I have to leave Dallas to do that, I'll do it without a second thought. I love you, Jayna."

Jayna was so floored, she was speechless. She knew she should say she loved him too, but she couldn't. Not that she wasn't crazy about him—she was. It was just that she didn't know if she believed in love, not the way he did.

But at the same time, she had to admit hearing him say those words to her made her feel warm all over. Tears suddenly welled in her eyes, but before she could reach up to wipe the embarrassing things from her cheeks, Eric's lips were there, kissing them away. His mouth quickly moved from her cheeks to her lips, and soon enough, she was having a hard time remembering why she'd been crying in the first place. It was amazing the way he could make her forget her problems with a simple touch. She had about a hundred critical decisions to make, but right then, she couldn't think of a single thing that couldn't wait until later…much later.

Pushing him back on the couch, she climbed onto his lap and kissed him with the same abandon he was kissing her with. Eric rested his hands on her hips, letting her take charge, though she could tell from the bulge in his pants that he was more than a little aroused.

He wasn't the only one. Knowing how excited Eric was got her going too. Dragging her mouth away from his, she sat back and slowly pulled her shirt over her head, then did the same with her bra. Eyes molten, Eric cupped her breasts in his big hands and leaned forward to take one stiff nipple into his mouth. Oh God, he could drive her insane with that mouth of his.

Jayna gasped as his slightly extended canines grazed her sensitive nipple when he sucked it into his mouth and feasted on it. The crazy combination of warm, soft tongue and hard, sharp fangs was unbelievable, and she wondered if it was possible for him to make her come just from teasing her breasts.

She didn't get to find out because Eric picked her up with a growl and carried her to the bedroom. After setting her gently on the bed, he slowly worked off her jeans, then her panties. It was funny, but she wasn't self-conscious at all in front of him, not even when she was completely naked and he was completely clothed. In fact, she rather enjoyed being naked in front of him. And she could tell that he enjoyed it too. He looked hard as a rock in those jeans of his.

Eric grabbed his T-shirt and ripped it over his head, exposing his delicious pecs and sexy abs. But when he reached to unbuckle his belt, she sat up and stopped him.

"I'm an alpha now too, remember?" she said with a smile. "That's my job."

Eric looked surprised for a minute, then returned her grin, letting her undo his belt and yank open his jeans. She shoved them down his legs, then slid off the bed and dropped down to her knees to help him step out of them, a position that left her face-to-face with the object of her affection, so to speak.

She couldn't stop herself from reaching out and wrapping her hand around the base of his perfect cock. Right then, she decided to do something she hadn't done in a long time. She leaned forward and dragged her tongue across the broad head of his shaft. The sexy growl he let loose as she did made her pulse beat that much faster.

One little taste wasn't enough though, and she scooted closer and licked him like a lollipop. He was so scrumptious, it was all she could do to keep herself from shifting out of pure pleasure.

In between those long, lazy licks, Jayna took his shaft in her mouth and moved up and down as slowly and sensually as she knew how. Eric growled even louder when she did, which only made her want to do it faster. She'd never gotten a chance to repay him for the oral pleasure he'd given her the other day, and now seemed like a very good time to do it.

She'd just added a little hand massage into the equation, falling into a nice, easy rhythm, when Eric weaved his fingers in her hair and gently guided her away from his cock. She tried to stay where she was, suddenly feeling very possessive about what she wanted. But he was insistent, and soon enough, he had her mouth off his shaft and had pulled her to her feet.

"What's the deal?" she demanded. "I was enjoying myself down there."

The look Eric gave her was hot and hungry. "I was enjoying myself as well—a little bit too much. A few more minutes of that and I don't think I would have been able to stay in control."

She looped her arms around his neck and raised a brow. "Who says I wanted you to stay in control?"

Eric chuckled and nudged her back onto the bed. "You're an alpha, all right. No doubt about it."

Jayna laughed and scooted higher on the bed. "I guess

you'd better watch out then, or the next thing you know, I might just want to be on top during sex."

Eric climbed into bed with her, a look of faux horror fixed on his face. "Anything but that."

She tackled him back onto the blankets, laughing as she scrambled on top of him. She straddled his hips, enjoying his expression as her very excited pussy came into contact with his very hard cock. She moved back and forth on him a few times, just to give him an idea of what it would be like with her on top; then she leaned forward and slowed things down a bit by kissing and nibbling his chest. She paid careful attention to the fresh scars there, reverently pressing her lips to them, knowing he'd gotten them for her.

His hand glided over her hair, caressing her softly as she kissed her way back and forth across his pecs and shoulders, sometimes moving lower to pay attention to his abs. She knew Eric enjoyed what she was doing because he let out the sexiest growls as she did it, but she wondered if she enjoyed it even more. Being able to do something for Eric after everything he'd done for her made her whole body come alive in ways it never had before.

Jayna would have been happy to spend the next few hours kissing every inch of his glorious body, but Eric apparently had other ideas because he suddenly rolled over and pinned her to the bed under his weight. His position left his cock pressing against her clit, and she gasped as he slid the long length of his shaft up and down her clit.

"Who's being the alpha now?" she groaned, looking up into his golden, hunger-filled eyes.

He chuckled. "We can take turns, if you want."

She tried to laugh with him, but it turned into another long moan as he slid his cock across her clit again, making stars explode in her head and her whole body shake.

"That's okay," she finally panted. "I'm good with you taking the lead for a while."

Eric growled and buried his face in her neck, his fangs nipping her there as he continued to torture her clit in the best way possible.

It didn't take long before Jayna felt her orgasm approaching. When she came, it was slow and drawn out, just like the movement of Eric's cock against her clit. She shook and moaned beneath him, digging her nails into his shoulders so deep she was sure she'd drawn blood.

"Best. Orgasm. Ever," she said.

The bed dipped beneath her, and she looked over to see Eric beside her, a condom covering his shaft. He lay beside her and slowly traced a single fingertip over her stomach, breasts, neck, and lips until she was moaning. And when she decided he'd teased her enough, Eric was right there to lift her up and gently sit her right down on his cock.

Jayna growled long and low as Eric's thick cock spread her wide and she felt him slide deep inside her. She leaned forward and placed her hands on his chest, smiling at him and the way he made her feel so good.

"Look at you," he said with a grin. "Riding on top now."

She pressed her breasts against his chest, burying her face in his neck. "I guess that means I'm an alpha for sure, huh?"

"I guess so." Eric's hands moved lower until he grabbed her ass, urging her up and down on him. "Hope you don't mind if I help you out a little bit?"

He was only plunging in and out a few inches at a time, but it felt so good that she was having a hard time thinking of a snappy comeback.

"Help is good," she breathed.

It was the best of both worlds, actually—getting to be on top, she could control exactly how deep he went, and was also able to enjoy the sensation of him thrusting up into her, slow and steady.

She was almost certain that after the huge orgasm she'd had earlier, there was no way she'd be able to come that hard again so soon. But she discovered she was wrong. Once Eric began to take her fast and hard, she felt that crazy tingling sensation deep inside her, and had no choice but to close her eyes and scream into Eric's neck as he roared and came with her. She bucked and ground down on him, loving how coming in this position felt so completely different. Maybe it was simply because Eric knew how to make love to her—a woman could definitely get used to this.

Later, she snuggled close to him, her head pillowed on his chest as she basked in the afterglow of what they'd just shared. For now at least, she didn't want to think about anything else but being with Eric. She only hoped he was right about finding a way for her pack to stay in Dallas, because the thought of leaving him hurt too much to even think about—and taking him away from his pack didn't make her feel any better.

~~~

"So what kind of work are Jayna and her pack looking for?" Mac asked.

She was sitting cross-legged on the couch in the

dayroom of the SWAT compound's training building, Gage on one side, Cooper on the other. Becker had dropped Jayna off at Mac's parents' house an hour ago, then came here. The rest of the Pack was gathered around the room, every one of them eager to help, and Becker appreciated their willingness to come up with a solution to Jayna's problem, especially after he'd lied to them.

"Something that doesn't necessarily require a high school diploma," he said in answer to Mac's question. "I think Joseph and Chris have one, but Jayna ran away when she was seventeen. And while both Moe and Megan were close to graduating when they turned, I don't think either one of them actually did. We can worry about them taking the GED later though. Right now, let's limit our search to jobs that don't require a high school degree. When I talked to Jayna and her pack about it last night, they said they're open to pretty much anything. But I don't think bagging groceries at the local supermarket is going to cut it. They need jobs that let them spend as much time together as possible. They don't like to be away from each other for very long."

"Damn," Xander muttered. "I thought our pack was tight."

"It's not really that strange if you think about it," Gage said. "As betas, they're closer to a real wolf pack than we are, so it makes sense for them to live together and work together. I'd be surprised if they didn't like to sleep together too."

"Huh." Cooper looked at Becker, his mouth twitching. "So, when you and Jayna are together, does the rest of her pack watch?"

Becker growled as Alex and Max both stepped

forward to fist-bump Cooper. Not that it mattered. The sound was barely audible above all the laughter.

Mac smacked Cooper on the arm. "Behave," she admonished. Digging her cell phone out of a purse that could have done double duty as an overnight bag, she turned to Becker. "Okay. Let me make some calls."

One by one, the rest of the Pack did the same, calling friends, contacts, and anyone who owed the SWAT team a favor. As they came up with possibilities, they posted them on the extra whiteboard Trey had rolled out of the conference room. If a job had potential, it went on the board.

In between, they fielded calls from other cops and law enforcement agencies in the Dallas area who'd heard what Becker and the rest of the SWAT team were up to. They didn't just call with job opportunities either, but about apartments for rent and a few cars for sale that didn't cost too much. Before long, the whiteboard was full on both sides. If Mac, Khaki, and the guys hadn't been there, Becker might have teared up. Hell, even with them there, he got a little misty.

By the time he left to head out to the Stones' place a few hours later, Becker had four pages of solid job possibilities and some apartments for Jayna and her pack to consider. He only hoped it was enough.

As the Harley's engine vibrated under him, he tried to tell himself it was all going to work out. It had to. Now that he'd found *The One*, there was no way in hell he was letting her get away. If that meant he had to move heaven and earth to find a good life for her and her pack mates here in the city, he'd do it. If being with Jayna meant he had to empty out his bank account and sell everything he owned, he was okay with that too.

He had friends in other places he could turn to. Family too. His parents owned a huge house and a lot of land outside of Denver. If he showed up with Jayna, her pack, and no job, his family would welcome them with open arms. Okay, maybe his mom would be a little shocked when she found out his girlfriend came with an extended family, but she'd overlook it if there was a possibility of a grandchild in the near future.

Becker was still daydreaming about kids with Jayna someday when headlights suddenly appeared in his rearview mirror. He glanced over, swearing when he saw two vehicles speeding up behind him and closing fast.

"Kathryn and Ethan are being really cool about us staying with them," Megan said as she set down another plate on the big dining room table.

Jayna followed her, placing a knife and fork on either side of each dish. "Yeah, they are."

Actually, they were amazing. College professors in their sixties, the couple had taken Jayna and the rest of the pack into their home simply because their future son-in-law had asked. But as kind as the woman and her husband had been, Jayna didn't want to overstay their welcome. The modest ranch-style home with its four bedrooms was never meant to house five adult werewolves. But finding a place of their own when none of them had jobs was going to be difficult.

Laughter coming from the kitchen was a welcome interruption from the dark place her thoughts were headed. When she'd gotten back to the Stones' house a few hours ago, Megan had told her the guys were in the barn with

Ethan, helping him clean out the stalls. Even though Kathryn and Ethan were full-time professors at Texas A&M, they both loved horses and had four beautiful ones.

Now the guys were in the adjoining kitchen, giving the older couple a hand with dinner. Jayna couldn't remember when she'd last had a home-cooked meal, and the aroma of lasagna and garlic bread made her mouth water.

She glanced at Megan as she placed a fork on another napkin. "Eric said he'd leave his pack and come with us if we leave Dallas."

Megan paused, the plate in her hand halfway to the table. "Wow. That's a big deal."

"Yeah," Jayna agreed.

A frown creased Megan's brow. "You don't seem happy about that. Don't you want him to come with us?"

"Yeah, of course I want him to. It's just…" Jayna hesitated. "I know Eric thinks that's what he wants to do now, but what if he changes his mind years from now and resents me for making him leave his pack? I'm not sure I could handle that."

Megan set down the plate she'd been holding and moved on to the next. "Maybe we won't have to leave Dallas."

Jayna gave her a sidelong glance. "Would you be okay with that?"

Megan nodded. "It'd be nice not moving around every few weeks."

That was one more vote in favor of staying. "What about the guys? Do you think they'd be all right with staying here? So close to another pack of werewolves, I mean?"

"Why not?" Megan shrugged. "They already have a serious case of hero worship where Eric is concerned."

Jayna smiled. Yeah, she'd noticed that too.

"And Eric would do anything for you," Megan continued. "You should have seen the way he stood up to his alpha yesterday. Eric told him he'd walk away from the pack to keep you safe. You've seen Sergeant Dixon, so you know how scary he can be. But Eric was willing to fight him and as many of his pack mates as he had to if that's what it took. He'd do anything for you."

"I know." Jayna swallowed hard, emotions welling up all of a sudden. "That's why I can't let him walk away from his pack."

Megan stared at her. "That makes no sense. If it's what Eric wants to do, then why not?"

Jayna looked away.

"It's because you're scared to death of letting Eric get too close, isn't it?"

Jayna looked up sharply. "Too close? I think it's a little late for that since we're already sleeping together."

Megan set down the last plate, then came around the table to take Jayna's hand in hers. "Sleeping with a guy isn't the same thing as opening your heart to him. It's about being willing to open yourself up and risk getting hurt for a chance at finding something real. That's not you, Jayna. You're really good at keeping people at a distance, you always have been. But I'm guessing Eric makes you feel things you've never felt for a guy, and it's freaking you out. And when you get freaked, you run."

"I'm not running from Eric," she said stubbornly.

"Aren't you? Can you honestly look me in the eye and tell me the only reason you don't want Eric to come with us if we leave is because you don't want to make him choose between you and his pack?"

Jayna opened her mouth to tell her friend exactly that, but the words wouldn't come—because they would have been a lie, and she didn't want to lie to the only person in the world who really knew her and liked her anyway. Well, the only person besides Eric.

"Okay," she admitted. "Maybe I am running. But I'm just so scared of getting hurt."

Megan put an arm around her shoulders. "I know you're scared. But why? I mean, I know your mom and stepdad weren't the poster couple for happily ever after, but you and Eric aren't your mom and stepdad."

Thank God for that. "I know. But, Megan, Eric believes I'm this mythical soul mate that werewolf legends talk about. That we're destined to be together. That he loved me the moment we met."

"So?" Megan said. "I still don't see what the problem is. You fell for Eric the second you met too."

Jayna started to deny it but couldn't. "Maybe. Probably. The first time we met in that warehouse full of werewolves shooting at each other, I couldn't think about anything because I was too lost in those beautiful blue eyes of his."

Megan shook her head with a laugh. "People are trying to kill each other all around you, and you're losing yourself in some guy's beautiful blue eyes. Sounds like a magical power at work to me. Again, what's the problem? If you and Eric are magically destined to be together, what are you worried about?"

Jayna gave her a small smile. "I'm worried that there really isn't any magical power pulling us together, that it's all in our heads. What if I'm not nearly as wonderful as he seems to think I am and he figures it out a few weeks after he's run off with us? What if he wakes up one morning and realizes he doesn't love me at all and that he screwed up his whole life for nothing?"

"Okay, I'm going to say this as gently as I can— you're an idiot."

"Thanks a lot."

"Jayna, I can promise you one thing for sure: Eric is never going to stop loving you. I've seen it in his eyes. He can no more stop loving you than he can breathe underwater. It's impossible. You'll never lose his love, but you can screw around and abandon it because you're too stuck in the past to see what's right in front of you."

Jayna could only stare at her friend in awe. "When did you become so smart?"

Megan laughed. "I'm no smarter than I ever was. I'm just bright enough to know something good when I see it. The question is—do you?"

For once, Jayna decided not to overthink a simple question. She was just going to say what her heart told her to say.

But before she could, a sound from outside caught her attention. The horses were stirring in their stalls and neighing, like they had when they'd first gotten a whiff of her and her pack of werewolves. She glanced at the doorway to the kitchen, checking to see if the guys had gone out to the barn again. After Moe, Joseph, and Chris had spent most of the afternoon in there helping Ethan, she didn't think the horses would still be afraid, but it was possible. All three guys were in the kitchen though, helping make dinner and laughing at some joke Ethan had just told them.

She headed for the kitchen before she even realized what she was doing.

"Jayna, what's wrong?" Megan asked.

She didn't know what was wrong. Something just…was.

Then, a scent she never thought she'd smell again hit her.

Crap.

Jayna ran the last few steps into the spacious country kitchen. "Ethan, do you keep a gun in the house?"

Everyone turned to look at her in confusion. She opened her mouth to ask again when the back door suddenly burst open. She whirled around with a growl to see Liam come sauntering in. He was followed by Kostandin and a whole bunch of nasty Albanians. They were all carrying weapons.

Liam didn't say a word as he aimed his pistol at her chest and squeezed the trigger.

Chapter 15

BECKER TWISTED THE GAS ON THE BIG HARLEY AND IT surged forward, but it didn't help. The two trucks behind him were moving too fast. They were going to hit him.

He swerved to the side, avoiding one SUV a fraction of a second before it could smash into his rear tire. The violent maneuver almost put him and his bike on the pavement, but he got control of it just as the vehicle sped past him. He turned to shout at the idiots, but his words froze as he recognized the driver. It was one of the Albanians. He should have figured it out sooner, since both the cars were big, black Escalades.

He was still trying to wrap his head around that when he was forced to slam on his rear brakes and swerve sideways again to avoid creaming into the rear bumper of the Escalade that had just zipped past him and slowed down.

The second car quickly moved in behind him. Becker didn't have to look to know it was another one of Kostandin's crew. If they slammed into his rear wheel, he was toast. Even a minor thump at this speed would send him flying and almost certainly get him run over. He wasn't sure even an alpha werewolf could live through something like that.

He darted a quick glance to the side, praying he could get off the main road before some unsuspecting driver came along and got in the middle of this mess. But that wasn't an option. The edge of the road along this stretch of highway was lined with barricades and steel guard-rails. Slamming into those would be as bad as getting hit by one of the SUVs trying to run him down.

The vehicle in front slowed down even more, making it easier for his buddy to get Becker from behind. Becker slammed his right foot down on his rear brake pedal again, putting the bike into a sideways slide, then let up on the brake and gunned it, slipping around the left side of the Escalade by mere inches. He would have been home free if the Albanian in the backseat hadn't leaned out the window and started shooting at him with one of those MP5 automatics the mobsters seemed to love so much.

Becker veered to the left but couldn't go far because of the guardrail. Most of the spray of bullets missed him, but one 9mm round hit him in the thigh and another clanked into something important-sounding on the bike. Blood ran down his leg at the same time his bike made a grinding sound and began losing speed. He twisted the accelerator as far as it would go. Nothing happened. So much for getting past the front car.

One look in the rearview mirror told him he was doubly screwed. And with the second SUV coming right up behind him, he couldn't drop back, either. He was completely boxed in with the first SUV on his left, the guardrail on his right, and the second truck behind him. On top of that, his bike wasn't running well enough for him to get ahead.

The driver of the first Escalade must have realized that at the same time because he immediately jerked the car to the left. Becker would either get crushed against the guardrail, or the jackass with the MP5 was going to get close enough to put a lucky shot through his head.

Becker decided to go for option three. He yanked the handlebars to the right, slamming into the side of the SUV. Before he could lose control of the bike, he was up and leaping off it, landing on the hood of the Escalade. His move caught the driver completely by surprise, giving Becker enough time to punch his clawed hand through the hood and get a grip on something before the stunned driver could recover and try to toss him off.

He tried not to listen as his beautiful, not-even-paid-off-yet bike hit the asphalt hard and was promptly run over by the second Escalade. But it was impossible to ignore the fact that these assholes had just destroyed a frigging work of art.

Becker shifted, cutting loose a growl and climbing the hood, his hands punching through the thin steel with every lunge forward. The guy in the backseat was trying to lean far enough out the window to get a shot at him, but the driver was swerving around so much that he couldn't get a clear pop at him. The same went for the guy in the passenger seat with the handgun. All he was able to do was hold the semiautomatic pistol blindly out the passenger window and shoot in Becker's general direction. A few rounds nicked him, but nothing that caused any serious damage. Having a partially shifted werewolf on the hood of his vehicle probably had something to do with his poor marksmanship.

As an added bonus, the driver's wild attempts at slinging him off were also keeping the second Escalade from passing, so Becker only had one vehicle to worry about.

The gunner in the backseat finally said the hell with it and tried to shoot him through the windshield. All the guy accomplished was pelting the driver with brass cartridge cases and getting the windshield out of Becker's way. The driver freaked out and almost lost control of the car when Becker reached through the shattered window and ripped the guy with the handgun out of the passenger seat and tossed him aside…where he was run over by the second SUV. Somewhere, the soul of Becker's Harley was growling its approval.

The move didn't come without a price though. The guy in the backseat shot him through the same damn shoulder he'd been hit in a couple days ago. *Damn.* It hurt like a son of a bitch. Ignoring the pain, he crawled into the passenger seat to yank the gun out of the guy's hand, then grabbed the asshole's arm and dragged him out too.

The driver kept yanking the steering wheel from side to side right up until the moment Becker ripped out his throat. Unfortunately, the dead man's foot wedged against the gas pedal, and instead of slowing down, the Escalade raced forward.

Becker swore and reached in to grab the wheel. He got the car going in a straight line, but it was still gaining speed. He needed to get the damn driver out of the way.

Thankfully, the driver hadn't been wearing a seat belt, so Becker just had to shove the guy out the door, then climb into the driver's seat.

Once he got control of the vehicle, he jerked into the left-hand lane, then immediately slammed on the brake, forcing the other SUV to swerve to the right. The moment that Escalade was even with him, he yanked the wheel to the right and smashed into it, causing it to hit the metal guardrail and slide along the barrier for a few feet, then crash through it and flip a few times before coming to a halt.

Becker slammed on the brakes, screeching to a loud, tire-squawking stop. He was out of the car before it stopped rocking. Jumping the guardrail, he ran to the other SUV. He wanted nothing more than to kill every last son of a bitch in there, but he controlled his rage. There might be more going on than just an attack on the SWAT officer who had taken down their crime family. If there was, he needed to know about it.

The Albanian who'd been driving was already dead, but the other one had gotten out and was dragging himself toward the tree line a good twenty feet away. When he realized Becker was following him, he rolled over onto his back and took a shot at him. Becker avoided the gunfire, then lunged forward and ripped the gun out of the man's hands.

Becker grabbed the Albanian's shirt and yanked him off the ground with a snarl. "I'm guessing Kostandin sent you, so you have one chance to tell me where he is."

The man's Adam's apple bobbed up and down. "Kostandin had us watching the SWAT compound, waiting for you to come back. He told us to follow and kill you, no matter what we had to do. The rest of us wanted to get the hell out of Dallas, but Kos said we had things to take care of before we left."

"That's not what I asked you." Becker bared his fangs, making sure the Albanian got a good look at them. "Where the fuck is he?"

"I don't know!" The guy swallowed hard. "He and Liam said they were going to some farm near here, that he was going to kill every one of those werewolves who betrayed them. That's all I know. Please don't kill me!"

Becker dropped the Albanian to the ground with a

growl. As much as he hated to let the guy go, Becker wasn't a cold-blooded killer, and he didn't have time to mess with him.

He jumped over the guardrail and ran to the Escalade with the shattered front window. He knocked the remaining pieces of glass out of his way before climbing in and speeding toward the Stones' house.

Digging his phone out of his pocket with one hand, he hit the speed dial for Gage. As the phone rang, Becker's gut clenched so tightly he almost couldn't breathe. He floored the gas pedal, but he still couldn't make the Escalade go fast enough. Something told him that he wasn't going to get there in time.

Jayna fell to her knees beside Megan, slapping her hand over the bullet hole in her friend's chest, trying to stop the blood from pouring out. But it was no use. It just kept flowing out between Jayna's fingers.

It had all happened so fast. One moment, Liam had been pointing a handgun at Jayna, and the next, Megan had been flying in front of her as the gun went off. She was breathing and her heart was beating, but her eyes were closed and she was getting paler by the second. Moe, Chris, and Joseph were at her side in seconds, begging Megan not to die, while Ethan and Kathryn were stunned into silence as they took in the gun-wielding men and the girl lying on the floor of their kitchen slowly bleeding to death.

Jayna glared at Liam. It was hard to see him clearly through the tears in her eyes, but he clearly didn't even care that he'd just shot a girl who had been like family to him.

"What the hell have you done?" she screamed.

His lips curled in a sneer. "Her fault for getting in the way. If she'd minded her own business and let me deal with you, I might have let her live. The guys too, even though they betrayed me just like you did."

"Betrayed you?" Jayna wiped the tears from her face with her free hand. "They never betrayed you, and neither did I. You're the one who sold your pack out to these pieces of crap." She motioned with her chin toward Kos, who was regarding them with amusement in his hard eyes. "We told you we didn't want to be part of this."

"You don't get to decide what you want to be part of!" Liam shouted. He took a step toward her, eyes flaring as he raised his pistol to point it at her head. "I was trying to give us a better life, something you would have realized if you and your cop boyfriend hadn't been so busy trying to take over my pack."

Jayna's heart began to race. Liam was about to kill her and there wasn't anything she could do about it—not without taking her hand off the wound in Megan's chest. And she wasn't going to do that.

So she knelt there beside the girl who was like a sister to her as Liam's face twisted into an animal snarl. Ethan and Kathryn were behind him, so they couldn't see the creature he'd become, but they must have heard the growls and had to know that something bizarre was happening.

"You always thought you were better than me, always looking down your snout at me when I asked you and the others to do the things that were necessary for us to survive," Liam sneered. "And then, when we get here, when we finally have a chance to be part of something that would let us stop scratching in the dirt for pennies and nickels, you decide you know better what the pack needs. You decide to betray me with that fucking cop! Well, his ass is dead now, and yours is about to be."

Jayna's heart thudded to a stop. Liam was lying. Eric couldn't be dead. She was so busy convincing herself of that, she didn't realize Liam had closed the distance between them and put the barrel of the gun against her forehead.

She held her breath, bracing for the bullet that would take her life, when someone shoved Liam aside. She blinked, staring up at Moe standing in front of her and Megan. Joseph quickly moved to stand at Moe's right, while Chris took up position on Moe's left. Jayna didn't have to see the guys' faces to know that they'd shifted. The look of shock on Ethan's and Kathryn's faces told her that. Not that it mattered. The Stones weren't going to make it out of there to tell anyone what they'd seen.

"Get out of the way," Liam growled as he altered his aim and pointed his weapon at Moe. "This is between Jayna and me. I know she's the one who turned you against me. She's the only one who has to die."

Moe didn't move. Neither did Joseph or Chris.

"She didn't turn us against you," Moe said. "You did that all on your own. And if you want to kill Jayna, you're gonna have to go through us."

Liam growled, but Jayna knew he'd shoot them without even thinking about it. She wanted to stand up to protect them, but she was terrified of leaving Megan's side. She looked down at her friend and was surprised to find Megan looking up at her.

"Stop him," she whispered. "Don't let him hurt anyone else. Please."

Fresh tears pricked Jayna's eyes. Typical Megan. Always so selfless.

"This is all very touching," Kostandin said. Stepping forward, he pointed his gun at Moe, then thumbed back the hammer. "But the she-wolf will not be helping anyone. Liam may have come here thinking he could take back his pack from her, but I came here to kill every last fucking one of you."

Jayna jumped up and lunged for Moe just as the kitchen door exploded off its hinges and disappeared into the night. Jayna was still trying to figure out what had just happened when a blur of movement caught her eye. Her heart surged as Eric's scent filled the kitchen, but before she could even blink, he'd grabbed two of Kostandin's men and disappeared outside with them.

Gunshots echoed in the night, making Jayna jump. Terrified shouts quickly followed, then a loud, menacing growl. After that, an eerie silence descended over the whole farm. Even the horses out in the barn seemed to be holding their breath.

Then, a single gunshot sounded from outside, and one of the Albanians over by the granite-topped island crumpled to the floor without a sound. The eight remaining Albanians aimed their guns at the row of windows over the sink and started shooting while Kos turned to fire at Moe.

Jayna knocked Moe to the floor, then threw herself at Chris and Joseph, taking them down too. She glanced over at Ethan and Kathryn. The couple was on the floor, wedged up against the other side of the island, Ethan shielding his wife with his body.

More bullets whizzed through the opening in the wall, sending Kos and his men scattering. Leaving the guys with Megan, Jayna used the distraction to herd Ethan and Kathryn toward the living room. Joseph and Moe showed up to take over for her before they got more than a few feet.

But then Kos caught sight of them. He shouted for two of his men to stay and finish them off. "The rest of you, come with me. We're going to kill that asshole cop right now."

Jayna froze. Eric may have been an alpha werewolf with SWAT training, but she was still terrified at the thought of him taking on Kos and the six Albanians by himself. But right then, she had to push her fears for Eric out of her head. If she didn't find a way to get her pack and the Stones to safety, she wouldn't be around long enough to worry about what happened to Eric.

But when she went back to grab Megan, all she found was a trail of blood leading out of the kitchen. For a moment, she thought Chris had gotten her to safety, but he was helping Moe and Joseph with Ethan and Kathryn. *Crap*.

That was when Jayna realized the front door was already wide open. She didn't have to get a whiff of the two distinct scents leading in that direction to know Liam had taken Megan.

Heart in her throat, Jayna jumped up and ran for the door, ignoring the bullets zipping past her head and missing by mere inches.

"Get everybody somewhere safe," she growled as she sped past Joseph and the other guys.

Jayna hoped the oldest werewolf in the pack was up

for the task because all she could think about right then
was saving Megan.

—⁓—

Becker had just cut the engine and was letting the
Escalade coast down the Stones' gravel driveway
when he heard the gunshot. He threw open the door
and was running for the house before the SUV came
to a stop.

He slowed and dropped to one knee, reaching for
his off-duty Sig 9mm he always kept clipped inside the
top of his motorcycle boot. And swore. Before going
undercover, he'd locked his weapon in his gun safe in
his apartment, and in all the craziness of the past couple
days, he hadn't gotten it out.

Cursing his stupidity, he headed for the front door of
the house, fully intending to kick it in and start tearing
people apart with his bare hands. But one glance in the
living room window stopped him. He could see Liam
standing in the kitchen, a gun in his hand and a body on
the floor, thick, red blood pooling beside it.

Becker's heart stopped. He couldn't see who'd been
shot, but his mind was filling in the blanks.

Jayna.

He grabbed the doorknob and started to turn but
forced himself to stop and take a breath. Even though
everything in his body screamed for him to get the hell
in there, he knew it wouldn't do any good to rush in
without a weapon or a plan.

As he paused, he realized the person on the floor
wasn't Jayna. He could hear Jayna's heartbeat going
nice and strong. *Damn.* It was Megan. She was too tiny

to take a wound that serious. He could hear her heart beating, but it was weak.

Becker could hear Jayna and Liam arguing about something. He'd hoped his pack would get here in time to set up some kind of entry plan. But when he heard Liam say something about Jayna betraying him to *that fucking cop*, quickly followed by a threat to kill her, Becker knew he had to move. There was nothing he could do on this side of the house though, so he darted around to the back.

He got there in time to see Kostandin with his Colt .45 aimed right at Moe's head. The look on Jayna's face told Becker everything he needed to know—Kos was about to start shooting.

The hell with a plan.

Becker dug his claws into the wooden frame of the kitchen door, then yanked, letting the rage he usually did a good job of controlling come out with a vicious snarl. Tossing the door aside, he reached in and grabbed the two Albanians nearest the door, pulling them out. He slung one across the gravel courtyard between the house and the barn, then turned back to deal with the second guy. The man twisted in his grip, pointed his MP5 at Becker, and fired.

Becker knocked the barrel aside with a growl, slashing his claws across the Albanian's throat, ignoring the gurgling noise as the man died. But he was so worried about Jayna and her pack that he didn't have time to think about it.

Becker spun around just as the first man was getting to his feet and lifting his weapon. For a moment, Becker contemplated diving for the MP5 the now-dead

Albanian had been holding, but he didn't have time. So instead, he flung the body at the first Albanian just as the man pulled the trigger. The move distracted the gunman, letting Becker close the distance between them, then put the Albanian down in the most efficient way he could, regardless of how much blood was spilled.

Snatching up the man's MP5, Becker checked the magazine, then flipped the weapon's selector switch one click up from full auto to single-shot semi. He quickly moved to the left, aimed for the first Albanian inside the house he could see clearly, then put a single shot through the guy's chest. Becker would have preferred to take out Kostandin or Liam, but they wouldn't oblige by making a nice target of themselves.

All hell broke loose in the kitchen as the rest of the Albanian thugs started shooting in his direction. Becker doubted any of them could see him in the dark, but he sure as hell could see them. He started peppering the Albanians with carefully aimed shots. He wasn't necessarily looking to hit them, just keep them from going after Jayna and the others.

His plan worked too well. The Albanians came charging out the recently renovated kitchen door, weapons blazing. Becker returned fire, dropping two of the men. But then his ammo ran out.

Shit.

One round clipped his hip, another his right thigh just above the knee. Becker bit back a howl as his leg fractured. The pain only got worse when he was forced to turn and fall back to the barn. He would have rather stuck a fork in his eye than turned tail on those jackasses, especially Kostandin. But trying to stand up against a group of well-armed thugs with nothing but claws and fangs was the definition of stupid, and he liked to think he was smarter than that.

He made it to the barn without getting his ass shot off—just barely. His leg hurt like hell and felt like it was going to give out on him any second.

His initial plan was to haul ass through the barn, slip out the back, then loop around to hit the thugs from behind. That plan changed as soon as he slipped inside the tidy four-stall structure and saw that it didn't have a back door or any windows.

Well, shit.

Becker could hear Kos's men reloading just outside the door and knew they'd be coming in soon. He glanced around, looking for a place to hide, but other than the stalls currently occupied by four terrified horses, there weren't any. Hell, there weren't even any decent sharp-edged farming implements hanging from the walls. What kind of frigging barn was this anyway?

He turned to face the door, his leg throbbing. He was going to have a hard time facing so many bad guys with his leg this screwed up. On the bright side, he'd gotten the Albanians away from Jayna and her pack. At least they were safe. That had to count for something, right?

Jayna was running full speed as she cleared the Stones' front porch. It wasn't hard to track Liam and Megan. The scent of Megan's blood was so strong it made Jayna want to cry.

The moon wasn't out yet, but she had no problem spotting Liam making his way through the rows of fruit trees along the left side of the property. He was moving slower than normal. Then again, he was dragging Megan with him. Jayna briefly wondered why Liam didn't just let Megan go and get the hell on his way. But the answer was simple: he was keeping Megan to use as a shield or a bargaining chip.

As if catching a whiff of her scent, Liam looked over his shoulder at her. Instead of continuing toward the main road like he'd been doing, he changed direction, heading toward the barn.

Jayna growled and ran faster. She could still hear Megan's ragged breathing and faint heartbeat. But she was getting weaker by the moment.

Oh God, please don't let Megan die, Jayna prayed. Not that—anything but that.

Thoughts like that should have made Jayna so weak in the knees that running would have been impossible. But she wasn't feeling weak. She was feeling furious— furious that Liam had shot the most fragile and gentle member of a pack he used to call his own, furious that he was running with her now like she was nothing but a disposable means to an end. Jayna wanted to kill him for being so cruel.

Liam was just up ahead. Jayna tensed to launch herself at him when she caught sight of Kos and his soldiers running into the barn. It didn't take a genius to figure out why. She assumed Eric had lured them out of the house on purpose. The fact that he was holed up in the barn didn't make sense. Wouldn't he just be trapped in there?

Gunshots sounded inside the barn. Her blood ran cold. Every instinct in her body screamed at her to run into the barn and save Eric.

But how could she do that and save Megan at the same time?

She was so caught up in the emotional tug-of-war inside her that she almost didn't see Liam stop and turn to face her. Jayna skidded to a stop just as he dragged a semiconscious Megan around in front of him like a shield. Blood soaked half of Megan's shirt and ran down her jeans. She looked so weak that if Liam hadn't been holding her, she would have certainly fallen to the ground.

Liam pointed his gun at Jayna and pulled the trigger. Jayna dodged to the side to avoid the bullets, depending on reflexes and speed she never knew she possessed. But Liam had some pretty fast reflexes himself.

While she avoided the first few bullets, the next one bit deep in the muscles of her left arm. The pain stunned her so much that she forgot to keep moving. That earned her another bullet through her leg, knocking it right out from under her.

Jayna tumbled to the ground, fully expecting Liam to put the next bullet through her head. When the shot didn't come, she looked up to find him glaring down at her over the barrel of his pistol, his eyes filled with hate.

"You brought all this on yourself, you know that, right?" he said in a tone so flat and emotionless she barely recognized the voice as his. The gentle and compassionate alpha who'd taken her off the streets and treated her like his little sister was long gone.

Between the sounds of fighting coming from the barn and watching the life drain out of Megan, it was hard to pay attention to what Liam was saying, but Jayna forced herself to try. She needed to figure out a way to get him to let Megan go before it was too late.

"I was taking care of everyone," he continued. "But you couldn't just be a good little beta and play your part, could you? You always thought you were better than me, questioning everything I said."

Jayna opened her mouth to tell him that wasn't true, but he cut her off. "I never understood why you kept asking why women couldn't be alphas, but now I do. You wanted control of the pack all along." He motioned at Megan with his pistol. "Well, you've been pack leader for all of a day now. Tell me, how's it working out for you? How's it working out for the rest of the pack?"

Jayna started to push herself to her feet, but she froze when he pointed the gun in her direction again. She held up her hands in a gesture she hoped would placate him.

"You're right, Liam. I did betray you. But I never wanted to be the pack leader. I just wanted us all to be safe and together. If you want to kill me for that, fine. But you don't need to hurt Megan. She, more than any of us, doesn't deserve this. She deserves to live."

Liam stared at Jayna so long that, for a minute, she thought she might have gotten through to him. But then he snorted.

"Still trying to act like the alpha," he sneered. "Saying anything you can think of to save your precious pack. But a real alpha understands that you can't always save everyone. Sometimes the pack has to pay for their alpha's bad decisions. What kind of lesson would it be for you if I let Megan live?"

Jayna shook her head as he turned the weapon away from her and pointed it at Megan's head. "I think it would be fitting if I let you watch me kill your precious little Megan before I shoot you. She was always more loyal to you than me anyway. That way, you can die knowing you completely failed as an alpha."

Tears stung Jayna's eyes. "Liam, don't! I'm begging you."

"Begging?" He let out a harsh laugh. "Yet another reason you could never have been a pack leader. An alpha never begs—ever."

Jayna held her breath as he pressed the muzzle of his handgun against Megan's temple. She curled her good leg under her, ready to launch herself at Liam even though she knew she'd never get to him in time.

Megan opened her eyes and looked straight at Jayna. She was obviously weak and in a lot of pain, but it was clear that Megan knew exactly what was about to happen.

A sudden howl of pain came from the barn, and Liam chuckled.

"Doesn't sound like it's going too well for your cop boyfriend. Maybe we should wait for Kos to finish Eric off so he can drag him out here for you. Then you can see two of the most important people in your miserable little world die before you go out. Or should I just go ahead and pop Megan before she bleeds out on me?"

Jayna knew she should beg some more, say anything to give Megan another minute to live. But she knew Liam would never grant that minute.

"You're a complete piece of crap, Liam, you know that?" she growled, her fangs extending farther than they ever had. The nearly uncontrollable anger coursing through her made her muscles vibrate and twist so much she was trembling. "And you were always a worthless alpha."

Liam laughed. "I guess that answers my

question—Megan it is." He cocked the hammer on the pistol still pressed against Megan's head. "Say goodbye, Megan."

—⁓—

Becker was hit more times than he could count, but he ignored the pain and threw himself into the Albanians' midst as well as his screwed-up leg would let him. They hadn't been expecting that and it limited their ability to shoot out of fear of hitting each other.

He tore into them with claws and fangs, letting himself slip further into his wolf form than he'd ever been. His claws ripped into clothing and flesh alike, shredding material and spraying blood. Their shouts of terror and panic mixed with his snarls as he fought for his life—and Jayna's. He couldn't let any of these men leave that barn, no matter what it cost him.

As tightly packed in the small barn as they were, the men still kept shooting. He ignored the stabs of pain as one bullet after another tore into him. He pushed the pain down deeper, thought about Jayna, and kept fighting, ripping out a throat here, breaking an arm or leg there. He even grabbed one of the men and tossed him into a stall with one of the fear-maddened horses, smiling to himself as the horse stomped the man to death.

Becker wasn't sure how long the fight took—everything blurred together—but at some point, he realized there weren't any more men to fight. And that he was bleeding a lot.

He dropped to his knees as a wave of weakness hit him and his broken leg gave out. *Oh shit*. He hadn't been hit in the heart, but it really felt like he was on the verge of bleeding out.

A sharp sound made his head snap up and he saw Kostandin leaning against the wall just inside the doorway, clapping his hands.

"That was impressive, Eric," Kos said. "I don't believe any of those omegas that Liam brought in, or even Liam himself, could have done that. It's a pity you had to be a cop. You could have been very useful to me."

Becker slowly pushed himself to his feet. He was unsteady as hell, but this wasn't over. Kostandin had to die, or the Albanian would hunt down Jayna and her pack purely out of revenge.

Kos regarded the forty-five in his hand, tossing it aside with a shrug. Then he reached behind his back and pulled out that big-ass knife he always carried. He held it so the blade caught the light, giving Becker a wicked smile. "Shooting you would be too easy. This is way more satisfying, for me at least."

Becker growled low in his throat and started forward, but the sound of voices outside the barn froze him in his tracks. It was Jayna. He'd thought she and her pack would already be far away from here. What was she doing outside the barn? Then he heard Liam saying he was going to shoot her and Megan.

Like hell.

Becker roared and lunged at Kos. The impact hurt so badly, Becker's vision went dark for a moment. But he fought off the wave of unconsciousness that threatened him and focused on finishing off Kostandin.

That wasn't nearly as easy as it should have been. If

he hadn't been so beat up, it wouldn't even have been close, despite how big and muscular the Albanian was. But in Becker's current condition, Kos was on equal footing with him.

Becker caught Kostandin's right wrist just as the wickedly sharp knife came at his chest. At the same time, Kos grabbed Becker's right wrist, fighting to keep his claws away from his throat. Becker tried to bring his right knee up into Kostandin's balls, but the broken leg refused to cooperate, turning what he had hoped would be a vicious strike into barely more than a stumble.

Kos took advantage of Becker's poor balance and slammed him into the wall of the barn so hard Becker heard the wood crack—at least he hoped it was the wood. Either way, another wave of blackness rushed over him as his head bounced off the wall like a Ping-Pong ball.

Fuck. He didn't have time for this. He needed to get out there and help Jayna and Megan.

But worrying about them came close to getting Becker killed as Kos yanked him away from the wall, bringing his head forward at the same time to head-butt him. Becker felt the bones of his nose crunch as blood went everywhere.

The big Albanian laughed. "You're barely making this worth my while. But I guess it's like I told you when we first met: for all your werewolf strength and speed, a knife through the heart will kill you as quickly as it would any man."

Mouth twisting into a smug smile, Kostandin drew back his knife hand to stab Becker through the heart.

Becker didn't try to grab Kostandin's hand this time,

but instead only blocked it partially. While he spared himself a thrust through the heart, he left a good portion of the left side of his chest unprotected. Kos took the bait, driving the blade into his left pec up to the hilt.

As incredibly painful as it was, it left the Albanian completely unprepared for a counterstrike. With a snarl, Becker grabbed a handful of Kostandin's hair and jerked his head to the side, sinking his fangs into the Albanian's exposed neck. He bit down hard, then violently twisted his jaws back and forth as he pulled away.

"And like I told you when we first met," Becker rasped. "It's tougher to knife a man knowing that if you miss, he's going to rip out your frigging throat."

He tossed Kostandin's body aside and ran for the door. God, please let him be in time.

Jayna knew she couldn't get to Megan in time, but she reached deep inside herself for every ounce of strength and speed she possessed anyway. If Eric was right and she really was an alpha, now was the time for those abilities to make their presence known.

And it happened.

Her legs practically hummed with power, propelling her forward faster than she'd ever moved. Her claws extended farther too, ready to tear Liam apart.

Then a roar sounded from her left, so loud and filled with rage it was impossible not to glance over to see what it was. She was shocked to see Eric racing out of the barn so fast he was nothing but a blur. But he was even farther away from Megan than she was.

Jayna turned back to see she wasn't the only one who

was distracted. Liam was staring at Eric with fear unlike anything she'd ever seen in his eyes.

Megan, on the other hand, was looking directly at her with eyes that were clear and bright and full of emotion. Nodding ever so slightly, Megan drove her elbow into Liam's chest.

The blow wasn't very powerful—Megan was too weak—but the move was such a surprise that Liam released her. She dropped to the ground like a rock. It gave Jayna the opening she needed, and she covered the last two yards separating her and Liam in the air.

Liam must have sensed her coming because he jerked his head up just before impact. Jayna slammed into him so hard that every bone in her body felt it. She landed astride him with a snarl and raked him with her claws, ripping the gun out of his hands and sending it flying across the graveled courtyard.

He took a vicious swipe at her with his claws, but she blocked him instinctively, like her arms just naturally knew what to do. In the same motion, her own claws— longer than Liam ever dreamed his could be—slashed across his face, cutting deep.

Screaming, he threw up his hands to protect himself. "Jayna, please. I'm begging you!"

Jayna hesitated. But all it took was one quick glance at Megan, crumpled motionless on the ground a few feet away, to remind her who she was dealing with.

Growling, she glared down at the werewolf who used to be her alpha. Now, he was nothing to her. The rage that filled her at what he'd done to her pack was almost too much to control. "Alphas never beg—ever. Isn't that what you told me?"

Liam's lips curled into a snarl, his eyes glowing. He took another swipe at her face, aiming for her eyes this time. She knocked his hand away, hearing bones break as she did. Liam howled and went at her with his other hand, going for her throat.

Jayna hated the idea of killing Liam, even after everything he'd done, but Megan needed her too much for Jayna to mess around with him anymore. Lifting her hand, she raked her claws across his neck, feeling them dig in deep. Then she was rolling off him before he even stopped breathing, leaping to her best friend's side at the same time Eric reached them.

Megan's eyes were closed and Jayna had to put her ear to her friend's chest to hear if her heart was still beating. It was, but very faintly.

She looked at Eric to ask what to do and saw him pulling Kostandin's big knife out of his own chest while he dialed his cell phone. He was bleeding from what looked like a dozen wounds too, and his face looked a mess.

"Oh God, you're hurt!" she cried, wanting to pull him into her arms but terrified of leaving Megan's side.

"I'm fine," he assured her as he tossed the blood-covered blade on the ground, then put the phone to his ear. "Keep talking to her. Help will be here any second. She needs to know you're here."

Jayna leaned over and grabbed Megan's hand, whispering in her friend's ear that help was on the way while keeping one eye on Eric. How the hell could he be okay after getting shot up like that and stabbed almost all the way through his chest?

She blinked back tears. She couldn't lose Eric. Or Megan. Not now. Not ever.

Jayna was kneeling beside Megan, holding her hand, Eric by her side, when Trey and Alex slid to the ground beside them. Jayna wasn't sure how long it had been since she'd killed Liam—maybe a minute or two—but it felt like a lifetime. Since then, she'd sat there holding her friend's hand and counting every beat of Megan's heart.

Eric took Jayna's free hand and held it tightly. "She'll be okay."

Jayna wasn't quite as sure, but she nodded anyway.

Trey immediately got an oxygen mask on Megan, while Alex ripped open her shirt and injected her with some kind of shot that made her heart beat stronger.

Alex carefully rolled her over to check her back, then gave Trey a pointed look. "No exit wound."

Panic gripped Jayna. "Is that bad? Is she going to die?"

Alex's face was glum. "I don't know. An alpha's body won't start the healing process while there's foreign material in the wound. If she were an alpha, we'd be going in for the bullet fragments, but with a beta, I don't know what to do. I'm not sure what would be harder on her—leaving the bullet in or the shock of taking it out."

"Take it out," a calm, commanding voice ordered from behind them.

Jayna looked over her shoulder to see Sergeant Dixon standing there, concern on his face. The rest of Eric's pack was gathered around too, but kept their distance. They looked just as worried as their commander.

Moe and Chris ran up then. Ethan and Kathryn followed behind, helping support Joseph. Blood ran freely down one leg of his jeans.

Could this get any worse?

"Take out the bullet," Dixon repeated. "She's a beta, but the same rule applies. The bleeding won't stop until you get it out."

The SWAT medics exchanged looks, like they really weren't sure about this, but after a moment, Alex reached into his bag for a pair of long forceps and gently eased it into the wound above Megan's bra. Jayna didn't want to watch, but she couldn't look away. She knew Alex was being extra careful because he didn't want to cause additional damage, but it was all she could do not to shout at him to hurry up.

"Heart rate is dropping," Trey announced urgently. "Get the bullet and get out of there before she goes into cardiac arrest."

Jayna squeezed Megan's hand. "Hang on, Megan."

Suddenly, Dixon was down on one knee on Jayna's other side. "Keep talking to her. You're her alpha. If you tell her to fight, she'll fight. But you have to be calm and you have to project confidence. She needs to feel your strength. Be the alpha she needs you to be."

Jayna wasn't sure she could do that. She looked at Dixon. Up close, he didn't seem as scary as before. "You're an alpha. Can't you do it?"

Dixon shook his head. "I'm an alpha but not her alpha. It has to be you."

Jayna looked down at Megan again. The bullet wound was bleeding even more now, and her face was pale and pinched.

"We're losing her," Trey said sharply.

The tears Jayna had been holding back ran down her cheeks.

Eric squeezed Jayna's hand, placing his other one on her back and making gentle circular motions. "You can do this, Jayna. You're stronger than you think."

Jayna looked into his eyes, amazed at the confidence she saw there. She swallowed hard. If Eric believed in her, she would believe in herself. He hadn't been wrong about her yet.

She glanced at Moe, Chris, and Joseph to see them regarding her with that same confidence.

She took a deep breath and turned back to Megan. "Hold on, Megan. Just a little longer, okay? Alex is almost done taking out the bullet. And when it's out, the pain will be gone and everything will be all better."

She waited for Megan to squeeze her hand, to give her some indication that she was listening, but her hand lay limply in Jayna's.

"We'll stay together and be a pack, Megan—you, Moe, Chris, Joseph, and me," Jayna promised, fighting back another rush of tears. "We're going to stay here in Dallas, and we're going to find an amazing place to live. Big enough for all of us—Eric too if he wants. You're going to have a room all to yourself, and my room will be right beside yours. We'll put Joseph in the room farthest away. I know his snoring keeps you awake at night."

Beside her, Eric smiled.

Jayna kept talking even after Alex had the bullet out and Trey announced that Megan was getting stronger by the second. Jayna had so many things to say that she couldn't stop talking. Jayna told Megan how important she was to the pack and to her especially.

When Jayna stopped to a take a breath, she realized

that both Eric and Megan were looking at her with tears in their eyes and smiles on their faces. Everyone else, including Moe, Chris, and Joseph, had moved away, giving them privacy.

"Wow," Megan said softly. "I don't think I've heard you talk that much since I've known you. When you get going, you don't stop, do you?"

Jayna bent and kissed her on the forehead. "I guess I don't."

"We're really going to stay here in Dallas, right?" Megan asked. "You weren't just saying that, were you?"

Jayna glanced at Eric to see him grinning at her, even though he looked like complete hell. He was still bleeding from nearly every part of his body. But he looked happy.

"We're staying if Eric still wants me to," she said softly.

He leaned close to kiss her. "Of course I want you to stay. I love you, remember?"

Jayna smiled. "That's good because I never want to leave. It took me a while to figure it out. I had a little help from my friends." She glanced at Megan. "But I finally realized that I love you too. So much it scares the hell out of me. But I'm ready to face that fear and be with you—to be *The One* for you. Because you're *The One* for me."

He kissed her again. "Good. And before you even say anything, I know you and your pack are a package deal. And I'm okay with that."

"Does that mean you're okay living with us too?" she asked. "Joseph really does snore a lot. And Chris listens to the most godawful country music."

Eric chuckled. "I wouldn't have it any other way."

Jayna felt the weight of the world lift from her shoulders. Loving her was one thing. Loving her pack was another. She was glad Eric was up for the challenge.

She pulled him in for another kiss, but Megan interrupted.

"Guys, maybe that should wait until Trey and Alex get a look at Eric. He's bleeding all over me."

Chapter 16

"YOU GUYS THROW THESE THINGS YEAR-ROUND, EVEN when the weather is this cold?" Jayna asked as she and Eric cuddled together on one of the picnic benches at the SWAT compound, watching Cooper work the grill.

"Year-round," Trey answered from beside Max on one of the other nearby benches. Alex was sitting opposite them, devouring a burger. "If it gets really cold, we move most of the party inside. Except for the grill, of course. Whoever's cooking gets stuck outside for most of the day."

Jayna shook her head. Yep, these SWAT guys were officially crazy. It had to be fifty degrees out here and most of them were in shorts and T-shirts. Heck, Cooper wasn't even wearing a shirt as he stood over the grill flipping chicken and ribs. But she had to admit, while he might be crazy, the man knew how to cook. The food was amazing! And watching Cooper run around with his shirt off didn't make her complain either. She was totally and insanely in love with Eric, but that didn't mean she couldn't appreciate a fine specimen of manliness when she had the chance to gawk.

She wasn't the only one. Tuffie, the pit bull mix and pack's resident mascot, was glued to Cooper's side as he cooked. Okay, the occasional piece of food the SWAT cop tossed her way may have had something to do with it, but Jayna was pretty sure the pooch didn't mind admiring those rippling abs of Cooper's. The girl was practically grinning, she looked so happy to be standing beside the hunky guy.

Eric had been planning to man the grill for the day, but Cooper had volunteered to do it instead, so Eric could spend most of his time with her and her pack. Even if Cooper was Eric's best friend, it was still a nice thing for him to do.

It had only been two weeks since that night at the Stones' place, but she and the rest of her pack already felt at home in Dallas—and at the SWAT compound. Mostly because everyone had gone out of their way to make them feel so welcome. In fact, Sergeant Dixon— Gage—had put on this cookout especially in their honor to officially welcome her pack to the area. If there was one way to win over her pack, Jayna knew it was with free food. The fact that the food was so good only made it that much better.

"So, how did the session with Internal Affairs go?" Xander asked as he and his girlfriend, Khaki, sat down at the table with them.

Both SWAT officers had their plates piled high with food, mostly of the meat variety. Jayna could understand why. Since becoming an alpha, she'd noticed a desperate hunger for meat more than anything else. But her body was stronger and faster than it had ever been, her senses were sharper, and her natural werewolf weapons—claws and fangs—were still filling out to their full size. She guessed all those changes took a lot of protein.

Jayna jerked her attention back to the conversation as Eric mentioned Detective Coletti. That was the nosy Internal Affairs guy who'd had Eric on limited duty ever since the situation out at the Stones' farm. As far as the district attorney was concerned, they had no problem at all with anything Eric had done.

According to Gage, the DA was only concerned about Frasheri, and after they'd flipped a few of the low-level Albanians, the case against the mob boss was moving ahead at full speed. With all the money, drugs, and weapons Eric had led them to in the self-storage unit, Frasheri was going away for decades. The DA couldn't care less about why Kostandin and his men had shown up at the Stones' house, but the detective from Internal Affairs was a different matter. He'd questioned Eric almost every day since that night. Gage assured Jayna that Coletti was just doing his job, but as far as she was concerned, the guy was a complete ass.

"He asked me the same questions we've been going over for the last two weeks," Eric said. "Why do I think Kostandin and his thugs attacked the Stones' home? Have Jayna and Megan ever had any dealings with the Albanians? How did Kos and Liam end up with their throats torn out?"

Eric had kept his story simple. Jayna and her pack were just some friends visiting from out of town. Kos and Liam must have gone out there looking to get some revenge against Gage's future in-laws, and Jayna and her friends had just gotten caught in the crossfire. Eric had suggested he was only guessing and that he didn't know why bad guys did what they did.

"Coletti might think there's more going on than I'm telling him, but he's got nothing to back it up," Eric added. "I finally think he's ready to give up and move on. Officially, he's waiting on the medical examiner's report to close out the investigation, but I heard she turned in her report this morning."

"You mean that hot blond in the lab coat at the Stones' farm that night?" Trey asked as he bit into a burger. "She was so checking me out."

Max frowned. "Why the hell would she do that?"

Trey grinned. "Because she finds me incredibly attractive, of course."

"Dude," Alex said. "She works in a room surrounded by dead people all day. I'm not sure her thinking you're attractive is a good thing. She could be measuring you up for a body bag for all you know."

Everyone laughed except Xander. He was regarding Eric thoughtfully. "And you're sure there's no loose piece of evidence floating around out there that can come back and haunt us?"

Eric shook his head as he slipped an arm around Jayna's waist. "Nah. We're okay."

That seemed to settle the issue, and everyone got down to some serious eating. Jayna was glad to see the guys from her pack joining in with the fun, ribbing and joking like they'd been part of the SWAT pack for years—just another sign that staying here had been the right thing to do. Chris, Moe, and Joseph were more relaxed and outgoing than she'd ever seen them. Hanging out with all these mature alphas was good for them.

She'd been a little worried about that, concerned the guys would be on edge all the time with alphas around to remind them of Liam. But that didn't happen because none of Eric's pack were the least bit like Liam.

Her bigger concern, however, had been finding a place to live and jobs for all of them. But all those fears had turned out to be as silly as all the rest. Eric's entire pack had busted their butts looking for jobs that would work for them, but it was Ethan and Kathryn Stone who had come through in the end.

The older couple had been a little freaked out when they'd discovered there were werewolves in the world and that their daughter was marrying one, but they'd gotten over it surprisingly quickly. And after seeing how well Chris, Moe, and Joseph had handled the horses, Ethan had talked to a few friends and gotten all the guys, Megan, and Jayna jobs working at a horse rescue and rehabilitation center. The facility took in wild as well as domesticated horses and racehorses that had been injured or mistreated. The place was privately funded, and while the pay wasn't great, it allowed them to all work together. The people who owned it had immediately picked up on the fact that the injured and abused horses were amazingly calm and relaxed around her pack, which was something that even Gage couldn't explain. Megan and the guys adored working there, and in the end, that was all that mattered.

Mac helped find them a really nice multiple bedroom loft apartment in a renovated furniture factory over by Baylor University's Dallas campus. The place had five bedrooms, a big, central kitchen, and best of all, allowed pets, so they'd not only be able to have Tuffie visit, but also get a dog of their own, something Jayna really wanted. With its proximity to the campus, the place would have normally been way outside their price point, but Mac had promised the owner's college-aged daughter an internship at the paper where Mac worked in exchange for reduced rent. Plus, Eric had moved in with them, so they were sharing the cost with more people.

Jayna had been afraid the rest of her pack would have an issue with Eric moving in so soon, but they hadn't even batted an eye. Jayna was still getting used to the fact that her whole pack knew every time she and Eric had sex though. It was a bit unsettling.

All in all, everything was going absolutely wonderful. If there was anything negative to pick out, it had to be what had happened to Eric's bike. Jayna had gone out to the highway with him the next day to find his precious bike in pieces. Highway patrol had been picking them up and putting them in cardboard boxes. Jayna had thought Eric was going to cry, and she still felt terrible about it two weeks later.

She'd been all ready to help him pick out another Harley, but he'd surprised her by getting an SUV instead.

"Your whole pack won't fit on the back of a Harley," he'd told her with a smile.

Yet another reminder of why she loved him. But she was glad he hadn't suggested a minivan.

Outside, a car pulled up to the fence. Eric immediately got up to unlock the gate so Megan could get in, but Max beat him to it, Alex on his heels. Jayna laughed. At least half the guys in Eric's pack had a thing for Megan. There was something very intriguing to them about the small, quiet werewolf that went way beyond sex appeal and pheromones. Megan had risked her own life to save her pack leader, something every guy in Eric's pack understood and respected.

But Megan had been busy recovering from the gunshot wound and working part time at the horse rehabilitation center, so she hadn't hung out much with the guys in Eric's pack. This would be her first real chance to socialize with them, and they were all more than a little eager to talk to her. It was like her debutante ball.

Eric's pack mates stopped as soon as they saw that Megan was holding hands with Zak Gibson, Mac's photographer and best friend. A person would have had to have been blind not to see the connection between the two of them. Megan was grinning from ear to ear, and there was a light in her eyes that Jayna had never seen before.

Jayna jumped up and hugged her friend. "I'm so glad you felt up to coming out today."

"Dr. Saunders said it would be good for me to get out in the cold air for a bit." Megan grinned. "Even if he hadn't, I would have come anyway. There was no way I was going to miss this cookout, not after Zak told me how much fun they are."

Saunders was a doctor Gage had developed a friendship with over the years. As crazy as it seemed, Gage had actually told Saunders they were werewolves, figuring they would need a doctor they trusted in case he or any of his pack ever needed serious medical attention. Jayna was already starting to realize the alpha of the SWAT pack was light-years ahead of her when it came to thinking of all the different ways to take care of your pack. She looked forward to learning from him.

"Sit," Zak said to Megan. "I'll go grab us some food."

Eyes twinkling behind his glasses, he flashed her a grin, then jogged over to where Cooper was working the grill.

"Seriously, Megan," Max said. "What's Zak got that we don't?"

Megan blushed but didn't say anything.

"A brain," Khaki said, and everyone laughed.

"Maybe it's as simple as Zak being *The One* for Megan," Eric said.

Megan's color deepened even more at that, but luckily Zak came back just then and saved her from any more embarrassment.

"One what?" he asked, setting down two plates on the table, then sitting down beside Megan.

"I'll tell you later," she said softly.

Jayna caught the flash of green in Megan's eyes as she hastily took the can of soda Zak held out. She hoped Eric was right and that Zak was *The One* for Megan. It would be like icing on the cake if her best friend could find the same kind of love she'd been lucky enough to stumble on with Eric.

"Hey!" Moe called from over by the volleyball net. "We're starting another game. Any of you guys want in?"

Trey downed the rest of his burger in one bite and eagerly headed over to play, along with Xander, Khaki, Max, and Alex.

Jayna looked at Eric. "Aren't you going to play?"

He leaned over and kissed her. "Nah. I'd rather make out with you instead."

She laughed, not sure how much making out they'd be doing with his pack and hers barely twenty yards away, not to mention Megan and Zak sitting at the other end of the picnic table. Although they were so into each other, they probably wouldn't have noticed what she and Eric were doing.

Jayna was the one who leaned in to give him a kiss this time. "Thank you."

"For what?" he asked.

She gestured with her hand. "For all this. I don't even

like to think where my pack and I would be if you hadn't gotten us out of the mess we were in."

Eric brushed her hair back from her face with a gentle hand. "You would have gotten them out all by yourself. That's what an alpha does."

Jayna wasn't sure about that, but it made her feel all warm inside to know that Eric thought so. She might be her pack's alpha, but Eric was hers. He saw things in her that she never would have seen for herself. But she guessed that's what happened when you found *The One*. They made you better than you could ever be on your own.

*Here's a sneak peek at book four in
Paige Tyler's sizzling SWAT series*

To Love a Wolf

IT MUST BE PAYDAY. EITHER THAT, OR GOD HATED him. As Cooper strode across the bank's lobby and got in line behind the twenty other people already there, he wasn't sure which.

He'd been so exhausted after work he hadn't even bothered to shower off and change into civvies at the SWAT compound like he usually did. Instead, he'd come straight to the bank in his combat boots, military cargo pants, and a dark blue T-shirt with the Dallas PD emblem and the word *SWAT* on the left side of his chest. He couldn't wait to get home and throw everything in the wash so he could grab something to eat and fall into bed.

He bit back a growl as the man at the front of the line plunked a cardboard box full of rolled coins down on the counter and started lining the different denominations in front of the teller.

"You've got to be kidding me," he muttered.

A tall, slender woman with long, golden-brown hair a few people ahead gave him a quick, understanding smile over her shoulder. He smiled back, but she'd already turned around. He waited, hoping she'd glance his way again, but she didn't.

He hated going to the bank, but his SWAT teammate had finally paid off the bet they'd made months ago

about whether his squad leader and the newest member
of the team would end up being a couple. Instead of
giving Cooper the hundred bucks in cash like a normal
person, Brooks had given him a frigging check.

When Officer Khaki Blake had walked into the
training room for the first time, every pair of eyes in the
room immediately locked on her—except for Cooper's.
Oh, he'd noticed she was attractive. But he'd been more
interested in watching how the rest of the SWAT team
reacted. While most of the guys had checked her out
with open curiosity, none of their hearts had pounded
as hard as his squad leader's, Corporal Xander Riggs.
Cooper had immediately pegged Khaki as *The One* for
Xander, and vice versa.

But just because Cooper accepted the concept of
The One didn't mean he bought into the idea that
there were women in the world for him and the other
remaining thirteen single members of the Pack.
Cooper wasn't jaded when it came to love, but he
wasn't naive, either.

The two people ahead of Cooper finally got fed up
and walked away. He quickly stepped forward and
found himself behind the attractive woman who'd
smiled earlier. He couldn't help noticing that she looked
exceptionally good in a pair of jeans. Or that her long,
silky hair had the most intriguing gold highlights when
the light caught it just right. She smelled so delicious he
had to fight the urge to bury his nose in her neck. Damn,
he must be more tired than he thought. If he wasn't
careful he'd be humping her leg next.

He opened his mouth to say something charming, but
all that came out was a yawn big enough to make his

jaw crack. The woman in front of him must have heard it too, because she turned around.

"And I thought I'd been waiting in line a long time," she said, giving him a smile so breathtaking it damn near made his heart stop. "You look like you're ready to fall asleep on your feet."

Cooper knew he should reply, but he was so mesmerized by her perfect skin, clear green eyes, and soft lips that he couldn't do anything but stare. He felt like a teenager back in high school again.

"Um, yeah. Long day," he finally managed.

What the hell was wrong with him?

Acknowledgments

I hope you had as much fun reading Becker and Jayna's story as I had writing it! When hubby and I met with Jayna over a dinner of spicy chicken at P.F. Chang's, we knew we needed to pair her up with a SWAT hunk who was the sensitive type. She had some issues to work through and needed the right alpha werewolf to help her do it. Becker immediately came to mind because he has this boyish quality about him we thought would be perfect for her. And when we found out how many pairs of yoga pants she owns, that sealed the deal. Because we all know how much Becker loves a woman in yoga pants. Luckily, Jayna and Becker fell hard and fast for each other from the moment we introduced them!

In addition to another big thank-you to my hubby, I want to also thank my agent, Bob Mecoy, for believing in me and encouraging me and being there when I need to talk, not to mention always having such great ideas; my editor, Cat Clyne, for loving this series and hot guys in tactical gear as much as I do; and all the other amazing people at Sourcebooks, including my publicist, Amelia, and their crazy-talented art department. I'm still drooling over this cover!

I also want to give a big thank-you to the men, women, and working dogs who protect and serve in police departments everywhere, as well as their families.

And because I could never leave my readers out, a

huge thank-you to everyone who has read my books and Snoopy Danced right along with me with every new release. That includes the fantastic girls and guys on my Street Team and my FB Groupies. You rock!

Hope you look forward to reading the other books in the SWAT series as much as I look forward to sharing them with you. Be sure to look for Cooper's book, *To Love a Wolf*, coming summer 2016!

Happy Reading!

About the Author

Paige Tyler is a *New York Times* and *USA Today* best-selling author of sexy romantic suspense and paranormal romance. She and her very own military hero (also known as her husband!) live on the beautiful Florida coast with their adorable fur baby (also known as their dog!). Paige graduated with a degree in education, but decided to pursue her passion and write books about hunky alpha males and the kick-butt heroines who fall in love with them.

Visit Paige at her website at www.paigetylertheauthor.com, where you can also sign up for her newsletter.

She's also on Facebook, Twitter, Tumblr, Instagram, tsu, Wattpad, and Pinterest.